James Calbraith is a Poland-born writer, foodie and traveller, currently residing in South London. His debut historical fantasy novel, "The Shadow of Black Wings", has reached ABNA semi-finals. It was published in July 2012 and hit the Historical Fantasy and Alternate History bestsellers list on Amazon US and UK.

Praise for *The Shadow of Black Wings*

"Fast paced and full of energy."
— Adrian Tchaikovsky,
author of the *Shadows of the Apt*

"This manuscript is full of highly crafted detail that will make readers shiver at times with fear and delight...a familiar yet highly original fantasy that is a worthwhile read."
— Publishers Weekly

"The real-world cultures are incredibly well-researched and truthful, and yet well-balanced with the fantasy elements. An intriguing and impressive series."
— Ben Galley,
author of the *Emaneska Series*

By James Calbraith

THE YEAR OF THE DRAGON
Book One: The Shadow of Black Wings
Book Two: The Warrior's Soul
Book Three: The Islands in the Mist
Book Four: The Rising Tide
The Year of the Dragon Books 1-4 Delux Edition

Transmission
Dragonbone Chest

Visit James Calbraith's official website at
jamescalbraith.com
for the latest news, book details, and other information
Or sign up for the newsletter at:
tinyletter.com/jcalbraith

The Warrior's Soul

Book Two of
The Year of the Dragon

James Calbraith

FLYING
SQUID

Published July 2012 by Flying Squid
ISBN-13: 978-83-935529-3-1

Cover Illustration: Yue Wang
Map Illustrations: Jared Blando
Cover Design: Flying Squid

TABLE OF CONTENTS

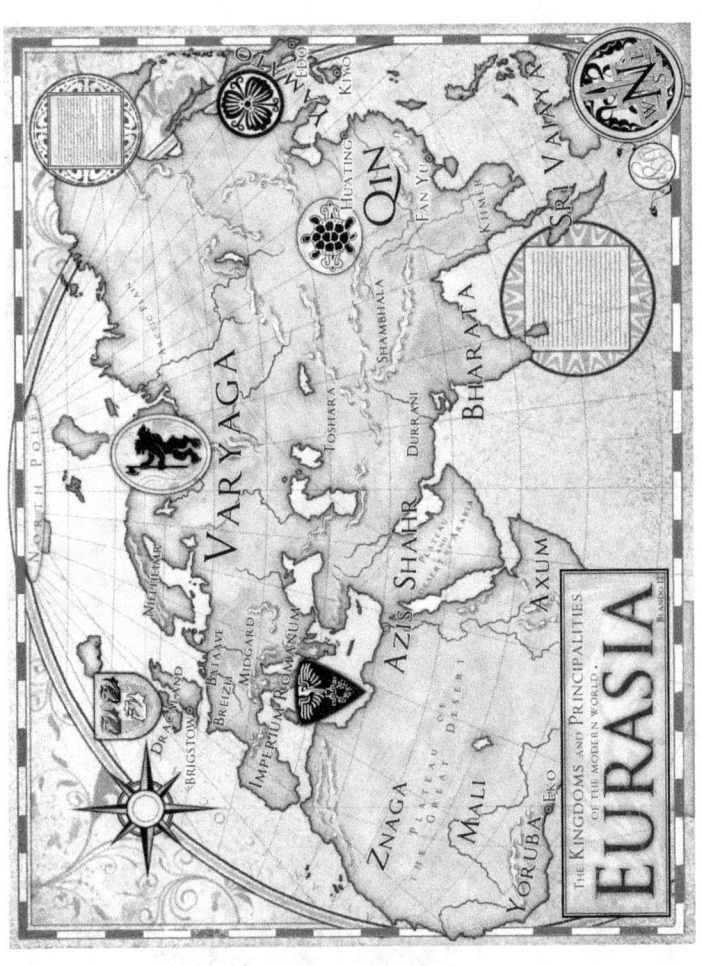

THE KINGDOMS AND PRINCIPALITIES
OF THE MODERN WORLD

EURASIA

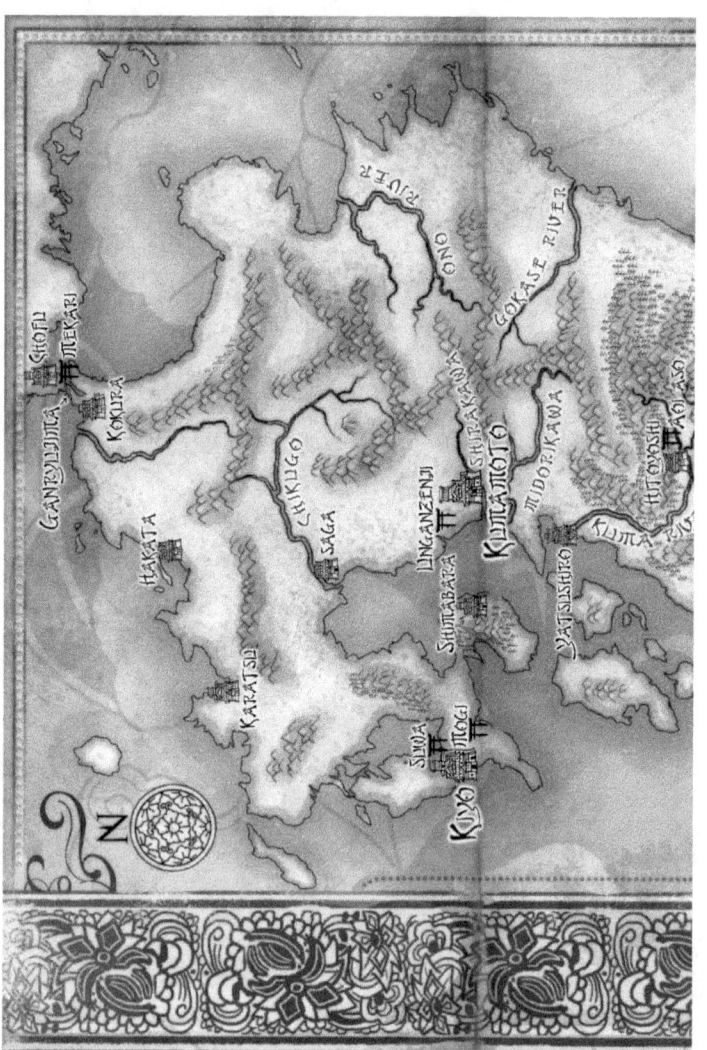

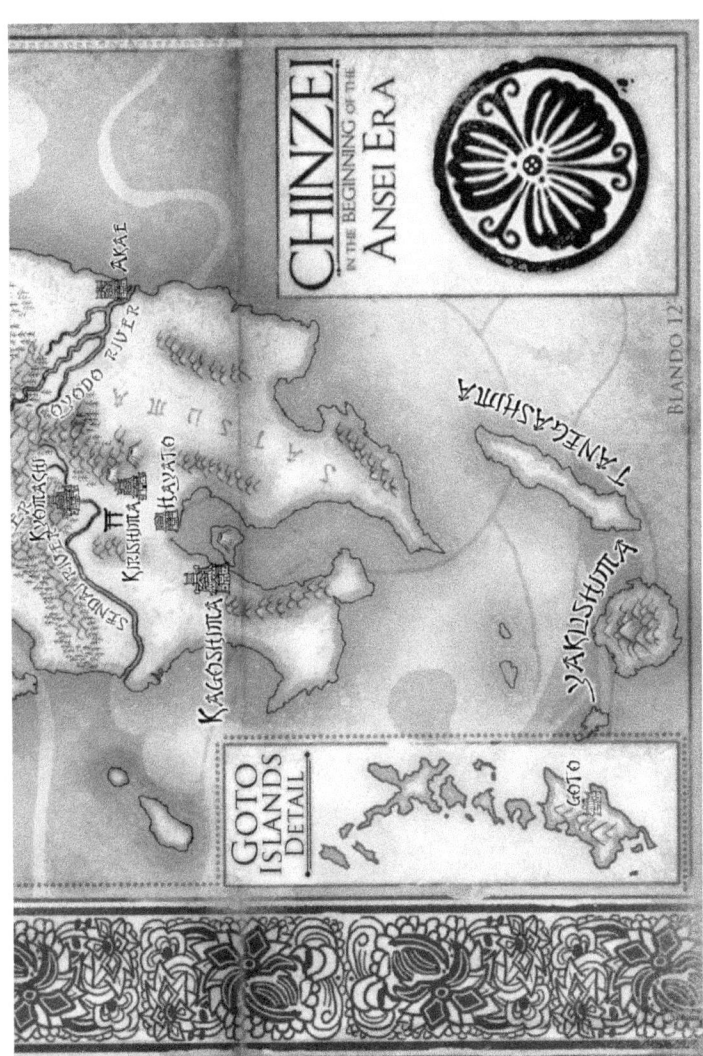

CHINZEI
IN THE BEGINNING OF THE
ANSEI ERA

BLANDO 12

AKAE
KYODO RIVER
KIRISHIMA
KYOMACHI
HITOYATO
SENDAI
KAGOSHIMA

TANEGASHIMA

YAKUSHIMA

GOTO ISLANDS DETAIL

GOTO

The same attitude is needed to defeat one man and ten million men.

Go Rin No Sho

PROLOGUE

The majestic brilliant globe of the sun ascended slowly out of the waters of Kinkō Bay, beyond the slopes of the imposing cone of the Sakurajima Mountain. The first fishing boats of dawn were scattered on the pastel blue ocean like dots of silver thread embroidered on an indigo-dyed kimono. From where Atsuko was sitting the entire scene – the great mountain, the sea and the boats, the rising sun – formed a living backdrop to the lush green garden, gentle hills covered with fresh grass and tall dark trees cut to form a frame for the moving picture.

"This is my favourite season in the garden," said Shimazu Nariakira, sitting beside her on the veranda of a small, perfectly proportioned teahouse.

"Surely the time of blooming azaleas or flowering hydrangeas is much more beautiful, Father?" she said, referring to the bushes lining a narrow pond winding at their feet. Atsuko knew her adoptive parent enough to know the answer to this riddle, but she also knew he enjoyed telling it. The great *daimyo* of Satsuma rose a little and leaned to her side.

"I have designed this garden to show the spirit of the Satsuma clan – for those who know how to look. Right now, gazing at the pond, we see the present. The azaleas are already past their prime, a reminder of glories gone by. But the hydrangeas are yet to sprout flowers – "

"A promise for the future," she said, finishing his thought. He smiled and nodded.

Once, at the height of their power, when the civil wars ravaged Yamato, the Shimazu had gambled to conquer all of Chinzei Island. They failed, but, unlike other defeated clans, were not destroyed. Allowed to live, but not flourish, like the early spring hydrangeas, the clan bided their time for revenge. Time and patience was what the Shimazu had in excess. Two and a half centuries had passed since their last unsuccessful gambit and it seemed like even more would have to pass before they could try again.

"All this beauty and refinement," said Nariakira, taking a long, sad look at the flowers, the maple trees and the framed landscape, "all this futile, fruitless effort is just a substitute for the power and action we are no longer allowed. Have you read of the eunuchs at the Qin emperor's palace?"

"I have, Father. An awful fate for a man."

"We are all like those eunuchs. The *daimyo*, the samurai... Castrated by the Tokugawas, rendered feeble and powerless by the system they've introduced. Like the eunuchs we concentrate our energy on the meaningless pursuits of art, philosophy and courtly intrigue. We concern ourselves more with the taste of tea and smell of cherry blossom than warfare."

Atsuko nodded politely. She was the only one Nariakira could discuss such matters with. He had no sons and he trusted none of his advisors enough to share the most secret plans with – except perhaps Torii Heishichi, his Chief Wizard.

"Appreciating fine art refines the swordsman's soul and skill," she said.

"What need is there for a swordsman's skill when he stands against a peasant armed with a thunder gun?"

She laughed. The thought was preposterous.

"That will never happen. No peasant could afford a thunder gun."

"It will happen sooner than you think. And the samurai, with all their elegance and comfort and refinement, will be caught completely unprepared – mark my words."

"The samurai are the world's greatest warriors."

"We were once – and we might be again… but under the Tokugawas we've become a mockery. All the neighbouring countries laugh behind our backs. All the Westerners are sharpening their teeth, ready to pound their ironclad fist on the gates of Edo. Even the commoners no longer respect their superiors."

"And do you plan to defeat them all with your smoking boat?"

Nariakira turned his gaze north, where the garden ended with a tall impenetrable hedge, and smiled. There, beyond the hedge and the cliff side, lay his secret wharf and in it his beloved ship – a black yacht with no sails.

"That's just a toy. A little more than a model."

"An expensive toy."

She knew he could afford it. After Nariakira's father's reforms, the Satsuma fiefdom was the richest in the country. The Bataavian machines had opened new lands for farming, the overseas trade – through 'smugglers' based on Nansei Islands, which Nariakira only pretended to fight – was more profitable than ever. The *Taikun*'s tax collectors had no idea of Satsuma's real income. Here, far beyond the Southern mountains, his word meant little, his spy network was non-existent. The province was so remote and inaccessible it was almost like a separate country. No Tokugawa ever decided to risk an all-out war to bring the impudent Shimazu to heel, and no Shimazu would ever dare to dream of openly opposing the *Taikun* and his many vassals.

"I needed to know I can build it without having to rely on the Bataavians in case they change their minds."

"And can you?"

Nariakira grinned. "The blueprints came from Dejima, but everything else was made by my men. Satsuma's shipwrights built the hull, Satsuma's engineers created the engine, Heishichi provided the fire elementals from a pit inside Kitadake Mountain as good as the Bataavian ones. I could build ten more ships like it before the end of the year."

"Ten more toys."

He chuckled. "Put a gun on each and we would already have a mightier fleet than all of the other *daimyo*s put together. And the ocean-going warship I have ordered will dwarf even that. But then what? Nobody ever won a war in

Yamato by the strength of ships alone. I would need something else to change the balance of power… something radical, something new."

There was movement in the bushes and Nariakira froze, his hand reaching for the sword. Atsuko drew breath. There wasn't supposed to be anyone in the garden at that time.

"*An assassin?*" she whispered, but Nariakira shook his head.

The man emerged onto the path in a hurry, making no effort at secrecy. It was one of the *daimyo*'s personal messengers. Nariakira frowned.

"What message is so urgent that it has to be brought to my private garden at dawn?"

THE WARRIOR'S SOUL

CHAPTER I

"So you're saying the neighbours saw nothing?"

"Nothing, *doshin* Koyata. The silk merchant from across the street heard some screams and noises, but that's all."

"What about the girl? We still can't reach her?"

"She's hiding in Suwa – outside our jurisdiction."

Koyata stood before the entrance to the Takashima Mansion's main building, squinting at the afternoon sun. This day was too long. The plain grey overcoat marked with the red pentacle badge of the Kiyō police lay heavily on his shoulders. His clues were as scarce as his resources – the precinct could only spare two men to help him. The bodies of the guards had disappeared before anyone could inspect them. The members of the household were all either dead or missing and, worst of all, nobody could investigate the scene of the crime.

"I will try again," declared Koyata, whose high rank of a *doshin* meant he was responsible for supervising all crime-fighting activities in the district.

"Be careful, Koyata-*sama*," Ishida, the shorter and fatter of his two subordinates warned him earnestly.

Dismissing their fears, he entered the building and climbed the narrow steps to the first floor. He stopped in front of the remnants of the broken sliding panel separating the ruined study from the corridor. He carefully reached into the room with the *jutte* truncheon. Nothing happened. Encouraged, he stepped forwards, crossing the threshold.

Lightning struck him in the chest, and he flew a few feet into the air before landing painfully on the other side of the corridor.

"Koyata-*sama*!"

The two policemen hurried to his assistance.

"I'm all right. *Kuso*! When is Sakuma-*dono* going to help us with this barrier?"

"He said he won't leave his son's bed as long as the kid is unconscious," explained Ishida.

"Such a tragic accident…" added the other.

"If it *was* an accident," Koyata said under his nose.

"You don't think – "

"I think it looks like somebody's targeting the *Rangaku* scholars, and I think that's why Sakuma-*dono* doesn't want to leave his house."

The only item found at the scene of the crime was an antique bronze dagger, covered with dried-up blood, discovered on the road a few yards away from the gate of the residence. Koyata recognised the pattern from his days in the forgery trade – he would not have progressed so high up in the hierarchy if he hadn't a keen eye for such detail. The dagger was at least two hundred years old, of the type used

20

in the Yōkai War. The bronze blades were manufactured with a singular purpose – to vanquish magical creatures, or users of magic.

He rotated the bronze dagger in his fingers. He could feel the barely noticeable buzz coming from the blade, a confirmation of the latent magical ability he did his best to conceal from his colleagues and superiors. He had always admired real wizards, in secret. Takashima-*sama*, Sakuma-*dono*… Those names meant much to him. It worried him greatly that somebody would wish to hunt them down.

"Well, if you ask me, I won't be sorry if they all go to hell," said the taller policeman. "Just look at all this barbarian junk on the floor," he added, pointing to the books and magical artefacts scattered all over the study. "I bet he just killed himself with one of these contraptions."

"There would at least be a body," Koyata replied, dismissing the idea outright.

"Exploded, melted, eaten by a demon," the policeman said with a shrug.

The *doshin* looked sharply at his subordinate and clapped his thigh.

"Hirata, you're brilliant!"

"I am?"

"We'll just say the wizard did it to himself! That will save us all the work!"

And keep the superiors off my back, he thought. Already the magistrate officials had contacted him regarding the mysterious attack.

"We are certain you will find evidence incriminating the Bataavians." The city bureaucrat's fat jowls shook as he spoke.

"I'm not so sure, *tono*. You know as well as I do that the Bataavians regarded Takashima-*sama* with great esteem. What possible motive – "

"I don't think you understand, *doshin*. You *will* find the necessary evidence."

"I… I see."

An accident – due to mishandling Bataavian technology. *You'll have your evidence, but good luck incriminating anyone with it. What do you say to that, you fat brush-pusher?*

"It's a good idea," Ishida agreed. "It's just as believable as an abduction by rival mages, or a *shinobi* attack, or any other mad theory spun by the folks back at the precinct."

"Are they really talking about a *shinobi* attack?" the *doshin* asked, laughing.

"Old Jūzō does. He sees ninjas and demons everywhere."

"He's been watching too many *kabuki* plays. The *shinobi* are extinct. Let's go back and write this one off; there's nothing more for us to do here."

Koyata grinned. His mood improved. He would still try to solve the mystery of the Takashima Mansion, of course – but now he could do it in his own time, by his own rules.

He shook off the doziness and yawned discreetly. He retreated behind the frame of a ground floor sliding panel and observed the courtyard outside through a hole in the paper. The hours of waiting paid off – somebody *did* appear at the Takashima residence.

An unmarked palanquin stopped at the gates. The night was pitch-black, illuminated only by a single paper lantern carried by one of the priests accompanying the vehicle. A youth wearing a wide-brimmed, face-concealing hat stepped out of the palanquin and limped towards the main hall, supported by the priest with the lantern. This must have been Shūhan's heir, Satō, Koyata realised. He had heard rumours the wizard's daughter preferred to wear male clothes – and a sword. In any other city this would have been reason enough to arrest and disgrace her. In Kiyō this was merely an eccentricity.

Koyata sneaked after the heir and two priests. As she climbed the stairs, the girl dispelled all the protective spells with a wave of her hand. She entered her father's study without a hindrance.

The residence, like all aristocratic houses built in times of the assassins, was full of hidden corridors and hideouts, and the *doshin* had all day to discover most of them. With the magic barriers gone he could now reach a small concealed alcove from which he had a good view of the entire study.

The girl gingerly touched the floor. The air crackled with remnants of a powerful spell. She gasped with pain, touching her shoulder.

"We did warn you, Takashima-*sama*," the priest with the lantern said in a worried voice, "the wound has barely sealed. If you will not rest now, it may never be healed completely."

"It doesn't matter. I have to take care of my legacy. Help me clear these up."

The girl and the priests gathered all of wizard's belongings into a great pile in the library. Koyata watched it in horror. Was she planning to burn it all? So much knowledge, so much research… If she did, the *doshin* would have to come out of his hiding place and stop the girl, he decided, even if revealing his continued interest in the case brought the wrath of his superiors upon his head.

The girl reached for a large black book at the bottom of the pile and picked it up tenderly. The cover and the edges of the pages were burned. Several pieces of paper fell out from between the pages, scribbled with composed writing.

"It's difficult to carry such a bulky tome," remarked one of the priests.

"I know." The girl sighed and threw the book back onto the pile. "I don't need it anymore."

I need to find out what that book is.

She lifted one of the floorboards and picked up a roll of golden coins. A fortune in gold! Koyata gulped. He had only ever seen so much money in the treasure houses of the gambling dens he had raided.

"There is nothing else I want to take," the girl said. "All these things…" she pointed to the pile of magic contraptions, books and documents, "I can neither carry nor leave to the robbers or magistrate."

Right, that's it. Koyata grasped the handgrip of his truncheon, ready to pounce, but the girl turned to the accompanying priests and said something which made him stop and let out a quiet sigh of relief.

"Throw it all into the dry well by the cemetery. Bury it deep. My father and I will come and retrieve it once this is all over."

She arrived at the servants' quarters dressed in the simple common uniform of a shrine attendant; a grey cloth *monpe*, pantaloons that ended at half-knee, and a brown jute tunic. It was itchy and chafing compared to silk, but Satō found it remarkably easy to walk, even run in the narrow trousers.

It was Lady Kazuko's idea for her to hide in the servants' quarters. Even though the shrine was probably the safest place in the city, its walls still could not provide a complete guarantee of safety.

"This will be the last place anybody would look for a samurai's daughter, and it will help you to pick up some of the language and behaviour of the lower classes in case you need to disguise yourself."

"Why would I need to disguise myself as a serf?"

"Do you not intend to look for your father?"

"Of course I do!" the girl blurted out.

Finding Shūhan was the only thing on her mind right now. No body had been found at the mansion, and she had

25

recognised the faint pattern of a transportation hex still lingering on the floor of the study. The thought of her father being still alive, somewhere, was the only thing keeping her from breaking down.

"Well then, you can hardly travel as Takashima Satō, as long as there's an unknown enemy waiting for you outside the shrine's gates."

"I suppose not," she agreed reluctantly, "but a *servant?* They are so uncouth and – and *smelly!*"

"Just try to see how they live," said the High Priestess, "they may surprise you yet."

The poor commoners were employed by the shrine to assist with the simplest menial tasks – carrying luggage for the guests, chopping firewood, transporting heavy goods. Satō entered the quarters with hesitation, holding her breath, expecting to find it in a state little better than the village of *eta*, the untouchables. But, though very poor and simple, the rooms were as clean as any and, to her surprise, everyone inside seemed rather cheerful.

Despite her being dressed like one of them, the servants immediately fell to their knees.

"I, uh... why are you kneeling? I'm just a commoner like you..."

One of the girls raised her face, smiling broadly.

"*Tono*, if you want to hide among us lowly serv'nts then by all means you can, but you ain't foolin' nobody 'ere just by wearing the garb of a common'r."

Satō winced on hearing the peasant's crude accent.

"Please stand up, all of you. I need to learn how to be more like one of you, and quickly."

The servants stood up slowly. The girl who spoke first approached the wizardess boldly.

"Please come, *tono*."

She led Satō to sit beside her on the bedding. Satō looked at the quilt reluctantly, expecting bedbugs and fleas to scurry off it the moment she sat down, but it too was clean and freshly washed.

"First off, you need to grime yerself. Ye'r not tanned 'nuff, yer skin's too pure. Any fool can see you come from a good 'ouse."

"What do you propose?"

"Lessee... Why don't you rub some walnut juice on yer skin? Not too much or ye'd look like an *oni*. There ain't that much sun now, so it needn't be much. An' maybe some lamp oil if yer don't mind t'smell."

"What else?" encouraged Satō, wondering how many other fugitive nobles before her had been through the same ordeal. The girl seemed experienced.

"Yer need to slouch, like this. See how every'un is bent, that's from carryin' all them heavy bags and such. Yer walk straight, proud. That's a samurai walk. Walk low, don't look at the high-up folk."

"I see."

"An' yer looking mighty grim, if you don't mind me sayin' so. You should always smile."

"How so?"

"If we don' smile, a samurai could think we don' like summat about'em, and that be trouble, so we smile. An' what's not to smile about? Our life's a good'un."

"*Eeh*! You call this a good life?" Satō cried out.

She looked around at the squalid dormitory full of people whose combined wealth was maybe less than a tenth of a golden coin, if that.

"Sure, *tono*, an' why not? As long as we do our duty well, we ain't got nuttin' to care about. T'shrine gives us food and a place to sleep. That's more than we'd'ave in our home village. We ain't be needin' no more than that and we're all in the same boat, so we don't fight or bicker with each other. Ye'll see if yer spend a day 'ere, this life's as good as it gets."

Satō pondered the girl's words for a while.

"What is your name?"

"They call me Ikō, *tono*," the girl answered, still with the same beaming innocent smile.

"And how did you come to live in the shrine?"

"I'm a *kambe*; a payment, like," she proceeded to explain. "When t'news of great famine came from up north, all villages in Saga ran to the priests like 'ens to a cock. Ours was a poor place and t'only thing we could promise to t'great shrines were t'first girl babies born after 'arvest. The famine never came after all, but a deal was a deal. On t'day after the 'arvest feast, me mom bore three daughters in one birth. When we were five, we each got sent to one of t'great shrines – 'ere, Karatsu and Kirishima."

"Have you ever seen your sisters?" asked Satō. The three shrines were quite a distance apart from each other, even for a wealthy traveller.

"Only once, we all came back to t'village for our brother's wedding five years back. But I know them's all taken care of well, just like me, and that makes me 'appy."

"And your parents?"

"Me mom's died a few years ago, but she lived a long and good life, bless her. Me dad perish'd with t'pox when I was but tiny. 'scuse me, *tono*, but I mustn't tarry no more, there's work to be done, always. Ye'll be arright 'ere, *neh*?"

The girl stood up, leaving Satō on the jute quilt alone with her thoughts. The wizardess found her gloominess had disappeared. If the girl managed to stay so merry despite the hardships of her life, what right did Satō have to stay depressed? She was healthy, well fed, a roll of golden coins she'd taken from her father's safe box – a real fortune by any account – tightly wrapped on her stomach. She had friends and allies. Her father was very likely alive, and even if not – such was the lot of a samurai. She would continue his legacy and rebuild the dōjō. Yes, she decided, there would be no more misery. Like Ikō, she would meet her fate with a smile.

There was some commotion outside and the few servants remaining in the room scrambled to the small window to see what was happening. Satō stepped up and they politely let her closer to the opening. She could see almost the entire main courtyard from here, as the servant quarters were built on a low prominence to the west of the main gate.

The High Priestess, accompanied by several other priests and attendants, was arguing loudly with a troop of samurai. The warriors carried themselves very pompously, their rich kimonos gaudily festooned with golden dragons and silver leaves, boasting wealth and prestige. A sign of mallow was embroidered on their collars, and their leader, wearing a wide-brimmed lacquered hat, frantically waved a narrow wooden paddle, the symbol of high status.

"It's *bugyō*, the *Taikun*'s magistrate!" Satō whispered, recognising the markings of high office. The magistrate was the highest ranking official in Kiyō, equal to the provincial *daimyo*s.

The servants at the window, and Satō with them, gasped audibly as one of the magistrate's retainers pulled out his sword by an inch. Lady Kazuko halted her protestations for a moment, before renewing them with even more vigour. At last the magistrate gestured his men to calm down, barked a few more words indignantly and turned away.

The High Priestess watched the officials march away down the stairs then turned her face towards the servants' quarters. Satō could not see her face clearly at that distance, but she could imagine the look of anxious concern in Lady Kazuko's eyes.

Even the Suwa Shrine was no longer a safe place.

Lady Kazuko had barely managed to confront the magistrate at the gate when Nagomi approached her with news that the Westerner suddenly grew very agitated.

"He keeps saying, "Kazuko-hime, Kazuko-hime"," reported the girl.

The priestess pursed her lips. What other unpleasant surprises would this day bring?

It took her priests an hour to find Tokojiro in some tavern by the harbour. By the time she finally called for the Westerner, he had managed to calm himself down.

"It's about my dragon. I didn't think there would be any need to mention this," the boy said apologetically. "We... I was separated from it in the disaster and I had little hope of seeing it ever again. However, I believe it has now been captured – somewhere in this land."

"How do you know this?"

"I have a... link, a mental connection with my dragon. I can tell it arrived on a beach somewhere – to the south of here, if I have my bearings right – and was captured by armed men."

The priestess closed her eyes and prayed for guidance. How could she have missed that? Of course a dragon rider would have a *dragon*. She was silent for a long while.

"This is all too much for me, especially considering the other events... I need to consult the Spirits."

"What other events?"

He does not know, the High Priestess reminded herself.

"Satō's house was attacked – by a man in a crimson robe," she said.

"Crimson robe... you mean – "

"With long black hair and eyes like nuggets of gold, apparently."

She let the news sink in as she observed the boy.

"I must leave this place." He stood up. "I am putting you all in danger."

The boy thinks, the priestess thought with satisfaction.

"Sit down, please," she said. "The shrine is still the safest place for you to be right now, if not for very long. The others are also under its protection. We can think of something together."

"But I need to find my dragon. It can't be kept in a cage for too long. It may even die if it's not taken care of properly. Besides, it... it's my friend."

A friend?

Lady Kazuko glanced at the interpreter. Tokojiro nodded and shrugged.

"Does your... *friend* pose any danger to others while in captivity?" she asked.

"I don't know." The boy shook his head. "It depends on how long it is kept imprisoned, and in what conditions... If it turns – "

There was a word that Tokojiro did not understand and had to have explained by the boy.

"Goes wild, breaks the link with me, its rider. A feral dragon will burn villages, slaughter livestock - kill people... Even a small one, like mine, can be terribly dangerous."

"I have heard enough," said the High Priestess, her hand raised. "We will help you, I promise," she told the boy, "we will find a way, we need just a little more time. Have faith. Make sure you stay out of sight – at all times. I predict further trouble coming our way."

And I don't need the Spirits to tell me that.

At the back of the shrine gardens, in the part most overgrown and unkempt, stood an old teahouse. Funded by one of the *Taikun*s of old, the small square building with walls of unpainted wood and bamboo was the quintessence of simplicity and aesthetics. These days, the High Priestess alone used it for her contemplations. Only she and a few gardeners even knew of its existence. The roof of dark straw badly needed repairing and the tea stove begged for replacement, but it was still the best place to meditate in the entire shrine.

A flock of blue-winged magpies darted, screeching, from among the pink azaleas growing wildly over the earthen walls of the pavilion as Lady Kazuko sat on the narrow veranda overlooking a small lotus pond with a cup of fragrant, frothy *cha* in her hand. She liked the cup. It was covered in a sky-blue glaze, spotted and cracked in a deliberate, yet seemingly random, pattern. She had bought it in Heian, a long time ago. The best potteries in the country were selling their wares on the approach to the great Kiyomizu Temple. An old frail woman had walked among the rich merchants trying to sell just this one bowl. She was blind, and this was the last vessel she had created before her eyes died.

THE WARRIOR'S SOUL

"You have a gift of seeing," the old woman said, touching Lady Kazuko's hands.

"I do," the priestess agreed. There was no point in asking how the woman knew.

"I could tell you this cup is mystic and will aid you in your divinations, but all I can say is that it will hold the *cha* without spilling, and that the glaze will not peel or lose its shine for many years."

"That is as much as I expect from a teacup."

Despite the old woman's words, Lady Kazuko did enjoy making her divinations while drinking from the cup. Perhaps the gentle blue of the glaze helped to clear her mind, or perhaps the amount of *cha* it held was just right.

She reached for the small round bamboo box and shook it vigorously. A single stick fell out. She picked it up and smiled. Forty-four - life is a game of *shogi*. All success depends on cunning and strategy.

The sticks were just a toy, of course, a souvenir from the Qin district, but in the shrine, where the air itself was permeated with spiritual energy, even children's toys could tell the truth. The sticks simply confirmed what she had already learned from all the other divinations - the yarrow, the compass, the bones, the Four Pillars, the Six Planets, even the *omikuji* ribbons... She had spent the better part of the day trying to pierce the veils of fate and, of course, she had visited the Waters. The Spirits were most obliging, providing her with many detailed visions, but little guidance as to which of the futures was the most probable one. It was often a problem with the Waters of Scrying. Only very rarely were they as straightforward as when they had presented Nagomi with her first prophecy. And clear answers were what she needed most on this day of decisions.

She could still have given away the foreigner to the authorities. She could say he had been brought to the shrine against her will, that she knew nothing about it. None would dare question the word of a High Priestess, not over that of a drunken unemployed interpreter and two children. This would be the clever, rational solution. The shrine would be safe, her duty to the *Taikun* fulfilled; but she did not need the bamboo sticks or twigs of yarrow to see that the boy's arrival was no accident. One did not give away the gifts from the Gods.

She had had ample time to observe the foreigner, ever since she had requested his presence at the shrine. The circumstances of his arrival, as reported by Nagomi, piqued her curiosity. Then the blue ring on his finger caught her attention - a shard of sapphire stone, like the ones Nagomi saw in her vision. The boy said at first it was just a gift from his grandfather, but then admitted that it, too, had come from Yamato. A coincidence? The High Priestess knew there was no such thing when it came to divination. The other parts of the puzzle started falling into place. The crimson robed enemy assaulting Satō's and Nagomi's houses, and now the boy's *dorako*...

The mightiest will fall, remembered Lady Kazuko. She was bound to serve the Edo court with wisdom and advice. In exchange, the shrine was given protection from the domain lords and city magistrates. But the prophecy was older than the castle of Edo, and it concerned more than just the *Taikun*. The priestess had to consider the fate of all Yamato

35

before making a decision. It was a heavy burden, but she was prepared to carry it.

Where did the foreigner come into all this? Would this boy bring the darkness upon Yamato, or deliverance? Was he just a harbinger of doom?

The situation required a decisive unorthodox solution.

"Cunning and strategy," reminded the bamboo sticks.

The High Priestess lifted her head and looked towards the top of the mountain, where the forest was the darkest and most dense. Sudden understanding dawned on her. For a moment she had gained a prophetic vision of the threads of Fate, all converging on Suwa, the Shrine in the middle of the tangled, glistening spider's web. Nagomi's apprenticeship and prophecies, Satō's escape, the boy's arrival - even Tokojiro's old, forgotten debt of gratitude, all played a part in the greater divine scheme.

The Suwa Shrine was not just a place where all these things had happened, she realised. The shrine itself was the solution.

I need to write a few letters.

CHAPTER II

The shrine bell struck nine times. The door to Bran's room slid away. The red-haired girl's slim, almond-eyed face was lit by a small flickering flame in her hand. He got up and straightened the creases on his new *kimono*, a deep, dark purple silk gown embroidered with the crest of a triangular mountain reflected in the water. The High Priestess had given it to him as a gift, and taught him how to wear it properly.

He pursed his lips and inhaled deeply in unsure anticipation.

"Kazuko-*hime*," the girl said, their limited mutually known vocabulary making it impossible to explain further what she wanted. "*Dōzo*," she added, giving him a rolled up piece of paper.

It was a letter from the High Priestess, written in the elegant, if oddly spiky and angular, handwriting that he guessed belonged to the interpreter, Tokojiro.

Please follow the girl.

Do not fear. Keep your mind clear.

I will help you find what you are looking for.

Trust us, we all want to help you.

This was all very cryptic and vague, and did not inspire trust in him at all. Why couldn't the priestess just send the interpreter to explain what was going on?

A whole day had passed since he had reported about the dragon and nobody had come to see him except the blind girl bringing him food and some strange moustached man who carefully studied his sword and then left without a word. What did they want from him now?

He looked at the girl, but she only stood, smiling shyly, in silence.

"*Dōzo*," she repeated, gesturing him to follow her outside.

They walked down the long winding corridors and then, after putting on uncomfortable wooden sandals, out of the building into the night. The moon was waning, but still bright. The garden was completely silent. They passed through a small gateway leading out of the main compound, walked across the bridge over a stream – here there was, at last, a sound, the trickling of a waterfall and the croaking of frogs – then the path started ascending steeply into a deep forest growing beyond the northern limits of the shrine.

The wood here was different from the cultivated orchard of the inner shrine. It was ancient, thick, not even a sliver of moonlight filtering through the dense canopy. There was something sinister in the darkness, giant gnarled trees brooded over the narrow path and invaded it with their black roots, covered with moss, vine and cobwebs.

38

"Where are you taking me?"

Bran was losing his patience. He had trusted the girl and the priestess so far, but his trust was running thin. Where was the translator? Why were they taking him deeper into the forest? Cold sweat trickled down his spine – what if they were going to sacrifice him to their Gods? He was, after all, in a temple, and he knew nothing of the religions of the locals…

"Kazuko-*hime*," the girl repeated, and from the helpless look in her worried eyes Bran guessed she knew as little of the purpose of their nightly escapade as he did.

At last they reached the end of the trail, the heart of the forest. By the light coming from the stone lantern standing between two enormous cedar trees, Bran saw a cross-beam gate of cinnabar wood and, beyond it, a little shrine, no bigger than a shed, made of round white stones under a thatched roof. The bargeboards of the roof crossed and formed a fork at the top of the gables. The structure was leaning a bit to the side, the stones covered with thick pillow moss, and the thatch was black with age.

The red-haired girl drew a sharp breath seeing the building. The inquisitive boy – Satō, the wizard's son, Bran remembered - and Lady Kazuko were also there, waiting for him. The boy's arm was bandaged. The High Priestess reached out her hand expectantly.

"What do you want from me? Where's Tokojiro?"

"Tokojiro-*sama dame*."

The priestess shook her head and crossed her arms.

"Forbidden?" Bran tried to guess, "Is the translator forbidden to come here?"

There was no answer. He looked at the red-haired girl. She tried to smile encouragingly, but the concern was still in her eyes.

Lady Kazuko said something and he sensed urgency in her voice. He took her by the hand at last and, lowering their heads under a thick straw rope hung across the entrance, the two entered the tiny shrine. There was barely enough room for them to stand here, slightly bending their backs. It was pitch black, cold and damp. He could hear water dripping somewhere far below. The air smelled faintly of sulphur.

When his eyes got used to the darkness, only faintly brightened by the stone lantern outside, he noticed a flight of steps carved into the rock, leading downwards, damp, slick and coated with lichen. Somehow he managed not to slip and tumble down, slowly following Lady Kazuko. Soon they reached a vast underground chamber filled with smoke and mist.

There was a wide lake at the bottom, its waters sparkling and shimmering with their own pale light as if the moon was trapped underneath the surface. The blue light dispersed on the whirling mist, carving fantastic shapes from the shadows. The smell of rotten eggs and ammonia was now almost unbearable. The rocks around the pool were coated in fine yellow powder.

Bran glanced at the priestess nervously.

"What now?"

She made a gesture he did not understand at first, but when she repeated it he realised she wanted him to disrobe and enter the water. This was not another hiding place. There was to be some kind of ritual performed on him, but the priestess was frail and unarmed, he couldn't imagine her wanting to harm him. There was something in the old woman's eyes that made him believe her good will. If only they could somehow communicate… There was only one way to learn exactly what it was she wanted to do with him on that mysterious night - obey the command and see the ritual through to the end.

Bran cast the dark robe to the floor and undid the loincloth. He was naked, but not cold. The warm mist surrounded and caressed his body, as if it had a mind of its own. He stepped forwards and touched the surface of the water with his toes. It was bubbling and hot, almost as hot as the water in the *Oyū* bath. He looked at the priestess and she nodded. He took another step. The stone bottom of the pool descended steeply and before long he was submerged up to the chest.

The experience was not altogether unpleasant. His muscles relaxed, his joints lost their stiffness. He could sense underwater flows and currents warming his thighs and calves, streams of heat emerging from cracks in the bottom of the lake. He stepped deeper and the water covered his shoulders. He inhaled deeply.

The mist around him became denser and thicker, now milky-white. The thicker it became the deeper breaths he had to take and the more of it he took into his lungs. He was starting to feel nauseous, and turned around to come out of the pool before it was too late. The priestess observed him intently, but made no move.

Suddenly the mist whirled around him again and some shapes appeared in the fumes, wisps of thicker yellowish smoke. For a second he thought he saw a human face looking at him curiously. Then another appeared, and now he was certain - there were eyes gazing at him from the steam, faces of all shapes and sizes, small, large, narrow and round, gentle female ones with sad eyes and fierce male ones frowning under bushy eyebrows - dozens of them, swirling around in silence, crowding and pushing each other to get nearer.

Some of the faces then grew necks, shoulders and arms. The hands of smoke started touching him, stroking and poking his flesh. He yowled as wandering fingers pinched him on the back, on the shoulder. He was surrounded by a crowd of hands, a forest of palms, now scratching and punching each other to get closer, and some of the scratches and punches would reach him by mistake. "Stop it!" he wanted to say, but the mist had enveloped his head and mouth, making it difficult to breathe or speak.

He was terrified. He could not get back to the shore. The ghosts were pushing and pulling him around in a whirlpool of limbs, fighting for the prize of a young body. He noticed the female faces had now gone from the immediate vicinity, as stronger, more virile Spirits of men took their places in the front. Some of the ghosts procured weapons of smoke and fog, swords of mist, spears of steam, and started fighting each other in a manner of warriors on a battlefield. Misplaced blows fell on Bran's arms and head. He raised his hands, defending himself from the strikes, and closed his eyes...

As suddenly as it had started, the chaos stopped. Bran opened his eyes. The ghosts were still there, a troop of grizzled warriors armed to their lucid teeth, but they were no longer fighting. The throng parted, making way for somebody coming in from the darkness - a Spirit of a huge man in full armour, wearing a masked helmet with a fan-shaped ornament. In his chest stuck an arrow, still trembling as if it had been shot mere seconds ago. The Spirit raised a great, narrow-bladed halberd and pointed it in Bran's direction. Other ghosts bowed in respect and pulled back.

The warrior Spirit roared and lunged towards the dragon rider. Bran's mouth and eyes were forced open by an unseen power. The Spirit transformed into several wisps of white smoke that entered Bran's body. The boy felt an exquisite pain, as if molten lead was poured down his mouth, nostrils and ears. He wanted to scream, but he couldn't.

After what seemed like an eternity, the High Priestess climbed up the stone stairs and out of the shrine carrying the Westerner's limp unconscious body on her back. Immediately, Nagomi jumped to her aid and, with Satō's help, took the burden off the woman's shoulders.

"Did it work?" she asked.

She didn't exactly know what was supposed to work, or how.

"We won't know until dawn," replied Lady Kazuko, catching her breath.

"Why, what happens at dawn?"

"Patience, child, you'll see for yourself. Until then, we must wait and pray. Let's take him back to the shrine then beg the *kami* for a happy outcome."

Nagomi helped carry the boy's body down the hill, through the dark forest and quiet garden. It seemed lighter than what she remembered from the beach.

"Take him to my quarters," the priestess commanded.

They laid the unconscious boy on the straw mat floor in the Crane Room and sat beside him. Lady Kazuko closed her eyes and started chanting a monotonous droning invocation to the *kami* of Suwa. Nagomi joined her quietly, still casting worried glances at the Westerner.

"What is going on, Kazuko-*hime*?" she asked at last, when the chant finished, "what happened in that cave?"

"I'll tell you in a moment, but let me start with what happened yesterday. This will help you understand why I had to do what I did."

"You mean the magistrate agents," said Satō.

"Yes. They came to search the shrine for a harboured fugitive. Luckily, the *bugyō* made a mistake – he came without a proper warrant, so I could refuse his request and buy us a little time. However, when he's back with the *Taikun's* seal I will have no choice but to let him in."

"The magistrate should be investigating my father's disappearance, not chasing after harmless Westerners," Satō said, clutching her fists.

"How did they know Bran-*sama* is here? Who betrayed us?" asked a worried Nagomi.

"I'm afraid they were not looking for the boy. They were looking for you, Satō. Your family has been outlawed. *You* are now a wanted fugitive."

"*What?*" Satō cried out.

The boy stirred on his bed and moaned.

"I'm sorry," she said, remembering her manners, "but... I don't understand..."

"I'm not exactly sure what is going on here, either," the High Priestess admitted. "Perhaps the magistrate decided to use this opportunity to finally get rid of the Takashima family... They claim that your father perished through his unlawful experiments and you, as his heir, are equally dangerous."

"At least the boy is still safe," Satō said, biting her lip.

"But you're not. I told them you have already left the shrine in search of your father. This is what you will do today, at any rate, before they return."

"Today...?" The wizardess looked outside. It was still dark, the sky in the east slowly turning grey. "But, I don't even know where to go – what to look for..."

"And you will take Bran-*sama* with you," continued Lady Kazuko, "he will help you and you will help him."

"How can he help me – he's just a lost boy," Satō scoffed, "and he'll be slain the moment he steps out of the shrine."

"He may be lost, but there is a reason why he became lost here, of all places. This is not the first time his kin has met with the man in the crimson robe. He told me his grandfather met a similar being once before."

"So he came here because of the crimson robed man?" Nagomi guessed, trying to make sense of the fast-changing events.

"That I don't know, but there is more. If it was only a matter of hiding from the man in the crimson robe, or the authorities, I believe I could manage this without going through today's ordeal. But the boy must leave the shrine and the city. There is something he must go looking for."

"What's out there that's so precious to him?"

"The boy's *dorako*."

"The beast? It's *here*?"

Satō could not contain herself again, rising from her knees, almost standing up with excitement.

"That's what the boy said. He can somehow sense the creature coming. He says it landed somewhere south of the city."

"*Monsters from without*," whispered Nagomi. Lady Kazuko gave her a sharp warning look.

"*Eeh*?"

Satō turned to her friend.

"Nothing," the apprentice replied quickly and shook her head.

46

"South... Father told me to go south if anything happened to him," said Satō, now remembering her own urgency. "Kumamoto, Kagoshima... If our family still has any friends left, that's where they would be."

"You have been brought together by Fate," declared Lady Kazuko prophetically. "I have meditated on this for long hours and I am now certain beyond any doubt. The boy, the dragon, your father, the Crimson Robe, the strange items in the boy's box... You must venture south together, to find out the solution to this puzzle."

"But how?" Satō still doubted. "Are we to wrap his face in bandages and pretend he's a leper? Are we to mime our way throughout Yamato?"

Before the High Priestess could respond, the first ray of dawn pierced through the latticed paper window. The Westerner stirred again, violently this time, agony twisting his face.

"It has begun," said Lady Kazuko. "Now you will have your answer. Observe!"

He dreamt of a battle, a siege of a great stone castle overlooking a raging sea, with walls smooth and curved, rising high towards the clouds. Horsemen charged against the sallying defenders with long swords and great bows and arrows. Footmen in black armour scaled the walls, rectangular banners flying on their backs. Bronze cannons roared, spewing cannonballs over the battlements.

A Bataavian man-o'-war of ancient design sailed up to the castle. A terrifying broadside from its guns shook the walls to their foundations. Still the defenders stood strong, jeering and mocking the hapless assailants for asking the barbarians' help.

The final charge, one last push against the keep was his last chance to prove himself as an apt commander before the *Taikun* relieved him of his duty. All men were ordered forwards, all guns screamed in unison. The assault was exhilarating in its totality, a formidable rush of battle fever. They climbed past the first rampart, the second, reached the third...

A stray arrow buried itself in his chest. He fell off his horse. His men rushed to him, but it was too late. A retainer leaned over to listen to his final words - the death poem of a dying samurai.

"Among the bullets,

At the start of the year,

The name of

Scattered flowers remains

The only certainty."

Satō was the first to notice the transformation.

"Look at his face!" she whispered, astonished. "What –"

Lady Kazuko silenced her with a raised hand then leaned over the boy.

"Now is the crucial moment. Everything hangs in the balance."

The Westerner's face started melting and changing. His features rounded, his eyes narrowed, his nose became shorter and wider, his skin pale. There was a faint creaking of bones and strained ligaments. The boy squirmed in pain, but did not wake up. Nagomi turned her eyes away, unable to look at his suffering. At last the metamorphosis was complete, and on the bedding lay not a Western boy but a Yamato one, not unlike any of the boys she knew from the streets of her city.

"It's not over yet," the High Priestess remarked quickly. "We must pray that the Spirit who is in Bran-*sama*'s body does not overwhelm him and take over. The boy is strong and the power of his will is great but anything may yet happen at this point."

She chanted another invocation. Her hand resting on the boy's forehead glowed up with white light and the Westerner started grunting in his sleep.

"He's waking up," Lady Kazuko noted. "Satō, dear, would you call for Tokojiro-*sama*? He should be waiting in the common room."

"Yes, High Priestess."

The wizardess stood up, cast a confused glance at the boy's transformed face and disappeared outside.

"I'm sure you have noticed the significance of the events we spoke about today," the High Priestess said.

"The Prophecy," Nagomi answered, not looking at Lady Kazuko.

She was focused on the unconscious boy, trying to understand what had just happened. The transformation was like nothing she had ever heard about. She had no idea the High Priestess was in possession of such power.

"Things are happening much faster than I expected," continued Lady Kazuko. "Bran-*sama* and Satō must leave the shrine and the city - that much is clear. I will have Tokojiro-*sama* accompany and assist them, but what shall we do about you?"

"Me…?" she asked, looking back at the Priestess.

"You were there when the boy fell from Heavens and I believe your visions from last year portended his coming. It is obvious you too are greatly involved in this matter. But their quest is a dangerous one and I cannot put this burden upon you against your will."

"Oh, I understand." Nagomi lowered her head Her heart sank. When the High Priestess had spoken of Satō and the boy venturing upon a journey south, she naturally imagined herself accompanying them. Had she been expecting too much?

"Of course, if my duties to the shrine…"

The High Priestess scoffed.

"There are many ways to serve the *kami*, child. No, I don't mean you are to stay here when your friend embarks on a perilous mission, but it is something you must choose to do of your own accord."

"Oh, Kazuko-*hime*!" Nagomi said, lifting her eyes in renewed hope. "Need you ask? Of course I will go. Wherever Satō goes I will follow. If I am allowed, of course," she added hastily.

"You have my permission, child, and I'm glad you've agreed. The quest could prove impossible for just Satō and the boy. With you, it will be merely difficult. They will need your protection."

"*My* protection? But… they are the warriors, the wizards. They have swords and magic. I can only heal …"

"You can do much more than this. There are perils that cannot be subdued by steel or spell."

What does she mean?

"I will do what I can – if there is anything I can do."

"You can be yourself, for a start," the priestess said with a smile. "Satō will need your cheerfulness, and Bran-*sama*…" She turned her head towards the door.

"I can hear Tokojiro-*sama* coming. Could you leave us alone for a moment?"

THE WARRIOR'S SOUL

CHAPTER III

He winced, opening his eyes. His face felt sore, tense, and there was something wrong with his vision, although he couldn't pinpoint what. He was lying in the Crane Room, the High Priestess and the interpreter, Tokojiro, sitting by his side staring at him intently.

"Why are you looking at me like that?" he asked the interpreter.

Tokojiro glanced at the High Priestess. Without a word she produced a small, round, mirror of polished bronze. He looked into it warily and then dropped it.

"*By Owain's Sword!* What... What trick is this...?"

The face in the mirror was not his - flat wide nose, narrow eyes, pale-yellow skin, high angular cheekbones. It was the face of a Yamato man. He knew now what was wrong with his vision. He was used to seeing the tip of his hooked Roman nose in the middle of his face. It was gone. He touched his skin. It felt alien, flabby, soft.

"What is this...?" he said, still in shock.

"You have asked me for help."

Tokojiro translated Lady Kazuko's words.

"If you want to seek your *dorako* throughout Yamato, you will need more than just a good disguise. Your current appearance is that of one of the Ancestors in the Cave of Scrying. I trust the ritual was not too painful for you."

"Seek my…"

This wasn't what he had in mind at all. When he had asked for help, he hoped the priestess would use her contacts to expedite his transfer to Dejima or at least let the Bataavians know of the danger posed by Emrys. He never considered actually *travelling* across the unknown alien land in search of the dragon. Certainly not looking like this…

"Can I – can I change back?"

Lady Kazuko smiled encouragingly. "Why don't you try?"

"How? I don't know…"

"Remember how you normally look. Focus your will. The change will come."

It wasn't easy to remember his own face. Bran did not yet shave, so he had little reason to be looking in mirrors. Even though he tried his best, nothing happened at first, but then several muscles in his jaw crackled and moved. He cried out with pain and surprise.

"It hurts," he moaned.

The transformation continued against his will, muscles and joints slithering underneath his skin like living creatures.

"It will get better in time," Lady Kazuko said, leaning over him and touching his face, "so I've read."

Her hand was warm and soothing, but her words were not.

"You've *read*? Then this was something you had never done before?"

"The ritual of the Caves had not been performed since the Civil Wars," the High Priestess admitted with slight embarrassment. "The Spirits in those days had turned... belligerent. It was getting difficult to conduct the ritual peacefully."

Spirits? he thought, trying to understand. *Ancestors? What kind of magic is this? What happened to me in that cave?*

"But you knew it would work for me?" he asked.

"I had prayed it would, but there was always a risk."

"Why didn't you warn me?"

"You told me the *dorako* was your friend. Would you not have faced the risk for a friend's sake?"

Bran thought carefully about the answer. Yes, the priestess was right. What good was notifying the Bataavians? Emrys was *his* dragon, *his* responsibility. He had to find it on his own.

"I would," he admitted at last.

The priestess's face wrinkled in a gentle smile.

"Remember about how you feel right now. Remember this conviction. It will help you go through the hardships of the journey."

Hardships?

"Your face has returned to normal."

The priestess presented him with the mirror again. It reflected his round, jade-green eyes in a Prydain, lightly olive-toned face.

"Try not to do that too often. If you forget to transform back and are seen in public, your life is forfeit," she warned him, and clapped her hands twice.

The door slid open and the two familiar youths came in.

"Now, I believe some introductions are in order." The High Priestess gestured to the two. "You will, after all, travel together."

"We will?"

Bran blinked. How much of this had the woman prepared beforehand? Was it really fine to trust her?

The boy approached first, looking at him slightly suspiciously. He bowed deeply and spoke in a bright tinkling voice. The interpreter tried his best to translate the formal noble manner of the boy's speech.

"I am Takashima Satō. My father is Takashima Shūhan, son of Takashima Shirobei. I am the heir to the Takashima-Ryū School of Western Magic. Pleased to make your acquaintance."

Bran nodded. School of Western Magic… Lady Kazuko had mentioned there were wizards in Yamato and Satō's father was one of them, but a whole *school*? Was Satō a wizard as well?

He looked at the red-haired girl.

"Itō Nagomi…" she said, shyly, "daughter of Itō Keisuke. I'm the apprentice here in Suwa, training to become a priestess. I was with Satō when we found you on the beach…"

Bran bowed back.

"I am Bran ap Dylan o Cantre'r Gwaelod." His name sounded strange to his own ears. "Graduate of Llambed College of Mystic Arts, dragon rider."

"You will all need new identities," declared Lady Kazuko, "and disguises – except Bran-*sama*, of course, he's already as disguised as is possible for a man…"

"Wait," Bran said, raising his hand, "this is all happening very fast, I need time to…"

"I'm afraid there is no time. You must leave today."

"*Today*! But…"

"We don't know when the magistrate will return with a search warrant, how long your *dorako* can stay in captivity. This all means our time is short – very short."

"*The magistrate*? I don't understand any of this."

With Lady Kazuko's permission, Tokojiro quickly explained to Bran the arrival of the magistrate officials at the shrine. The news shook him. Focusing on his own problems he had forgotten of the risk his presence was posing to the others. He glanced at Satō's arm injured arm; the boy was hurt because of him. And the High Priestess – what could happen to her if she was discovered disobeying the laws of the city? He still did not fully understand the situation, but he could clearly sense the overwhelming sense of danger.

"Now you see why we must hasten," the High Priestess said.

"Still – " he replied slowly, hesitating, "is it really safe for me to go outside? I may look like one of you, but I can't yet speak your language, don't know your customs…"

"You have sworn the vows of silence," declared Lady Kazuko, and Bran again wondered how much of this she had planned ahead. "Tokojiro-*sama* has agreed to come with you – as translator and guardian."

"Guardian?"

Bran looked at the young interpreter doubtfully. He noticed Satō doing the same.

"I have the reputation of being as skilled with the sword as with the tongue," Tokojiro said, bowing slightly and smiling. He then repeated it – Bran guessed - in Yamato, for the benefit of incredulous-looking Satō.

"Let us pray your reputation never needs to be tested," said the High Priestess. "If you should encounter on your journey anything you're not capable of dealing with, send word. As long as I'm alive, Suwa will assist you to the best of its abilities. Now, let's not dwell too long on this. Bran-*sama*, a bath is ready for you."

Bran agreed, still a little dazed. He was conscious of the smell of sulphur and sweat that his body emanated and for some reason he was growing increasingly ashamed of it. Nagomi and Satō bowed and left the room hurriedly. Bran stood up, his head spinning slightly, and headed for the door.

"You will need to tie your hair in the samurai manner," Tokojiro said after consulting with Lady Kazuko. "I will help you with that, and with the proper way to walk. Playing dumb will only get you so far if you don't learn a few basics."

What's wrong with the way I walk now?

"*Hai* – yes."

"I'm sorry everything's so sudden," the High Priestess said, pursing her lips. "I know it must be difficult for you."

"It's fine," he replied, though he wasn't certain it was. "I understand it is for the best."

"I'm glad somebody thinks so," she said.

He made sure all the elements of the dark kimono were properly adjusted, the mountain crest on his shoulders – he was now a member of an *Aoki clan*, he reminded himself, like the man whose kimono he was wearing – in plain view. He then felt to see if the newly tied knot of hair at the top of his head was in place, buckled the leather satchel tightly and thrust his Prydain sword into the silk sash. The metal scabbard was painted black and the shrine blacksmith – the moustached man from earlier – had prepared a rough replacement hilt, a long wooden handle wrapped in black cord, that made the cavalry blade look almost like the swords he had seen other Yamato men wear. The proudly sculpted dragon-shaped handgrip, far too elaborate for the simple local style, was hidden in the satchel.

He was trying to wrap his mind around what was happening to him. His face and body changed. He traced the still unfamiliar features with his fingers. The intricacies of the magic involved evaded him – maybe he would understand it better if he knew thaumaturgy. The transformation was perfect, seamless; after the initial odd sensation had passed the new face felt as if it had always been there.

His thoughts… There was something going on there too, something the priestess had not told him about. When he had been given a bowl of breakfast rice, after his bath, his fingers reached for and deftly grasped the quaint bamboo chopsticks. His hand brought morsels of food to his mouth without hesitation, without mistake.

The many-layered robe felt much more familiar than before. The bowing seemed more natural than handshaking. *Something* was happening to him, and he wasn't sure he liked it. The High Priestess didn't know all the details of the ritual. What if the Spirit within was slowly taking him over?

He looked out through the door at the pouring rain. There was no more time to linger. According to Lady Kazuko's plan, Satō, Nagomi and Bran were to leave the shrine one after another at intervals and meet inside an inn at the bottom of the long stairs. Bran was to go last, accompanied by Tokojiro. The interpreter waited impatiently outside under the grey-tiled eaves. It was their moment to leave.

The dragon rider gingerly touched the cold red scabbard of Satō's sword, lying on the straw mat floor. As the Yamato boy was disguising himself as a commoner, he could not bear a weapon – it was decided that Bran would carry it for him. Bran had already noticed that most noblemen in Kiyō walked around with two swords at their belts, so it made sense for him to do so as well. Curious, he pulled out the blade for a few inches. It was of damascene steel of great quality, razor sharp, with a rich hardening pattern and a blacksmith's signature carved near the circular guard.

His Prydain weapon, a sturdy heavy blade of ancient design, was more a mark of his graduation from the Academy than a martial tool. A proud sign of an age-old legacy going back ten centuries to the times when wild dragons roamed the land and brave warriors stood in their way, and later, when dragon riders flew to battle alongside regular horse cavalry against humans cast in steel and mail. A little more than a decorative piece of iron, although the edge was still sharp enough to cut through muscle and bone. Yes, it could maim and, in skilled hands, kill. The runes carved along the fuller shimmered with gentle magic at the touch. They enabled the sword to break through magical shields and armour. Bran was taught how to use it to hack and slash with great force, like a carving axe or, in a bind, thrust.

A sword was never the primary weapon of the dragon rider – Soul Lance against the scale, magic against the shield, dragon against everything else. This was what the Academy had taught him. Other than the symbol of prestige, the sword would only be used in self-defence, when all else failed. Some young riders even went as far as to forgo the sword and replace it with a lightning pistol or pneumatic rifle. They would certainly prove more useful in this age of mistfire and thaumaturgy.

Looking at Satō's sword Bran recognised a weapon designed with just one purpose in mind – to kill a man with a single, fast, precise strike. It was sharp enough to cut through a falling piece of paper. It was well balanced, swift and strong, flexible enough not to snap and hard enough not to bend. The steel was of fantastic quality, the craftsmanship involved incredible – but there were no ornaments on the hilt other than a butterfly crest on the handguard, no superfluous carvings on the scabbard. This was the product of a culture that still esteemed swords as the main armament of a warrior, and knew their value. The boy was certain the blade could easily slash off a man's arm, leg, or even, with enough skill and strength, a head. But there was no magic about it. A simple *bwcler* would hold the deadly edge back. This was the most interesting bit of information, and Bran made sure to remember it well.

He thought again of the two men duelling in the streets of Kiyō and wondered whether Satō had also been trained to so ruthlessly destroy a human life. He must have been. The Yamato boy was of a soldier's age and bore the sword effortlessly. Admiring the blade, Bran was glad to have its owner on his side.

I owned a blade like this once, he thought. *It's a Matsubara if ever I saw one.*

"No, I didn't," he corrected himself immediately, startled. "I have no idea what a Matsubara sword is."

He waited for a moment to see if the strange memory would return but there was nothing but silence inside his head now. He sheathed Satō's sword, stuck it in the sash beside the Prydain blade and went outside.

Dear Tokojiro

How have you been? Edo is cold and wet right now. How's the weather in Kiyō? Oh, how I miss the sun of Chinzei!

Did you like the salted beef I sent you? It's of the same cattle that feed the Taikun's army. I hope it was to your liking. Not as good as Kuma horsemeat, I bet!

Regarding your question – no, unfortunately the court is still not looking for an interpreter of the Seaxe tongue. I assure you, if there is any need I will recommend you for a position at once.

Please take care of yourself,

Einosuke.

Tokojiro crushed the letter in his hand and threw it into the corner of the room in anger. Damned Einosuke - always so nice, always so proper.

"*Did you like the salted beef?*" He mocked the letter aloud. "The pox on you and your beef! Why don't you give me your *job* instead?"

Eight years had passed since the fourteen of them had met for the first time in Black Raven's little class, sitting around the cage in which he had been imprisoned. The mysterious Barbarian, who looked and spoke like a Yamato man, was teaching them Seaxe, the language of Dracaland, a nation of which they had only heard sometimes in Bataavian reports.

"They will come," he had been telling them, "one day. They are already at your doorstep, in Qin, and their ships are big and fast. Not only the Dracalish – others will come too - the Midgardians and maybe even the Gorllewin, all of them understanding Seaxe much better than your Bataavian. Nobody speaks Bataavian except Bataavians. When they all come you will be sent out to greet them, trade with them and negotiate with them. Your ability will be priceless."

They believed him, why not? With his almost-Yamato narrow-eyed face and almost-Yamato speech, he seemed to them like a messenger from the Gods. As the Gods had brought humanity the skill of planting rice and casting iron, so did Black Raven bring new forbidden knowledge to the chosen few. They were his disciples, his apostles. They were young and full of dreams.

And then everything turned to ruin. Black Raven disappeared and his students were accused of aiding his escape – treason of the highest order. Ten of them were executed. Two managed to run away, to vanish without a trace. Tokojiro fled to the Suwa Shrine, where the High Priestess agreed to hide him until the scandal quietened down. And Einosuke...

Einosuke was already safe in Edo by that time, as the official Seaxe interpreter to the *Taikun*'s court. And there had only ever been one interpreter needed. Despite Black Raven's warnings, the Dracalish never came. Tokojiro, his name blemished by the *bugyō's* accusations, equipped only with the knowledge of an unusable language, could find no employment. His samurai stipend was only enough to keep sobriety at bay. At the age of twenty six his life was as good as forfeit.

Now, though, it seemed the Gods took pity on him. With one stroke of luck, the hapless interpreter had gained a chance to prove his loyalty to the *Taikun* – which would no doubt be rewarded – and humiliate the *bugyō,* who had persecuted him so wrongfully.

He put a straw cloak on top of his brown kimono and walked out into the rain. It was time for him to accompany the Western boy on his strange adventure.

The gardens of Suwa Shrine exploded with mounds of purple, blue, pink and red. All the flowers opened to drink the most of the first strong rain of the season. Bran didn't know the names of most of them. A storm of lilac icicles hung from the eaves, frayed balls of crimson and mauve burst on the bushes below. Late magnolias still clung to the green branches, like great white and scarlet butterflies frozen in time in their finest hour. Spiral fireworks of icy white erupted along the walls and streams. Heaps of otherworldly pinks and reds exploded with a dizzying sweet smell. The air was so dense with fragrance that it turned almost tangible, edible; an air one wished to drink, or bathe in like perfume.

The lanes and avenues of the shrine were being decorated for some upcoming event. Along every path were strung ropes of colourful paper ribbons, fluttering in the wind in their hundreds. There were few people on the shrine grounds at this time of day, in this weather.

At first Bran was apprehensive – he had been hidden for so long, he was used to skulking and creeping along the eaves. Unnoticed, he passed towards the main gate, a great, heavily ornamented construction of gilded wood. He

65

stopped for a moment, ostensibly to admire the intricacies of the carvings, the workmanship involved in the building. In truth, passing this threshold was a difficult decision. Outside was an unknown dangerous world, a world where the only protection he could trust would be his own wit and strength.

There were dragons carved upon the gate, winged and wingless ones, and horses and fish with dragon heads. The craftsmen who had built the shrine seemed obsessed with the creatures. Bran wondered again about the Yamato dragons. He had seen them painted and sculptured throughout the shrine, but no live ones. Then again, he had not seen much of Yamato outside the shrine and the nurse's house, either.

Tokojiro coughed, urging him to hurry. Taking the presence of dragons on the gate as a good omen, Bran stepped forwards. He looked down and his heart froze. Up the stairs marched a troop of armed and armoured men in rich clothes. The *samurai*, Bran remembered the interpreter's explanation, the knights of Yamato. He was to pretend to be one of them. They were led by a grim-faced official in a wide-brimmed lacquered hat, accompanied by a standard-bearer. There was nowhere to hide at the top of the long empty stairs. He had to pass them.

He tried to look inconspicuous, which seemed to work at first – but after a few steps one of the samurai turned towards the boy angrily, waving his little wooden paddle like a sword, and launched into a furious tirade. One of his men drew his weapon halfway out of the scabbard, threateningly.

Bran started panicking. He had no idea what he had done wrong, or how to appease the angry man. He looked at

Tokojiro, pleadingly. The interpreter suddenly grabbed the boy by the shoulder and cast him forcefully to his knees. He spoke to the samurai, bowing deeply. Bran caught the word *Karasu* spoken several times – it was the name he had taken as part of his disguise, meaning "Crow", a name written on hastily forged identity papers he had been given by the High Priestess. The men laughed and sneered. One of them kicked Bran playfully then the group moved on upwards.

"Apologies, Bran-*sama*," said Tokojiro when they continued down the stairs.

"I don't understand, what happened?"

"The *bugyō* holds the highest office in the city. Above him is only the *Taikun* and the divine *Mikado*. You have insulted him greatly by not bowing first. Even if you did, you would probably still insult him."

"How come?"

"It's important how low to bow before whom. In this case, a long bow, bent in half, and you wait in this position until he responds."

"Why did they leave us alone?"

The interpreter smirked.

"I told them you were my cousin who was dumb and weak in the head. If I hadn't been with you, they would have cut you down on the spot."

"Cut me…" Bran remembered the two swordsmen, "for not bowing properly?"

"Of course," Tokojiro scoffed. "You must learn these things if you wish to survive. For now, just observe me and

67

play dumb." Saying this, he bowed slightly in the direction of another samurai passing them by. Bran repeated the nod. "That was my equal, a mid-ranking samurai, so we only needed a little more than a nod, and it didn't matter who bowed first. Never bow first to one lower than you, and *never* bow to a commoner."

"How did you know what rank he is?"

"In this case, I knew the man personally, but you can tell by the way men dress, walk, speak, if you're observant. Now be quiet," Tokojiro warned him, as they reached the bottom of the stairs and found themselves at a crowded street running along a narrow canal, in front of what Bran guessed was an inn.

It was Nagomi who found them, as Bran was looking for her fruitlessly. He would not have recognised her easily with her jet-black hair tied in a bun and the simple travelling clothes she was wearing instead of the shrine uniform.

She exchanged a few questions with the interpreter then they went towards the stables.

"The hair…" Bran whispered, reaching out a pointing finger. Tokojiro translated.

"I dyed it with a mixture from Kazuko-*hime*. It would be too conspicuous otherwise."

"I… I liked your real hair better," he said with a honesty which surprised him.

The girl blushed slightly and looked away.

"Let's find Satō."

They could not find the boy anywhere.

"Where is he? The rain is getting stronger."

Bran was growing irritated. He still could not shake off the edginess brought on by the incident at the gate and the nagging feeling of something odd happening to his mind. There were too many people around, too many men, armed and scowling. They needed to move on.

A street boy, all bent in polite bows, clothed in the stained cotton jacket of a commoner, torn at the elbows, approached Bran trying to sell him a tattered paper umbrella. The dragon rider waved him away, but the boy insisted, pushing against Bran with his wares. Annoyed and frightened that he would be recognised, he tried to evade the peddler. At last he looked at the boy's face, dirty under the straw conical hat.

"Sa-!" he started, but the boy put a hand on his mouth.

His face beamed with a wide smile, showing milky-white teeth, contrasting with the colour of his skin, bronzed with soot.

"Good, we're all together now." Tokojiro appeared between them glancing around nervously. "Let's get out of here."

Bran followed the others into the criss-crossing network of narrow streets of the merchant district. They were slowly directing themselves towards the southern borders of the city.

An endless array of tiny shops, workshops and dining establishments lined the thoroughfares on both sides. It seemed almost every house had some kind of mercantile enterprise going on at the ground floor, with sliding doors opened wide invitingly under a piece of green or blue cotton. The whole district was one big market. Nobody here afforded a moment of idleness. Entire families of owners worked in these businesses, from pretty young girls inviting clients in, to shrivelled old grannies dusting the shelves.

The wide avenues lined with peach and plum trees soon gave way to the winding paths of the residential area sprawling over the low hills south-east of the city. The houses here were small and narrow, with open windows and doorways staring at each other across the street. As the hills rose and the buildings grew more scarce, all the roads eventually combined into one highway leading towards a mountain pass. Rows of meagre narrow houses, covered with thin thatch, lined the road.

"Who lives here?" Bran asked.

"Servants, cleaners and seasonal workers," answered Tokojiro. "Those who keep the city working."

Beyond the pass the road descended slowly into a narrow canyon, its banks covered with dark unkempt conifer forest. The landscape here, in the low mountains surrounding the city, was one to which Bran was more accustomed.

"These woods look just like the ones in Gwynedd, my homeland," he remarked.

They didn't speak much as they walked down the road, keen not to draw attention to themselves. There were crowds moving in both directions along the thoroughfare and he had to pause between sentences whenever a stranger was passing them by, waiting until Tokojiro translated his words. All the questions crowding in his head had to wait for when they were alone.

"It seems most of the world between here and Dracaland is covered by jungle or desert."

"You must have travelled a lot?" asked Satō.

"It was my first journey." Bran smiled, pleased to talk about something other than the urgency of his plight. "Six months sailing from the port of Brigstow to Fan Yu in Qin. Twenty thousand miles, over three oceans," he added, proudly.

"I have never even been out to sea," said Nagomi, chuckling at herself. "A Kiyō girl, can you believe it?"

"I have never been farther out than Naniwa," said Satō, "and that was a long time ago, before my father's arrest. I only remember waiting for the tides to change at Tomonoura…"

"I've only been a passenger on the ship," Bran said. "I didn't do any sailor's work. Walking is challenging enough for me. How far do we have to go today?"

There was no answer – the interpreter was silent. The boy looked up. Tokojiro was looking back towards the city, not paying him any attention.

"Sir?"

"Ah, yes, I'm sorry." Tokojiro turned back towards Bran. "You were saying?"

Bran repeated the question and this time it was promptly translated.

"Mogi is our first stop – a fishing harbour on the eastern coast," the Yamato boy replied. "We should reach it easily before sunset if nothing slows us down. Beyond this valley it's just one *ri* downhill, along the river. Lady Kazuko mentioned a *Butsu* temple that can accommodate us."

"I hope she's right," added the interpreter. "there are only few inns in Mogi and the harbour may be crowded today."

"Crowded? Why?" asked Bran.

"Tomorrow is the great festival of rice planting at Suwa," explained Tokojiro, "and there will be many pilgrims arriving to Mogi from the big cities on the other side of the bay."

"I see," Bran said, nodding.

He glanced back to see what Tokojiro was looking at, but could see nothing except the narrow road winding among the trees.

CHAPTER IV

When he awoke, Shūhan found himself lying on a cold stone floor in a straw-padded chamber. The setting sun's red light penetrated through a narrow window fortified with sturdy bamboo bars. He was gagged with a piece of cloth, his arms and legs tied tightly with a single length of rope, his fingers bound stiff to bamboo sticks so that he could not cast even the weakest of enchantments.

The burn wounds he had suffered from magical energies and the dagger cut in his side had been treated roughly to ensure he would not die, but not enough to diminish the pain. He was stripped to the loincloth and shivering from the cold.

A door opened and into the cell came his adversary in the long crimson robe, hair tied neatly in a ponytail. His face was gaunt and pale-yellow like old paper, once handsome but now twisted perpetually in a mocking scowl. A crest of a black eight-headed serpent adorned his chest. He crouched before Shūhan with a mocking smile. The wizard winced at the strong odour of blood and death surrounding the creature.

"That was quite a trick you pulled off there. I had to port us out of the city to break down your defences. Almost ruined my plans, that."

Shūhan closed his eyes, relieved. He had bought Satō enough time to reach safety.

"But I've got you, and that should be enough. I'm sure you can tell me everything I need to know. Don't look at me like that!" the man protested. "We are both noblemen. I won't dishonour you with torture. I don't need to torture people to learn their secrets," he continued, his smirk revealing sharp, blackened teeth. "At least not anymore, not since I have my Tetsu."

He rose and called out. A creature of nightmares stepped slowly and hesitantly into the cell. It was clad in the orange robes of a *Butsu* monk. Black, parchment-like skin barely covered the bones and joints. Its face was a skull covered with thin leather, with gaping holes where the eyes and nose would be and an eternal creepy smile of gumless lipless jaws. It moved slowly, feeling its way with a claw-like hand. The smell of forbidden alchemy and arsenic surrounding the monstrosity was overwhelmingly nauseating. Shūhan jerked back in horror, but the ropes held him in place.

"Isn't he remarkable?" chuckled the Crimson Robe, guiding the mummy to its place in front of Shūhan. "I found him twenty years ago at Yudono. I didn't even know anyone still practised the art of *sokukamibutsu*. Don't mind him, it will take him a few minutes to warm up," he remarked as the mummy settled uneasily on the floor.

74

"When alive, he was a celebrated monk at the Chūren Temple. I have observed him for three years. Do you know what they do there? It's really quite admirable. They starve themselves for years, living on nothing but berries and nuts. Then for a thousand days they only drink tea made from the sap of the lacquer tree. That mummifies them from the inside. Imagine the pain! After that, they seal themselves in airtight tombs until they finally die."

"The disciples wait for another thousand days before opening the coffin and venerating the mummy, but I did not wait that long. I opened the tomb after five hundred days, just enough for poor Tetsu to attain the Third Power, the Knowledge of Minds. That's when I turned him into my slave." He patted the mummy with a smile. "It was easy enough, as he was already dead anyway!" He chuckled, boastfully. "It looks like he's almost ready."

Shūhan looked at the creature before him with deep compassion. Here was a monk of such rare piety and devotion that he had managed to fully perform the deadly *sokukamibutsu* ritual. If left undisturbed, he would no doubt have become a living incarnation of *Butsu* and now be venerated in a temple of his own. Instead, the wretched creature was suspended halfway between mortal life and Enlightenment, a fate a hundred times worse than simply dying.

As he reflected on the sorry state of the monk, the wizard felt a probing presence in his mind. He could do nothing about it. The mummy stared at him with the gaping eyeholes, reading his every hidden thought with such ease as if his mind was an open book.

The Crimson Robe spoke again, this time addressing Tetsu.

"Where is the *Gaikokujin*?"

In his head, Shūhan saw a kaleidoscope of random scenes from the recent past as the mummy browsed through the memories searching for the ones that would best answer the question. Eventually the wretched monster opened its ever-smiling jaws and produced a croaking struggling sound that could hardly be recognised as speech.

"In a large shrine on the mountain top."

"Suwa. I thought so. What is he doing in Yamato?"

There was another quick browse through the wizard's memories and the creature croaked again.

"He is cast away on a beam of light. Lost. Alone."

"What do you mean *on a beam of light*?"

"It has been said so."

"How odd. Does he know anything more about the *Gaikokujin*?" the golden-eyed man asked, nodding at Shūhan. "Tell me all. What are his plans?"

"It is not known."

"What about the Shard?"

"It is not known."

The monk jolted back as if startled by something in the wizard's mind.

"What is it?"

"It has been said the boy flies on a *ryū*."

"A dragon rider? Now that *is* interesting, but where's the dragon?"

"It is not known. The boy is alone."

"You don't really know much, eh?" The Crimson One leaned over Shūhan. "All right, no point in torturing poor Tetsu anymore. You may go."

The mummy rose slowly and made its hobbling way to the exit.

"Now, that wasn't so bad, was it?" The Crimson One smirked at the wizard. "I think I'll keep you here. If you play nicely, I may even ungag you and we can have a proper conversation."

The wizard was left alone. He was satisfied with how the interrogation had gone. It had been wise of him not to let Satō babble too much about the Westerner. He didn't even know the boy's name. That the dragon rider was hiding in Suwa was obvious. This was where Nagomi lived – and if the enemy knew so much, he must have known about the young apprentice too – and this was where he hoped Satō had escaped. Something was telling him the Crimson Robe would not strike at the shrine. Not yet, at least.

The girl was safe. Nothing else was important.

The sun was almost set beyond the mountains when they finally reached Mogi, nestled between a line of low forested hills and a narrow inlet of the Amakusa Bay. Tokojiro halted for a moment, taking in the view. Even though Mogi was a mere half-day's walk from Kiyō, he had not visited it in years.

What have I been doing all this time?

"What is this blossom?" asked the Westerner, as the road led them down among palm-like trees, heaving under the weight of large, stacked white flowers. The orchard was filled with the low droning hum of thick hairy bumblebees and the intermittent buzz of honey bees, dizzy with the abundance of nectar.

When will his questions stop? It had been like this ever since they left the shrine. The boy was curious about everything he had seen in the city. Tofu curd, *cha*, fish, brooms, fans, even roof tiles and details of clothing. He kept asking, keen to learn new words, new things. Once Tokojiro would have found it endearing. He used to be such a curious boy too, a long time ago. There was no harm in trying to learn about the world, was there?

"*Biwa*," he explained, sighing, "the town is famous for it. In summer it produces sweet yellow fruit. I believe it came from Qin."

She used to wear it in her hair.

The first two small inns in the village were both full, just as he had predicted.

"There's no point in looking any further," the Takashima girl decided, "it's going to be like this everywhere. Let's go and see that temple."

"I agree," said Tokojiro, absentmindedly. He looked back towards Kiyō again.

The Shiomisaki Temple of the Merciful Bodhisattva was built on a narrow peninsula jutting out into the bay on the south-eastern end of the village. A sandy path through the bamboo grove led to the top of a low rolling dune, overgrown with tall, wind-tattered pines, just as Tokojiro remembered.

The old wooden hall of the merciful Goddess Kannon emerged from among the black pines. One of the orange-robed monks was just finishing his evening prayers. He jumped off the veranda with agile keenness, bowed with hands put together and looked at the travellers curiously.

"We bring greetings from Kazuko-*hime* of Suwa, and humbly request a place to spend the night," said the apprentice girl, bowing.

"From Suwa? Of course, of course, follow me!" The monk led them to the white building. "I'm afraid we cannot offer you the comforts of a guesthouse, but there is a roof above and a straw mat below."

"That will be more than sufficient," replied the apprentice graciously.

Having eaten what small packed meals they had brought from the shrine, the travellers were accommodated in two neighbouring rooms separated by a thin paper wall – the girls in one, Tokojiro and Bran in the other.

"There is only one *futon*," said the interpreter, sliding open a cupboard sunken into the wall, "you can have it."

"You mean a mattress, don't you?" the Westerner guessed. "What do you call the blanket?"

'*Mōfu*,' Tokojiro replied, sighing heavily. He was standing by the narrow shutterless window, peering outside discreetly. "*Kakebuton* if it's a winter one."

"So how did you learn Seaxe so well?" the boy asked, preparing his bedding. "Who is this Black Raven of whom you spoke?"

Tokojiro turned away from the window and stared at the boy. Now there was an interesting question at last. He sat down cross-legged.

"I was eighteen when I met him… He came from a distant land across the Great Sea – one we did not know from Bataavian maps. A castaway like you, except that he had been cast off a beach in the northern island, Ezo. He was eventually brought to Kiyō, but along the way he had learned our language well enough to teach us his own."

"Black Raven is an unusual name."

"He was not a usual man. In his land he was a great prince, or so he said. He looked like one of us… He believed his people had come from Yamato. That's why he had sailed here, to find the land of his ancestors. We greatly respected him for that – we, the Yamato, worship our ancestors like the Gods. He was imprisoned in Kiyō, near Sōfukuji, but allowed to have visitors. He would teach anyone who wanted to learn."

"What happened to him?"

"Black Raven's gone," Tokojiro said with a shrug.

"Executed?"

"No, he was too precious to be killed. He just… vanished from his cage one day."

"I could be precious…" the boy said quietly, thinking about something.

Tokojiro laughed, somewhat more bitterly than he intended. If only the boy knew how precious he really was… He stood up and glanced through the window again. "If you'll excuse me, I have to check something outside. You should probably go to sleep now. It would be good to move out as early as possible."

"We don't even know where exactly to go…" said the boy, yawning, "but I suppose you're right. You can have this… *mōfu*, it's a warm night."

Tokojiro accepted the blanket with an embarrassed bow.

He's not a bad boy. More's the pity…

The moon shone faintly from beyond the clouds, but Tokojiro did not need much light to find his way to the back of the white-washed building where they had been accommodated, down a sandy path among the black pines and up a low grassy mound overlooking the sea, where a few monoliths of black stone marked the graves of those who had died in the service of the temple.

He lay a twig of *biwa* flowers on the top of one of them and bowed, silently.

THE WARRIOR'S SOUL

You would not approve of what I'm about to do, he thought. *You'd find a way to convince me I was wrong.*

But it was too late. The wheels had been set in motion. Turning back towards the temple he saw a faint shining dot of a lantern moving stealthily among the trees.

It was a night of unquiet slumber. Bran dreamt of ancient conflicts, of great, multi-tiered castles of whitewashed stone under siege. He dreamt of the samurai warriors charging against stone ramparts, brandishing long sharp blades under a hail of arrows. Of destruction and death, bodies filling up the moat, floating down a river red with blood.

He then dreamt of women in silk flowery robes, their faces painted with white lead and lips daubed with crimson, young and old, all beautiful and eager to please their lord with their dance and song – and their bodies, pale and soft to touch.

He dreamt of falconry and hunting, of drinking expensive *cha* and sniffing precious incense, of reading poetry and writing calligraphy, of tasting refined food and admiring meticulously arranged flowers.

Bran awoke in the middle of the night. For the most part the visions quickly perished from his memory, the details difficult to retain, but the overwhelming feeling of their *reality* remained. These weren't just dreams – these were somebody's memories. And now they became *his* memories.

As a boy of barely sixteen, he had seen only a few dead bodies at family wakes. He saw some soldiers of the Second Regiment wounded in fighting. He had kissed a couple of girls, he had *played* at war. But as the Spirit whose memories he shared in his sleep, he had lived and loved, killed and died – all within a span of one night. Who was the mysterious man from his dreams? A warrior – a leader of men, a general without a name…

His head hurt and he felt nauseous. He shuddered. The night was cold after all. He now wished he hadn't given the interpreter the blanket.

The boy's eyes tried to pierce the darkness to find sleeping Tokojiro, but he couldn't see him anywhere in the room. He was too sleepy and tired to wonder about it. He fell asleep again, and his dreams were again haunted by memories of another man. He was back in some courtly mansion among poets, warriors and philosophers.

It was the last night before the great battle. They all watched him dance a slow methodical dance. He sang a majestic measured chant, the words of which he – dreaming Bran – could not understand.

Saké wa nome nome, nomu naraba

Hi no moto ichi no kono yari wo

Nomitoru hodo ni, nomu naraba

Kore zo makoto no Kuroda-bushi

He finished and gulped a great cup of saké, given to him by an attendant. Everyone cheered. A woman came up to him, smiling, inviting, her brocade robes smelling of rosewood and cherry blossom.

"Shigemasa-*dono*," she said, bowing, before leading him to her bedchamber.

As she lay on a silk futon, he started to disrobe himself, but his arms became entangled in the sleeves of the kimono. He stumbled clumsily over his *hakama* skirt and fell onto the futon. The more he tried to wriggle out, the more the bed sheets and layers of clothes wrapped around him. He wanted to scream, but couldn't, his mouth refused to open. He struggled in panic, unable to make a sound. The woman disappeared somewhere in the darkness.

Bran woke up. He was still bound. He was lying on the straw mat with a rope tight around his hands and legs, a cloth gag in his mouth. Tokojiro was standing above him with a paper lantern, watching.

"Good, you're awake. The *Taikun*'s men should be here any minute."

"Mmrph?" Bran muttered through the cloth.

"Why?" the interpreter guessed. "I may be destitute and unemployed, but I'm still a samurai. I'm loyal to my masters, and to the *Taikun*. You're a wanted fugitive; did you think I would let you go simply because some priestess told me to? I just did not wish the magistrate to lay their hands on you. The *bugyō* doesn't deserve such a prize." He glanced through the window. "They're coming. Don't try to transform back to your Yamato face," he advised.

Bran realised he had slipped back to his usual looks while he slept.

"I'm not sure how that will work with a gag in your mouth, and I need a way to prove it's really you."

Bran thought fast, desperately. Gagged and bound he could not invoke the power of dragonflame – even if his link with Emrys was strong enough. The Soul Lance was also out of the question. He could maybe surround himself with a *tarian*, but what good would it do him?

That he was not yet dead meant he was worth something to his captors. Perhaps he could negotiate… Perhaps Nagomi and Satō could help him…

He had forgotten all about them! He turned his head towards the thin paper wall. Tokojiro noticed this.

"They can't help you. I took care of them in the same way. Don't worry, these men are only coming for you, they're not interested in your companions – although the magistrate might be, I suppose…"

Bran started wriggling desperately, trying to release himself from the bonds, but Tokojiro put his foot on the boy's stomach.

"Please stop. You're only hurting yourself. I know how to tie ropes; the more you struggle, the worse it will get."

"*He's bluffing,*" a voice spoke suddenly in Bran's head.

"What… Who is that? Is that you – the Spirit?"

"*A child could get out of these knots.*"

"You – you are Lord Shigemasa, aren't you?" Bran remembered the name from his dreams. "I can understand you!"

"*I am Taishō Itakura Shigemasa of Mikawa,*" the voice in his head grew louder and stronger, "*our souls are bound, it seems we can talk without words.*"

"Can you help me?"

"*Only if you let me. Open your mind, so I can reach you - your joints, muscles, limbs… then I can try to release us from this amateur's trap.*"

"How do I do that?"

"*I don't know, Barbarian. I've never done this before. Improvise, but be quick about it.*"

Not really sure what it was that he was supposed to do, Bran imagined himself floating away into the recesses of his consciousness. Immediately, the general's Spirit jumped forwards, pushing the boy's mind even farther back, giving Bran a glimpse of what it felt like to be a ghost attached to someone else's body.

Bran's muscles momentarily went limp, and the rope fell loose off his limbs. Before Tokojiro could react, Bran's body jumped upright, shaking the interpreter off. Tokojiro drew his sword and tried to strike the boy, but Shigemasa, in full control of Bran's movements, reached with his hand, grabbed Tokojiro by the wrist and twisted. Everything happened too fast for Bran to see clearly. Within moments, Tokojiro was lying on the floor, clutching his face. Blood spurted from between his fingers, from a cut dealt with his own blade, now in Bran's – the general's - hand.

"*Thou art no warrior.*" Shigemasa spat out the gag and scoffed through Bran's lips. "*Thou art naught but a craven coward.*"

The door slid open loudly and four other samurai rushed inside, all wearing a mallow crest on their clothes, brandishing long silver swords, ready to fight.

Bran could sense the general calculate his chances. Shigemasa decided to flee.

"*No!*" the boy cried into the void. "We mustn't leave the others alone!"

It was too late. The general kicked his way through the outer wall of thin bamboo and straw, and leapt outside into the darkness.

Something was very, very wrong.

The moment Satō awoke, sensing her wrists and ankles tied up, she understood what had happened. They had been betrayed. Dryness and a bitter taste in her mouth told her they had been given a sleeping herb in their evening *cha* – skullcap leaf, most likely. That's why she hadn't woken when the interpreter was tying her up.

She looked around. Nagomi was still sleeping. The light from a small lantern was seeping from the room on the other side of the paper wall. She could see the silhouette of a man leaning over something – she guessed it was Bran, no doubt bound like they were. The boy must have been Tokojiro's main target and the reason for betrayal, but why now? Why not give them up back in Kiyō?

There was no time to think about such things. She had to set herself and Nagomi free. Luckily Tokojiro was not only a traitor, but also a fool. He had forgotten to gag her. Did he not know that all a wizard needed to perform magic was his mouth?

Without a blade to focus or fingers to weave patterns, all she could do was cast the simplest of spells. She hoped it would be enough.

"*Ijslaag!*" she commanded the elements.

Her hands, the only conduit she could use, were covered with a layer of ice – thin at first then growing thicker as the spell sucked moisture out of the humid air. Her skin was freezing, but so was the rope. The jute fibre became brittle. Her training made her endure the horrific temperature long enough for the rope to reach snapping point.

"*Genoeg*," she whispered with blue trembling lips.

The ice dissipated. The remains of the shattered broken rope fell from her wrists. She felt around the floor and found her dagger – another reckless omission on the part of the traitor. She cut the knots between her ankles and stood up.

There was a commotion in the room next door. She saw silhouettes of four men jump inside, swords in hand. She saw Bran steal the interpreter's weapon with an amazing agility and then disappear through the wall. The four men followed. Tokojiro screamed in a shrieking panicky voice.

Nagomi stirred awake. Satō cut her binds with the dagger.

"What's going on?"

The apprentice looked around her, numb and bewildered.

"*Get up*," the wizardess commanded sharply, "we've been attacked."

"Bran-*sama*?"

"He ran away – I think. Stay here. I'll see what's going on."

Satō slid open the paper panel dividing the rooms. The first thing she saw was Tokojiro crawling on the floor, blood pouring from between his fingers smearing the straw mats. A hole was torn in the outer wall. All Bran's things were still there, including the Matsubara sword Satō had entrusted to his care.

She picked it up and pointed it at the interpreter. Tokojiro only now noticed her presence and the tip of the blade aimed at his head. He reached out his hand in feeble defence. An ugly bleeding scar ran right across his face through his left eye – now rendered useless – nose, corner of his mouth and chin.

"No, please… Don't kill me…" he begged, gurgling through blood.

"What have you done? Why? Who are these people?"

Satō spat out the questions in quick succession.

"*Taikun*'s men… I only wanted to… prove my loyalty…"

The wizardess lowered her sword. This was a sentiment to which she, daughter of a samurai, could relate. At that moment Tokojiro shrieked and leapt at her with surprising swiftness. She fell to the floor. The interpreter's one healthy eye looked at her with an odd combination of gratitude and hatred and he scrambled hastily on all fours outside.

Nagomi ran up to her.

"Are you all right?"

"Yes. Quick, he must not get away…"

"What about Bran-*sama*?"

Satō hesitated. They had barely left Kiyō and she already had to make a decision on her own. She glanced at the corridor where the interpreter had disappeared, then at the hole torn in the wall through which the Westerner fled, pursued by the swordsmen. She nodded to herself.

"Let's go."

They hurried through the pine forest, lighting their way with the paper lantern, Satō in front, trying to track the foreigner and the men who had attacked him.

It wasn't easy to follow the tracks in the darkness. Soon she lost all trace of the boy and could only spot the four sets of footprints left by his assailants in the sandy floor of the forest.

She kept thinking of Tokojiro's betrayal. How could they have made such a mistake? How could the High Priestess have trusted the interpreter so blindly? She should have guessed a true samurai would keep to his old loyalties.

It's a wonder we are still alive – but for how long? She shook her head. It was not the time to fall into despair. There was a clear task before her. One thing at a time.

"They separated here," she said, kneeling in the dirt. "I think they lost him as well. He was running really fast!"

Typical Barbarian, better at running than at fighting.

"Where did you learn to track?" asked Nagomi, catching her breath. "I can't see anything."

"My old man took me hunting on Mount Inasa a few times, testing the airguns. That was when mother was still alive and we would..." She stopped talking and raised her hand. *I can hear them*, she mouthed silently, and pointed to her right, from where the faint sound of conversation was coming. *Stay here*, she gestured, and started creeping through the undergrowth.

In the faint moonlight she saw three of the four *Taikun*'s samurai. One was lying dead, his blood staining the sand scarlet. Two others were standing over him, uncertain.

"Nobody told us the boy was good with a blade," said one, looking around warily.

"Don't be absurd, Tendō, he just got lucky," replied the other.

"Are you blind, Saotome? That's a masterly cut." The first one pointed to the dead body with the tip of his scabbard. "Where did he learn to fight with katana?"

"It doesn't matter. There are three of us with Hibiki, and one of him. We just need to stick together."

"And where is Hibiki?" The first samurai's voice was increasingly shaky. "He was supposed to be here by now."

"He'll come, don't worry, and the boy can't be far away. We'll catch him before dawn."

Satō listened to the conversation with increasing amazement. What were they talking about? Bran – master of the sword? It didn't make any sense. He had no samurai training. He may have been a soldier back in his homeland, but she had held his Western sword in her hands – it was a heavy, unwieldy, badly balanced hatchet, there was no way somebody familiar only with that blade could handle a katana with ease.

Suddenly the bushes parted and the fourth warrior appeared in the glade, clutching his stomach.

"*Hibiki!*"

The other two ran over. The samurai slipped to his knees, gasping for air.

Satō could not comprehend what she was witnessing. She considered Bran amusingly helpless, a nice boy who could tell her about dragons, but was generally useless, like most foreigners. It seemed she couldn't have been more wrong.

She slowly crept back to Nagomi who was crouching under a big larch, trying to hide herself as best she could.

"Bran-*sama* is here somewhere. He's alive and free," she told the apprentice, whose face lit up with joy and relief. "Let's try that way."

She had to find him. She had to learn his secret.

CHAPTER V

There was darkness at first, and emptiness. No sensations, nothing to touch, smell or see. He was *nowhere*. Cut off from the reality around him, from his own body, he found himself in a hollow featureless void.

Slowly some shapes began to emerge from the darkness all around him. A red light pulsed in the distance. As the veil lifted, he found himself lying on a vast barren plain of red-brown dust, with a tall spire of grey stone rising on the horizon. It was from the top of this spire that the red light was coming, like the beacon of a lighthouse.

He heard a voice booming, God-like throughout the strange domain - the sound of General Shigemasa's thoughts. Was this how the Spirits experienced the reality? Was this what Shigemasa's world was like ever since his soul fused with Bran's in the cave?

Or was he still dreaming…? There was no magic that could rip the consciousness straight out of one's body and cast it into this empty realm of nothingness. There couldn't have been. It was all a nightmare. Soon he would wake and everything would be back to normal.

Something appeared in the sky, coming from the direction of the tower. A speck at first, bright green against the auburn clouds, it grew into the familiar silhouette of a jade dragon.

"*Emrys?*"

The dragon landed gracefully on the dust and chirped welcomingly. It seemed real enough… Even the faint smell of brimstone and methane was there. Bran touched the beast carefully. In an instant, he was flooded with images and emotions, just as if he was using Farlink – but far stronger than ever before. The cage, the hunger, the bewilderment… he let go of the dragon and breathed out.

He was beginning to get the idea of what was happening to him. The world around him was, somehow, an image in his mind. The dragon represented the Farlink connection. The pulsating, beckoning red light remained a mystery, but there was no other feature in the landscape. Was this where he had to go to regain control over his body?

Bran looked doubtfully at the jade dragon beside him. Would it accept commands from him, just like the real Emrys? Was there such a thing as a Farlink to the Farlink? He climbed upon the dragon's body as he would normally. Emrys lowered its head and spread its wings ready to fly.

So far so good.

He could hear Shigemasa's loud euphoric thoughts. The general was overcome with joy at having a body of his own again. The red light projected images from the Taishō's eyes upon the auburn sky, the red clouds serving as an enormous screen – a samurai emerged from among the pine trees, sword lowered, unwary. The general cut him down with one stroke, without mercy. Blood stained the sand.

Emrys launched into flight. They were heading straight for the spire of grey stone. There was nothing but the featureless plain before him. If the general was at all able to notice him approach, he was too busy enjoying his newfound perceptions and senses to do so.

A great cry echoed throughout the realm of Bran's soul.

"*Life! How I've missed you!*"

"It's not *your* life!" cried Bran defiantly, surprised by the strength of his voice which echoed throughout the dust plain. "Give it back!"

This finally drew the general's attention. The red light turned straight on him. Shigemasa began to defend his dominion. First, a stone wall rose from the ground between Bran and the grey tower, but he managed to fly over it before it grew to tall. Next, some horrible demonic minion launched from the tower's balcony, a creature of nightmares, creation of a twisted mind, with shadowy body and wings of night clouds.

This was something Bran knew best – aerial combat. He swooped his Farlink dragon towards the creature. Claw clashed against claw and tooth against tooth, but the demon stood little chance against Emrys and its rider. With a thrust of its powerful limbs, the dragon shoved the creature tumbling towards the ground and then dived after it, spewing bluish fire until it made sure the demon perished, its shadowy body razed to ash.

"Is that all you've got?" Bran shouted.

"*No!*"

An invisible shockwave spread from the tower, casting Bran and his dragon away.

"I have waited for two centuries for this, I am not letting go!"

A deluge of images and sensations flooded Bran's mind as the general raged, waves of memories and pent-up emotions washing over the boy: painful death from a heretic's arrow; awakening to a ghostly existence in the Cave of Spirits; hopeful expectation that a spy, scholar or poet would descend into the misty sulphuric waters to merge its soul with Shigemasa's; centuries of pitiful existence, after the closure of the caves, shared with innumerable other Spirits trapped for eternity, with no chance of ever solving the riddle of their entrapment, and hesitation when the filthy barbarian had submerged his stinking body into the Waters. Had the general really sunk so low as to possess this long-nosed half-animal, this hateful, devious *Gaikokujin*? Finally an acceptance of fate and firm resolution. He had no trouble exerting his dominance over the other rivals. They were no match for him, the Taishō of the *Taikun*'s armies.

"The old witch had no idea what she had unleashed," Shigemasa said, chuckling boastfully, '*say farewell to your body, Barbarian – I will find a much better use for it!"*

Bran spurred his spectre dragon back into flight. He was not giving up that easily. Suddenly he felt a burning sensation on his hand. The blue ring – it was also here, in this phantom world! But why…? It blazed brighter than ever before. The light grew stronger and soon it was brighter even than the red beam coming from the tower. Bran raised his hand and the ring shone like a little sun on his finger.

"What – what is this?"

Bran could sense Shigemasa's bewilderment and pain.

"I'm coming to get what's mine."

"*No... No! You cannot send me back into the darkness — you can't...*"

In the blue light of Bran's ring, the grey tower started to crumble like a melting candle. By the time Emrys had reached the stone bulwarks, it was all but reduced to rubble. Only a single floor around the gate remained standing. Bran bade his dragon land in front of the massive wooden door and banged his fist against it. The gate dissolved into dust.

"*I won't let you — I won't... Two hundred years...!*"

Before entering the gateway Bran turned around and touched the scaly neck of the dragon one last time. He linked through to the real Emrys — the beast was half-sleeping, dormant, imprisoned somewhere far away, but at least it was still alive.

He crossed the threshold of the tower of his mind and the dirty red world around him disappeared.

He panicked at first, fearing something had gone wrong. He was again surrounded by impenetrable darkness. And then he remembered to open his eyes.

The pines rustled above him in the morning breeze. It dawned. He stood up slowly, staggering, dizzy, his right hand still clutching the hilt of Tokojiro's sword.

The air in the forest was cool, fresh and aromatic, smelling of resin and sea salt. Bran's head was clear. He could sense the general very faintly somewhere far at the back of his mind, cursing and thrashing about helplessly. He could feel his shame and despair, but he did not care.

Something rustled in the undergrowth. Bran grasped the sword – it was a bit lighter than his cavalry blade, and oddly balanced. He tried to swing it like he would his own weapon. It almost flew out of his hand. The rustling in the bushes repeated. Bran retreated against a large tree trunk, holding out the sword before him defensively. He summoned a *bwcler* to shield his left hand. Whatever was coming, he was ready.

"Bran-*sama*!"

The apprentice girl ran out of the bushes crying with joy. She stopped a few steps short of hugging him and pulled back, embarrassed. Satō followed warily, looking at Bran with anxiety.

"Good, he's alive," the boy said, nodding with relief.

"W–what do we do now?" Nagomi said. "We have no way to communicate without Tokojiro-*sama*..."

"We'll have to think of something. For now let's try to go back to the temple, avoiding the *Taikun*'s men if possible."

Bran listened to their conversation with increasing bafflement. Was he still dreaming, or trapped within his mind? The youths seemed to speak perfect Prydain. He understood every single word.

"I – " he started.

They turned to him swiftly.

"I comprehend thee."

"How…?" Satō opened his eyes wide. "What magic is this?" he questioned, holding out his sword threateningly.

"I do not know." Bran shook his head. "'Twas the Spirit from the cave – somehow, the ritual must have…"

"Oh, who cares *how*? Isn't it brilliant?" Nagomi clapped her hands. "We don't need an interpreter now!"

"Are you *really* you, Bran-*sama*?" the boy was still suspicious. "Did you cut those samurai who were after you?"

"I understand thy trepidation," he said, suddenly aware there was something odd about the way he spoke. "It was not me who did the slayings, but the Spirit within me. I do not possess the skill with this blade."

He presented the sword to Satō.

"Leave it," the boy said, "I don't want anything that belonged to that traitor."

"We can discuss everything on our way back to the temple," said Nagomi.

"You're right." Satō nodded solemnly. "Let's move. It seems we have a lot to talk about. Oh, and Bran-*sama* – your face…"

"I understand."

Bran nodded and turned around reluctantly to focus on the agonising transformation back into his Yamato disguise.

The warmth with which the monks of Mogi Temple had greeted the travellers the previous day was gone. The head monk stared at them coldly as they emerged from the pine forest.

"You are wanted by the government," he announced, "you have brought violence under the roof of this temple. If it weren't for the debt we owe to the Suwa Shrine, we would not let you go free. As it is, we can only request that you leave promptly."

He nodded at one of the monks, who dropped their travel bags to the floor in silence.

"You will find the boats at the pier. Now go, before I change my mind and report you to the guards."

"Thank you, Sir," said Nagomi, bowing.

Bran also bowed. They picked up their belongings and departed towards the harbour.

"Shouldn't we go back to Suwa?" asked Nagomi as they stood on a low hill overlooking the harbour, trying to decide their next move. "We can't possibly go farther on our own…"

"Why not?" Satō shrugged. Going back was the last thing on her mind. The entire shrine may have been swarming with traitors like Tokojiro. "It's not like that interpreter would have done us any good. He was all talk. He said he was good with the sword, but Bran-*sama* disarmed him in one move."

"Th-that wasn't me," protested Bran.

She stared at him, still surprised that the boy could talk.

"It doesn't really matter," she said, waving her hand at last. "What matters is that we're just as fine without him, now that you can speak our language. The three of us will be less conspicuous anyway."

"Those samurai who pursued me," said Bran, 'shall they not return, with more men? Now they know who to look for…"

"This is why we must move on." Satō was adamant. "The roads back to Kiyō will be swarming with guards by now. We can only go forwards as far away from the city as we can."

"And as far south as we can," reminded Bran, "that is where my *dorako* is."

"You're right," she said, nodding, "let's go get that boat."

It was early morning and there was only one ferry ready to depart in the harbour, a narrow vessel with a single sail and a square of canvas stretched over the deck as the only protection from the elements. A single samurai in a dark purple hooded cloak had just disembarked, paid the fare and hurried into the village without giving the three travellers a glance.

"Can you take us to Kumamoto?" Nagomi asked the ferryman.

"Kumamoto? That's too far for this tiny thing. I can take you across the bay to Shimabara, where the big ferries are," said the helmsman. "In fact, that's just where I picked up that gentleman," he added, nodding towards the fast disappearing samurai.

Satō watched the shoreline fade away as the small boat, barely big enough to fit the three of them, travelled eastwards at full sail. The westerly wind blew strong. The clouds receded a little and the rain stopped.

Of the three travellers only the foreigner was used to sailing. Poor Nagomi, first time at sea, sat on the bottom with her eyes closed, praying, her face a delicate shade of green. Satō made a valiant effort of trying to stay on deck, but, as the little vessel entered the wide waters of the bay and started rising, falling, bobbing and rolling on the high waves, she also had to sit down near the edge of the boat. In the end, the Westerner joined the girls, settling on the wet bench under the canvas windbreak.

The sea calmed down after an hour, and Satō stopped leaning over the side of the boat. Her skin returned to a healthy colour and she could pick up a conversation with Bran. She still could not get her head around the fact that the boy was suddenly speaking fluent Yamato.

"Not even the Overwizard can talk our language so effortlessly."

"I wish I knew how it happened," the boy admitted, "it would be a most valuable secret to any scholar."

"Or a spy," added Satō, observing the boy carefully. The High Priestess had never mentioned he would gain such an ability after the ritual. What if he had understood them all along and only pretended not to?

She realised her stare was rude and turned her eyes towards the west, where the easternmost cape of the Mogi

Peninsula, jutting out into the sea like the back of a great whale, was slowly disappearing beyond the horizon. It reminded her of the few sea journeys she had taken with her father and tears started welling up in her eyes. She focused on the more recent past.

"I wonder what he meant," she said.

"Who?" Bran asked.

"That monk, what did he mean when he said they owe the Suwa Shrine a great deal?"

"He means the Sun God rebellion." Nagomi spoke softly without opening her eyes, her lips trembling with nausea. Satō turned to her in surprise. "The priests at Suwa protected the monks and treasures of the Mogi Temple when it was attacked and razed to the ground by the rebels."

"Tell us more!"

Satō moved closer to her friend. She loved tales of old times, even more so if they were bloody and violent.

"That's all I know... I saw this written in the shrine chronicle. It was in the fourteenth year of the Kan'ei era."

"*I remember that year,*" said Bran unexpectedly. His eyes turned from green to black, gazing towards the western horizon. There was a melancholic sadness in his voice. "*The muskets of the heretics poured lead like rain on our heads; their arrows turned the day into night; their spears were like blades of rice in the field. From hamlet to hamlet they went, ravaging the shrines, plundering the altars and melting the sacred mirrors into weapons, saying their God had conquered our Sun Goddess, and all other Gods were just demons in disguise. They burned the temples and slew bald monks by the*

dozens. A youth of mere sixteen summers led them to their doom –
Messenger from Heavens they called him. On these shores the mutineers
clashed with the samurai army, overwhelmed them and chased the
recreant cravens all the way back to Kiyō."

He finished and mused at the waves in silence. At last his eyes turned back to green. The boy snapped back to the present.

"What just happened?" Satō asked suspiciously. If it was just a performance, it was a very convincing one. Perhaps he was telling the truth after all...

"It's..." Bran hesitated. "The Spirit's memories o'erpowered me..."

"Is it dangerous?"

"I... don't think so," he replied.

She sensed he wasn't telling the whole truth.

"What was this vision?" he asked. "Who were the heretics?"

"Those who shared the religion of the Westerners," explained Nagomi.

"The Vasconians," added Satō. "The Bataavians were on our side."

"The Sun Priests!" the boy said. "They had reached even here?"

Nagomi only shrugged.

"I don't know much. The heretic beliefs were banned a long time ago. The rebellion you spoke of was their last stand."

"That Spirit inside you…" Satō looked into Bran's eyes, trying to discern a trace of the alien entity. "Do you know its name?"

"He calls himself Itakura Shigemasa."

The wizardess thought carefully. The name sounded vaguely familiar.

"What else do you know about him?"

"He styles himself *Taishō*. What does that mean?"

Satō opened her eyes wide and gasped.

"*Chief Commander!*"

"I dreamt of leading a great multitude of men to their deaths," Bran said, nodding solemnly. "I thought 'twas merely a nightmare…"

Now she remembered. Itakura was the name of a clan of famous warriors and *daimyo*s from the northern province of Mikawa.

"He must have fought at the Shimabara siege," she guessed.

"It may yet be a good thing that you have bonded with such a powerful and wise Spirit," said Nagomi.

Or very dangerous, Satō tought.

"I would gladly be rid of him," replied Bran.

"You would not be able to talk to us then," Nagomi said and smiled.

"However jarring your manner of speech sounds," added Satō.

"Be it truly so strange to thy ears?"

"It's… outdated, archaic. I suppose it's how Shigemasa spoke two hundred years ago."

Or how a Vasconian spy would know it.

"You can understand *everything* we say, can't you?" the wizardess asked.

"I do, although sometimes it sounds to me…" the boy hesitated, "rude, uncouth. Some words I even feel are… *obscene.*"

Satō chuckled. She knew that, disregarding some boyish quirks, she spoke the most ornate style of the language, as befitted a daughter of an aristocrat. She had been taught that nothing ever changed in Yamato. The islands, as the poets, scholars and court historians told about them, were ageless, set in their ways forever. Any transformation, any progress was simply unthinkable. The system imposed by the *Taikun* was supposed to be as unalterable as the sky above and the earth below. This is what everyone had been telling her – everyone except her father.

"Our people have always changed and adjusted to the circumstances," he had once told his daughter, "Since the earliest days. We've learnt from the Qin how to plant rice and grow silk. We've learnt to build houses that withstand earthquakes and typhoons. When the Horse Lords invaded, we had to learn their strategies to beat them back. When the Westerners came, we learned from them anything they were willing to teach us and more – their magic, their technology, we've even tried their religion – but we saw it did not fit our needs… This is how Yamato grew to such greatness –

through evolution, not through stagnation, no matter what the courtiers at Edo would want us to believe. The Yamato should be like water, and the *Taikun* had frozen us into ice – but ice can break."

"For now we can pretend it's an accent from Mikawa," she said. "I will try to teach you the modern manner, or you will draw too much attention."

"I shall endeavour."

"*I will try*," she corrected him, and chuckled again as the boy winced hearing her "uncouth" words. "You can practise with the commoners, they won't know any better."

CHAPTER VI

The boat turned north around the tip of another peninsula, and entered a narrow inlet.

"Be this Shimabara already?" Bran asked the boat's steersman, looking at a rather disappointingly tiny village at the end of the inlet through his telescope.

The device drew the man's attention, and Bran had to explain he had bought it at the great market in Kiyō.

"No, kind *tono*, that's Kuchinotsu. It takes two days to sail to Shimabara and we're not likely to reach another port before the sun sets."

"I trust they have inns there."

"There's a guesthouse by the pier that a cousin of mine runs."

"I see. How very shrewd of thee," said Bran.

The old steersman grinned, exposing his toothless gums. His smile was contagious.

Satō looked jealously at the instrument, but was too polite to ask outright. Bran noticed the boy's stare and gave it to him.

"We don't get things like that at the market," he said, admiring the craftsmanship and power of the lenses. "Keep it safe," he added, reluctantly giving the spyglass back, "in the wrong hands something like this could start a war."

"It's just a small hand-held," Bran replied. "The case has more magic than the spyglass."

"Why, what's in the case?"

"It is made of a selkie skin, so it shall never sink."

He remembered Samuel saying these exact words at the birthday party. His face must have reflected his mood, for Satō asked immediately:

"What's wrong?"

"The man who gave it to me is now dead," Bran replied with a sigh.

"I'm sorry."

"It's all right." He shook his head slowly. "I had only known him a few months. He was one of the crew on *Ladon*."

"What was it like on the ship?" the boy enquired.

Bran rotated the barrel of the telescope in his hand and put it back into the selkie-skin case before answering, slowly and carefully rolling the words of the new language off his tongue.

"Crowded... Dirty... Noisy... Smelly. The food was bad, the water stale. Most of the time, nothing happened. For days and days the sea passed underneath and clouds above, and that was the only change, but then we would get an order and the ship would alter its course. There would be some sea battle or a landing, or just a diplomatic visit, and we would see another part of the world, completely different to what we had seen a few weeks before. My father told me no two harbours look the same."

"That sounds amazing…" Satō whispered.

Bran nodded in silent agreement.

The boat rocked, bumping into the wooden pier.

"*Kuchinotsu*!" announced the steersman.

Bran and Nagomi settled at the guesthouse for the night while Satō had to stay in the servants' room by the stable. At nightfall she smuggled herself into their quarters through the garden veranda.

The night was still young. They drank *cha*, sitting for a moment in silence. At last Satō found the courage to ask the question she had longed to pose ever since she had learned who the foreigner really was.

"Bran-*sama*," she started, "I'm sorry to keep asking you questions…"

"It is understandable," he replied, "I have many questions as well."

"What's it like to fly a *dorako*?"

Bran put down the half-empty teacup and pondered the answer with his eyes closed, remembering.

"Imagine thou… *you* are standing on the top of the highest mountain," he started carefully. "You canst – *can*,

111

sorry, see all the way to the horizon, for a dozen *ri* or more. The fields, the pastures, the forests, a lonely village in the valley… the people and animals below are as tiny as ants. Rivers are as thin ribbons of blue, crossed by ribbons of brown dirt roads. A strong cold mountain wind is howling around you, tugging at your clothes, forcing tears into your eyes. Imagine now that the mountain beneath thy feet starts to move," Bran continued. "All the fields and pastures and forests become splashes of colours, blurred as thou fliest past. The wind grows stronger, but it's not cold anymore – the dragon's breath blows around thee, keeps thou warm. Thou holdst onto the reins as it goes ever higher and ever faster. The mountain is gone and there is nothing but the blue sky all around thee, the Earth a forgotten memory somewhere far below…"

"Can you reach the clouds?" Satō asked dreamily.

"Oh, aye, easily, if it's a day such as today, when they hang low o'er the land. The clouds are cold and wet, like a very thick mist. When the day is cold and overcast, thou could even fly through the clouds for a short while, where there is always sun, but it's difficult for a human to last long at that height; not enough air to breathe."

"How long did you have to learn before you could fly?"

"I was flying with my dragon before I joined the Academy, but that was because my father showed me how and looked after me – when he was not on one of his expeditions, that is. Otherwise thou needst to first learn some navigation and special spells that slow one's fall. One can easily lose one's head in the clouds. When we find my *dorako* I will take thee for a flight," Bran said unexpectedly, and Satō jumped in surprise and disbelief, her eyes growing large and round.

"*Eeh*! Really?"

"Verily," the Westerner said, nodding, "thou art light enough, there should be no trouble, and thou, of course, if thou wishest," he said turning to Nagomi, who also listened to his tale.

The girl smiled and waved her hands.

"Oh, there's no need to trouble yourself. Sacchan's the one who's crazy about *dorako*."

"I sure am! I'm going to dream about them again tonight… but it's getting late. I should go back to the servants' quarters," said Satō.

She forgot about her suspicions for the night. What did it matter if the boy was a spy, after all? Her father might have worried about the intruding foreigners, but she didn't care. All that she cared for was that, thanks to Bran, for the first time in days she dreamt of something else other than the man in crimson robe and her father's agonising screams.

The simple breakfast served at the guesthouse surprised Bran. He was growing used to the strange familiarity with which Yamato began to greet him at every corner since his struggle with Shigemasa. It felt almost as if he had come back to a country where he had been born and raised, after a fifteen-year-long journey to Gwynedd.

This, however, was new. He could not recognise the dishes from the memories he shared with the general. A basket of tiny fish and prawns deep-fried in crispy batter was a taste unknown to him, as were the slices of sweet yellow potato and firm-fleshed orange pumpkin. The rice was too white, the fish too raw and the soy sauce too refined and watery. Everything tasted exquisite though, no matter what it was called or from what it was made. The boy wondered if having the Spirit inside him affected his taste buds as well, or was this food really as perfect as it now seemed?

He was trying not to think too much of what had happened to him back at the pine forest. It was too bizarre to contemplate, trying to make sense of it was like trying to understand a dream. Why was the land of his mind empty, dry and red? Why had the blue sapphire ring appeared in this outlandish scenery, why had it lit up and crumbled the tower of grey stone? He looked at his finger. The stone was calm, quiet, dark. Nothing peculiar about it, he remembered Doctor Campion's words. The ring's appearance in the red darkness must have been merely some figment of his strained imagination.

"Is the food not to your liking, dear guest?" the girl serving the food, the guesthouse keeper's young daughter, enquired with a concerned voice, seeing the straw basket still full of fried fish. "I can bring something else…"

Her extreme politeness towards him contrasted starkly with what he remembered of the *tafarn* wenches in Gwynedd. At first he thought she was kind to him because of his noble status, but he observed she behaved that way to all other guests.

There was nothing here that resembled the sleazy, noisy, dirty western taverns with which he was familiar. The common room was spacious and clean, the guests – mostly – quiet and well-behaved, the food delivered promptly and without fault.

He was awed and humbled by all this civility, until he noticed the sharp swords most men in the inn carried. He remembered the dead samurai he had seen in the street of Kiyō and the warnings of the interpreter. Suddenly the smiles and bows of the guests and the staff no longer seemed as genuine as before.

"We know little of such delicacies in Mikawa," he answered with a practiced smile and a nod.

"Delicacies, *tono*?" The girl laughed coquettishly, partially covering her mouth with her hand, but exposing teeth daubed with black ink – in the fashion he had seen on some women in the city and which repulsed him at first but was now becoming oddly appealing. The long sleeve of her kimono fell loose, revealing a shapely forearm. "It's only some *tenpura*. Surely you eat better food in the north, so close to the capital?"

"Ah, yes, well." Bran coughed. "Maybe in the *daimyo*'s castle, but I come from a small village in the mountains," he bluffed.

"What brings you all the way to Chinzei?"

Bran had no ready answer. He was too busy staring at the girl's impeccably white neckline – surprisingly attractive for a village girl – to think of his new identity. He turned to Nagomi in slight panic – Satō, in his servant's disguise, was not allowed to speak in the presence of "superiors".

The apprentice gave him an odd look before speaking.

"Karasu-*sama* is on a pilgrimage to thank the *kami* for saving his village from the famine."

"Ah, then you've been to Suwa to pray to the Morisaki, god of harvest!" the girl said, beaming approvingly.

"Aye, that is correct." Bran nodded, sighing quietly with relief and smiling gratefully at the apprentice.

Impeccably white neckline, he thought, astonished at himself. *What am I thinking about? What do I care for how a woman's neckline looks?*

He praised Nagomi when the servant girl left them alone.

"That was swift thinking. Thank you."

"I've seen enough pilgrims coming to the shrine from all over Yamato. The ones from the countryside always pray to give thanks for something – salvation from a famine, drought or plague. It's only the rich ones who ask for more."

He leaned over the bowl, preparing to wash himself before sleep. An unfamiliar face stared at him from the reflection in the water. He blinked his narrow eyes, furrowed his flat nose and pulled a couple more funny faces, to make sure it were really his own features.

"*Did you not like the girl?*" a voice in his head enquired.

"I... Eh?" Bran was taken aback by the Spirit's sudden forwardness. "I suppose... she was *comely*... What's it to you, anyway?"

"*Then why did you not take what she was offering?*"

"I ate as much as I could…"

"*I don't mean the food!*" the voice in his head mocked him. "*Did you not see how she revealed the nape of her neck, how she loosened her sleeves? Why, I do believe she would have given it to you for free if only you had asked!*"

"I… I do not understand…"

"*Oh! Don't tell me…*" The general paused. "*You've never had a woman, have you?*"

Bran realised what Shigemasa was talking about. Serving food and drink was not the only source of income for the guesthouse keeper's daughter —and she was, apparently blatantly, offering him her services.

"*Did your father not introduce you into the ways of the floating world?*" the Spirit prodded.

Bran felt his face turn bright crimson and hot. The situation was embarrassing in itself, but *talking* about it made it even worse.

"I… I hope I did not offend anyone…" was all he could say.

"*Eh,*" he could almost sense Shigemasa shrug, "*you're still a* wakashū - *she probably just thought you were inexperienced with women.*"

"I… I am," he admitted shyly, not wanting the conversation to continue.

"*Just my luck, to find myself an unbroken youth,*" Shigemasa said, sighing with exasperation. "*Your school must have been like one of those Satsuma samurai places, right?*"

117

"I suppose…?"

He decided to just go along with everything.

"*I guessed as much*," Shigemasa said, grunting, and with that the conversation seemed to have ended, leaving Bran in total confusion.

In the morning, the little boat took Bran and the others to the harbour town of Shimabara, where they caught a ferry across the bay to a place called Kumamoto. It was a much larger vessel, a broad merchant boat with a tall mast and great piece of cloth for a sail, slow, heavy and stable.

"Good of thou to join us," Bran said, seeing Nagomi climb out from below the deck.

"It is not as bad as the other one," the young apprentice replied, although her face was still pale and she visibly struggled with dizziness. "Is all sea travel so tough?"

"This? 'Tis nothing!" he said and laughed. The ship barely rocked on the low waves. "Out in the open sea there are waves that would cover this whole vessel, and the ships ride them up and down like… like…" He couldn't think of an analogy that the girl would understand. "Like leaves in a mountain stream."

"How can people survive this?" she said, turning even paler at the thought.

"It takes some getting used to," Bran admitted, "but there is little else more exhilarating than sailing the open sea. It's almost as good as flying. Of course, on dragon-back it would take us less than an hour to cross this bay."

"Can you still sense your *dorako*?" Satō asked.

He closed his eyes and focused on the Farlink. The ring on his hand warmed up slightly.

"Yes. Somewhere over yonder." He pointed to the south-east. "What is there?"

"You have the map, Bran-*sama*," the boy reminded him.

"Ah, of course."

The dragon rider was the only one who knew how to read Western maps, so it was him whom Lady Kazuko had presented with a rolled up piece of linen cloth she had found in the shrine's library. It was a copy of a Vasconian navigation chart, three hundred years old and badly inaccurate, but it did help Bran to get his bearings in this strange land.

"Where are we…? Ah, I see Kiyō." He was no longer surprised with his ability to read the ink squiggles that formed the Yamato writing. "If this be Qin," he said, pointing to a grey blot on the western edge of the map, "then my ship was somewhere here when it… perished. Flying straight eastwards, the dragon would land ashore somewhere – *here*."

He laid his finger on a crescent-shaped bay on the southernmost tip of Chinzei Island.

"*Hioki*." Satō deciphered the runes and thought for a moment. "That's Satsuma," he said, frowning.

"Is it far?"

"Farther than I thought we would need to go - across the mountains."

"A week?"

"Maybe more. But it's south and we will go through at least two big cities where we can find help and information, if my old man's name still means anything in these parts."

"Does that interfere with the search for thy father?"

"Until we find some clues, we can only hope the Crimson Robe will show himself again. So far all we know is that he's looking for you."

"Kazuko-*hime* said your honoured grandfather had met him before," noted Nagomi.

"It is merely a conjecture. He would be very old now if it were indeed the same person my grandfather saw when he came here on board a Dracalish vessel."

"A Dracalish ship?" Satō glanced at him sharply. "You mean *Phaeton*?"

"Yes, he was a midshipman on board the *Phaeton*."

"My father saw it when he was very young," Satō said. "It inspired him to study *Rangaku*."

"All is bound together by Fate," Nagomi added piously, "just like Kazuko-*hime* said."

"How did your grandfather get the black box? Who's the woman in the medallion?" Satō continued prodding.

Bran explained what little he knew and guessed about the contents of the box, and briefly told the story of his grandfather's life. He could sense Satō did not trust him fully since the incident with Tokojiro and decided hiding the truth would only make this distrust grow.

"What about the dragon figurine?" Nagomi asked when he had finished. "You didn't mention that."

"Oh, it has naught to do with my grandfather. I got it from my father a few months ago."

"Can I see it one more time?"

"It is Yamato work, isn't it?" the dragon rider asked, giving her the figurine.

"Yes, you can buy these things in Kiyō. The Bataavians from Dejima like them."

The man my father got it from must have once been here, Bran realised.

"Then it's not really significant?"

"I don't know, maybe." Satō shrugged. "It seems everything about you is somehow significant."

"I wish it were not so," he said, looking grimly at the steel-grey horizon.

The ferry entered the mouth of a large river and followed it upstream before reaching a harbour and a tall bridge. A massive castle loomed over the city, similar to the one Bran had been seeing in his dreams, but even greater. Its robust stone walls rose upwards in a maze of broad spiralling terraces, culminating in a colossal keep, six storeys tall, its white plastered walls covered with black wooden boards. It was an impressive construction that seemed able to withstand even a barrage of modern cannons, but it was completely exposed from above. Bran could not help thinking how easy it would be to capture it with just a few dragons.

If he needed any more confirmation that there were no dragons in Yamato, this nigh impregnable castle's lack of aerial defences was it. All he had seen of the creatures so far were carvings and paintings. What had happened to them all?

"Did Kazuko-*hime* advise anything about this place?" he asked, turning his eyes away from the ramparts.

"She mentioned a *Butsu* temple to the north of the castle," replied Nagomi, removing a tightly rolled piece of paper from a bamboo container at her belt. "The monks there are aware of most of what goes on in the Southern provinces, and have a great library of strange stories and legends."

"I knew a man in Kumamoto," recalled Satō, "a friend of my father's. If he's still here, I could try and contact him."

"We shall go to the temple first," said Bran.

What was supposed to be a proposition came out as an order, rather forcefully. Satō raised his eyebrows, but said nothing.

"Do you think we're far enough from Kiyō for me to stop disguising myself?" the boy asked.

"It would be safer if you would keep it until we at least move out of the city," Nagomi said, biting her lower lip in thought. "There must be many merchants and samurai from Kiyō coming here on business."

Satō sighed, picked up his heavy bag and headed north. Bran gave one last look to the castle walls – he couldn't shake the feeling of being watched from the tapering towers – and followed after the Yamato boy.

THE WARRIOR'S SOUL

CHAPTER VII

By the time they reached the temple compound, the sky had already turned a gloomy grey. Thick evening fog rolled down from the hills. Nestled between a shadowy mountainside to the west and half-abandoned fields to the east, the temple's dark curly roofs loomed over the poor desolate neighbourhood like a flock of crows.

"Be this really the place?" Bran asked.

"*Honmyōji.*" Satō pointed at a sign carved in a wooden plank above the gate. "Unless there's another one in Kumamoto…"

"We shall need lodgings. It is getting late. Let us enquire this man."

Bran approached a white-robed monk working a small radish patch just beyond the gate.

"Good monk, pray tell us whether thy establishment can provide us with accommodation?" he asked.

The man straightened himself, lifted the brim of his bamboo hat and looked at Bran, bemused.

"He means, can you find us a place to sleep," Nagomi said swiftly.

"Certainly, honourable guests." The monk bowed. "The *shukubō* is in the fifth building to the left, just before the Munatsuki stairs," he said, pointing in the direction of a long stone staircase that disappeared into the menacing darkness of the hillside. Flickers of stone lanterns marked its further path among the pines and cedars. "I don't think there are many other guests today."

"Thank you," Bran said, bowing graciously.

They walked down the stone alley, lined on both sides by clusters of granite gravestones. The monk was right: the *shukubō* – temple lodgings – were almost empty apart from a couple of tired pilgrims dozing on the floor of the dormitory hall, and two monks taking care of the place.

"More visitors!" rejoiced one of them as they entered the dormitory. "A noble samurai among them! We are truly blessed today. *Ingen*!" he shouted down the corridor, "Make sure your broth is at its best, we have fine guests!"

"Oh, that is quite unnecessary, we only need a place to stay," Bran protested after he realised the "noble samurai" was himself, but the monk shook his head, laughing.

"Ingen loves cooking, and I can only eat so much." He patted himself on the belly, which was flat and taut. "He'll be delighted to have a chance to show off his skill. We don't get many visitors here, and most of the pilgrims – well, they are certainly pious, but not what I'd call appreciative of proper cuisine."

From the dining room Bran could see the cook opening boxes and pots with a variety of mysterious ingredients, mixing, slicing, chopping and throwing them into one of the two huge clay pots bubbling away on the stone stove. The guests and the talkative monk, who introduced himself as Itsunen, watched his movements in silent awe. There was no doubt Ingen was a crafty cook. The delicate scent of the vegetable and seaweed broth filled the room and made Bran realise how hungry their journey had made him.

He had discovered early on that the Yamato ate plenty of kelp and laver, something he had not tasted since leaving Gwynedd, and it made him like their cooking even more. He now watched with eager expectation as the monk searched the kitchen for more ingredients to mix into the broth.

Ingen turned to the other monk with an accusing look.

"We're out of tofu," were the first words he uttered.

Itsunen shrugged with an innocent smile.

"The pilgrims ate it all."

"There should always be fresh tofu!" The cook's face turned fierce. "We are monks of Kumamoto, how am I supposed to make *dengaku* now?"

The two monks stared at each other for a moment like some avatars of light and darkness. At last, Ingen slumped.

"You will have to make more at dawn."

Itsunen looked dejected, but agreed.

"The soup is ready," the cook announced without joy, "but I'm not happy with the result. Maybe I should throw it away and start again…"

"*No!*" the three guests cried in unison.

Bran received a steaming bowl of the broth, with plenty of cut vegetables, mushrooms and kelp. It seemed to him the best soup he had ever tasted.

"What, no *noodles*? That's stingy!" Itsunen moaned.

"We're also out of noodles," Ingen replied coldly. "Are you a monk or a gluttonous merchant? You don't need that much food before sleep."

"It's perfect," Nagomi said, and Bran grunted agreement between one mouthful and another.

He was holding the bowl close to his mouth as he saw the others do. It was a much easier way to drink the thick soup.

"It is acceptable," the cook admitted, slurping the broth himself. "Not as terrible as I expected. Alas, I cannot offer you our specialty because *somebody* forgot to restock the cupboard."

He glared at the other monk.

"What brings you to Honmyōji at such a late hour, if you don't mind me asking?" enquired Itsunen after they had emptied their bowls – and asked for second helpings.

"We come from Suwa to speak to Father Ipponin," Nagomi mentioned a name given her by the High Priestess, "to ask him for advice and information."

Both monks turned serious.

"What is it?"

"The Reverend Ipponin passed away a few months ago. We have a new Abbot now," replied Ingen.

"However, I'm sure he will be just as happy to provide you with advice as the old one," the other monk said with a smile.

"We shall see him tomorrow," Bran said, nodding.

"Well, I'm finished," said Satō, standing up. "I can't eat no more. I'll better go where my place is."

He leaned over to Bran's ear and whispered. "I hope the stables here are a bit cleaner than in that poor excuse for a guesthouse we were at yesterday."

"As soon as we're out of the city, thou shall join us in the guest rooms," Bran assured him.

"You bet I will!" he said. "I won't stand another night at the stables. I think I'm starting to get some bugs crawling over me."

White custard-like rectangles of freshly pressed tofu curd simmered on the grid of a grill. Bran eyed them with suspicion. All he knew about the dish was the name, but that knowledge gave him no indication of the taste. Foods like soup, rice or fried fish were straightforward enough, but at times the local cuisine stumped him with dishes like the one Ingen was preparing for breakfast; grilled tofu skewers covered with a brown paste of fermented beans. How could it possibly taste?

Everyone else seemed to enjoy them greatly, praising the cook, so Bran gingerly put a small piece into his mouth. At first it seemed to taste of absolutely nothing, but the soft, sponge-like morsel was warm and full of the energy he needed that early in the morning. He tried another bite, and was now almost sure he could detect a faint aroma of wood from the grill and a savoury sweetness that had to be coming from the beans. He bit again, this time trying the red-brown sauce. The paste was sharp and salty, complimenting the blandness of the tofu cube.

Like most of the food he had been eating since waking up in Yamato, the breakfast in this inconspicuous temple was subtle and refined, only hinting at tastes and aromas. Bran appreciated the skills that went into making all those fine dishes, but he was yearning for a haunch of mutton or a slice of cheese – strong, simple, punchy tastes. Even an apple would have been nice, something he could really stick his teeth into.

"What lies beyond yonder staircase up the hill?" he asked Itsunen, reaching for another skewer, this time of aubergine.

"That's the Jōchibyō, the grave of Kiyomasa-*dono*," the monk explained, "founder of the Kumamoto castle. If you wish, noble guest, we can take you later to pay your respects at his shrine."

"His shrine…?" Bran hesitated, but noticed Nagomi's frown and barely noticeable shaking of her head. "Oh, aye, certainly, I'd be most delighted."

Another monk entered the dining hall, one they had not seen before, and greeted them with a deep bow. Ingen and Itsunen looked at him apprehensively, but said nothing.

"The Abbot wishes to see you as soon as you are ready," the monk said.

"The Abbot – " Bran looked at the man in the white robe in surprise. "We were just going to look for him."

"I know," the monk said, smiling mysteriously, "I will take you to him. All three of you," he added, nodding in the direction of the stables.

"What did they mean *his shrine*?" Bran asked Nagomi on their way to fetch Satō.

"You do not know? I'm sorry, I keep forgetting you're not yet familiar with our customs."

"Not all, it would seem. I guess using chopsticks is easier knowledge to absorb than spiritual matters."

"I see. I'll try to… I never had to explain this to anyone. We pray to the Spirits of our ancestors, great men from the past. This Kiyomasa-*dono* the monk mentioned must have become a worthy ancestor to be enshrined in such a place."

"So his Spirit is still somewhere up there? Like all those souls in the Cave of Scrying?"

"That's different. Those souls, like Shigemasa-*sama*, were never properly purified, so they are stuck to this plane until the day they can move on, but an enshrined Spirit becomes one of the *kami* and watches the world from the Heavenly Plane, answering our prayers - if we are deemed worthy – "

"I knew it. I leave you alone for one night and you've already started talking about Gods," Satō interrupted the lecture, coming out of the stables to meet them. "Where are you off to?"

"Apparently the Abbot wants to see us. *All* of us," Bran added.

The Abbot, a small plump man, surprisingly young for his position, welcomed them in a golden-roofed building off the main path. His guestroom opened on to a huge library filled with old scrolls and newer bamboo-bound books.

"I believe you've been expecting us," noted Nagomi after they sat down at a low table.

"Don't be so surprised, little apprentice," the Abbot replied, laughing and pouring *cha* into black cups. "You priests of the Old Gods are not the only ones who can peer beyond the veil."

Nagomi gasped.

"You're a Scryer?"

"I dabble in divination," the Abbot said, nodding humbly. "This temple has a reputation to keep and we can't afford as many spies and informants as we used to, so we have to resort to other means of keeping up to date."

"Thou knowest what we are here for then?" asked Bran, catching Nagomi's worried glance.

"Only vaguely; divination is not a precise method, as you well know." The Abbot smirked at the apprentice. "You are looking for something, *tono*…"

"Karasu." Bran nodded.

"You have lost something of great value, Karasu-*dono*. I can help you locate it, but I will need time… and resources.

132

The temple has many needs. The roof of the main hall needs a new coat of gilding, for example."

"I understand." Bran glanced at Nagomi. The apprentice was biting her lips in anxiety and staring back at him with alarm. "Let us consider thy proposition, Reverend One."

"It is you who are short of time." The Abbot shrugged. "You know where to find me."

"Thou seemed mightily uneasy, Nagomi-*sama*," Bran remarked when they went outside, "what is the reason for thy apprehension?"

"The *Butsu* monks are banned from using divination," the apprentice explained.

"I thought they're just priests like you."

Nagomi shook her head vigorously.

"They brought their God from Qin, a long time ago. Their rituals and beliefs are different. They have neither healers nor Scryers – at least they shouldn't. There's something very disturbing going on here."

"Didn't the High Priestess say this place is where we should come for help?"

"You heard what the monks said. The old Abbot is dead. This one doesn't seem like somebody Kazuko-*hime* would trust."

"He already knows too much," Satō joined in, 'so the less we tell him, the better."

"There is something menacing about this place," Bran agreed. "I would be loath to share too many secrets with this man. We should leave as soon as possible." Bran turned to the wizardess. "How long is it before that friend of thine arrives here?"

"I have not heard back from him yet, so not before dinner, if today at all."

"Is he to be trusted?"

"I'm not sure of anything now, but he was one of my father's closest associates in Kumamoto – and he despises the *Taikun*. He certainly seems more trustworthy than some fat monk."

"I came as soon as I could. I'm so sorry for your loss, Takashima-*sama*…"

Just as Satō had remembered, the most striking feature in the man's long narrow face were his large flaring nostrils. They gave him the appearance of being constantly agitated. The lips did not help – they were always slightly apart, and quivered as he spoke. The eyes under thin eyebrows were, however, serene.

Satō wore her black and vermillion attire of a Rangakusha for her meeting with the scholar. Master Yokoi was one of those old-fashioned scholars who only knew her as a boy.

"Thank you, Yokoi-*dono*," she said, bowing before the guest, "but my father is still alive."

"What? But we've heard the news – an experiment gone wrong…"

"It's a lie. My father was abducted. I saw it happen."

"I knew I shouldn't have trusted the official channels. Tell me, tell me all!"

The samurai listened to the girl's tale, breathing noisily. Absentmindedly, he straightened creases on his vest, embroidered with the triple dragonscale crest of the Hōjō clan. When she finished, he banged his fist on the floor mat.

"This is exactly the kind of thing that shows how weak the government has become. They allow one of the greatest scholars of our era to simply disappear and do nothing about it! I assure you, I will do what I can to help you find out what's happened to your father – and believe me, I can do plenty."

"You have my eternal gratitude, Yokoi-*dono*."

"What are you doing here in Kumamoto?" he asked, picking up a tofu skewer from a square plate. "In this temple, of all places?"

"We had to flee Kiyō. The magistrate outlawed my entire family. This temple was recommended to us by the High Priestess of Suwa."

"Outlawed? *Preposterous!*" He spat out bits of tofu. "You must come with me to the *daimyo*'s castle, you'll be safe there."

"I… I'm sorry, Yokoi-*dono*, but we have to keep moving south."

Satō glanced at Bran nervously.

"You're not telling me everything, child," guessed the scholar, also looking at the boy with interest.

"No, Yokoi-*dono*," the wizardess admitted.

"You're just as secretive as Shūhan," the samurai said, laughing and slapping his thigh. "We never knew what new spell or device he would come up with! Be that as it may," he turned serious, "I will not prod further. I know you have your father's brains, so I trust your judgement."

"Thank you for understanding."

"My humble means are at your disposal, if you need anything for the journey. I still think you should stay at the castle, though. This place – " he looked around, "it sends shivers down my spine, especially when the mist comes down like tonight. People say these hills are haunted."

"That's why a priestess is with us," said a smiling Satō.

"Thought of everything, eh?" The samurai laughed again. "Are you leaving soon, then?"

"At dawn, if we can't reason with the Abbot."

"I see. Do try to keep in touch, child. I will find out what happened to dear old Shūhan, of that you can be certain."

"I will try."

"Give my regards to the cook; this is some fine *dengaku*. I have to go now. Darkness is coming and I don't fancy going down these hills by night."

"Of course. You understand that all that we've talked about must remain a secret... Even the fact that I'm staying here."

"My boy, I have been conspiring since before you were born!" He put his hand on Satō's shoulder and looked her seriously in the eyes. "As far as I'm concerned - we've never met."

"Maybe we should have gone with him after all," said Bran as they watched old man's palanquin clamber down the hill path.

"We wouldn't be any safer there," replied Satō, "imagine how hard it would be to keep any secrets in a castle."

"The mist descends from the hills," noted Nagomi, wrapping herself up tightly. "Let's go back inside."

Satō entered the guest stables, almost bumping into the groom.

"What ye doin' 'ere?" the boy asked in a rude manner.

"I am..." Satō started politely, but quickly corrected herself, "What d'ye think? I'm off ta sleep."

"Spendin' night in the temple? Are ye daft?"

"Why, what's wrong wi'dat?"

The groom gave her a look one gave to village idiots.

"The mist is a-comin'! I ain't stayin' 'ere wi' the mist comin' down! You'd be'r come wi' me if ye have any brains left!"

"No, I–I'll stay'ere..."

"As ye wish," he said with a shrug, and passed her by, heading for the temple gate in a great hurry.

There was only one horse in the stables, used to send quick messages to the city below. Satō gave it a wide berth. Horse riding, along with archery, was one of the few samurai arts she had never managed to learn. Her father did not keep horses; there was no point in a crowded city. Large animals frightened her. She suddenly felt ashamed of her fear; Bran's dragon must have been far larger and more threatening than this horse, and yet the Westerner was not afraid to ride it – to *fly* it.

An owl hooted in the distance. Satō shivered. *It's cold here in the evenings*, she told herself, trying to explain the goosebumps that covered her skin. She stepped outside and looked towards the gloomy hillside, from which the mist descended upon the compound. Suddenly a dot of light flickered in the darkness then another. Soon there were dozens of them, a line of dancing flames zigzagging like a fiery serpent down the hill, and they kept coming closer.

Ghosts, thought the wizardess, *will-o'-the-wisps*? She felt around and her fingers found a large heavy stick. It would have to do, as her sword was still with Bran. Perhaps she should warn the others – the lights were ever nearer. Would she make it to the guesthouse? What kind of danger would she have to face? She gripped the stick harder...

A lonely, grey-robed monk emerged from the mist, glanced at her with slight surprise and proceeded to light another of the stone lanterns lining the temple's main thoroughfare. Satō breathed out and shook her head.

138

Fool! Scared of the lanterns! she scolded herself. *I've been pretending to be a servant for so long I'm turning into one!*

She waved the wooden stick. It was roughly the size and weight of a *bokken*. It had been a while since she had practised with one. She assumed a stance and performed a few basic exercises. The stick swished through the air with a satisfying whistle. It felt good. She had not lost any of her skill.

The temple precinct was shrouded in gloomy darkness, pierced only by the flickering lanterns. Deep into the night, the wizardess didn't feel sleepy at all. She was also no longer wary of the mist. Nothing out of ordinary had happened since the coming of dusk. Satō continued her practise with the stick, adding a little magic to the sword exercises. The horse looked at her curiously with big brown eyes and yawned.

She noticed a movement near one of the buildings – the Abbot's house. She sneaked closer. Everyone should have already been asleep at this time of night...

A thin bald man wearing loose black robes knocked on the wall quietly with a staff topped with jingling bells. A panel in the wall slid open, and the Abbot appeared in the opening, lighting his way with a large paper lantern. The bald man grunted something. The Abbot nodded, looked around and, not noticing Satō hidden in the shadows, headed towards the path leading up the hill with the bald man.

The wizardess hesitated. She was intrigued to see what the Abbot was up to, but she was more curious about what she managed to glimpse inside the building, in the light of the lantern, before the little monk slid the secret door shut.

Books — hundreds of books.

The night was thick, dense and humid, the fog seeping through the cracks in the thin wooden walls. Nagomi stood by the window of her room, looking out into the pitch black darkness of the garden, covered in the mist descended from the hills.

She was alone in a room much bigger than she required; she didn't like being alone. Back home, she could always feel her parents and Ine beyond the thin paper walls. At the Shrine she had shared her dormitory with a dozen other apprentices. Here, she could sense no other souls in any of the rooms adjacent to hers. It was an overwhelming sensation.

She raised the clay beaker to her lips and blew. The orange spirit appeared in an instant, flickering merrily. She hummed a made-up melody and it jumped and danced. Heaviness rose from her heart. The mist seemed to float away from the light, revealing a little of the garden. Only now could Nagomi notice the sleeping hydrangeas and a slender sakaki tree near her window. She sensed the tree's young spirit. It was grateful for the orange light which released it briefly from the hold of the dark fog.

There were other spirits in the garden, floating past from the graveyards around the temple and from the forest, not paying her much heed. She felt them all, and she no longer felt so lonely.

There was a rustle in the hydrangea bush and a black pony-tail bobbed up and down underneath her window.

"Nagomi? Is that you?"

Bran dozed in half-sleep. He tossed from side to side, too tired to wake, too restless to dream. He tried to clear his mind of racing thoughts. He could sense Shigemasa, deep inside his soul, louder than usual, babbling like a mountain brook in the distance.

"Please, just be quiet!" he shouted at his thoughts. In frustration, he punched the thick beam in the wall. The pain seemed to quieten the general, who continued his brooding in insulted silence.

Moments later, Bran felt the ring on his finger heat up and a new vision overwhelmed him. It had been a while since he had made contact with Emrys. It was as if his mind could only cope with either Shigemasa's or the dragon's presence at any one time. Once the general retreated from his immediate consciousness, the Farlink connection re-emerged.

This time the dragon was calm, sleepy, sedated. There wasn't much detail to the vision, mostly a smell – a faint, sickly sweet smell, oddly familiar. The dragon could not stretch its wings, confined in some tight space.

A man stood before the dragon, a lanky thin man, observing Emrys with great curiosity through horn-rimmed glasses. A crest of a crossed circle decorated his shoulders.

"We can't keep this up much longer," the man said to somebody out of sight. "If we don't find a better method of keeping it sedate, I'm afraid we'll have to – "

The vision was suddenly broken by the sound of rapid knocking at the door.

"Bran-*sama*!"

It was Nagomi, sounding urgent.

"Please, wake up."

He slid the door open and peered carefully into the darkness of the corridor.

"What is it?"

"Sacchan asked us to come outside. Are you alright?" She looked at him with concern. "You seem shaken."

"It's nothing. A bad dream."

Satō was waiting for them under the long eaves of the stables. The boy explained briefly what he had seen and what he wanted them to do.

"You would have us sneak like thieves?" Nagomi asked.

"I know it's not honourable, but I must see what's inside that room," the boy said. "That fat Abbot seemed very knowledgeable, so his archives must be a treasure trove of information."

They crept along the wall of the Abbot's residence. Thick fog concealed their movements and dampened the sound of their feet.

"It's here." Satō slid open a wooden panel slowly and quietly. "The servants sleep on the other side of the house, so we should be safe, let's just try not to make too much noise."

"What if the Abbot comes back?" Bran asked.

"We'll run," Satō said with a shrug, "he'll never catch us on those short fat legs."

They tiptoed into the hall. Bran sneezed into his sleeve. Satō lit a small iron lantern and raised it up to illuminate the room. The bookshelves were covered with a thick layer of dust and cobwebs. The new Abbot did not seem concerned much with the state of the temple's archives.

They found a pair of copper candlesticks in the corner and lit those as well. Now Bran could fully appreciate the number of volumes gathered by consecutive Abbots.

"What are we looking for here, precisely?" he asked, opening one of the volumes and reading by the light of a flamespark.

"Anything that could guide us to the crimson robed man," Satō decided. "It's a long shot, I know, but it's worth a try. This library is huge," he said, admiring the long stretches of cabinets, stacked with silk-stitched volumes and bamboo-bound scrolls, "there must be something here."

"Yes, but how will we find it?"

"Some of the cabinets are marked," Nagomi said, dusting off markings on the shelves, "*'Financial records'* – I think we can omit these."

"There must be a main chronicle somewhere…"

Satō browsed through scrolls.

"*Tale of Heike*…?" Bran picked up a hefty, silk-bound tome. "*The bells of the Gion Temple*…" he started reading aloud.

"No, not this one, leave it."

They searched for a long time, opening book after book, browsing through a few, opening pages and putting them back again if they turned out to be accountancy registers or well-known tales of days past. A few volumes were set aside for further reading.

"*Ach-a-fi!*" Bran exclaimed in Prydain.

"What is it?"

Satō ran up to him.

"Oh, it's… n-nothing," he stuttered.

It was a collection of erotic stories and drawings, the illustrations so explicit that he felt his face immediately turn scarlet with embarrassment. He put the book away on the shelf – but then, when he was sure nobody saw him do it, he took it again and hid it under his sash.

Several hours of fruitless searching later he was all but ready to give up, when Nagomi called him and Satō over.

"Look, I think I've found something."

She was holding a large folding scroll, long and densely written with ancient script.

"It's some kind of lexicon of monsters and magical creatures," the apprentice said, "look at this page."

"*In a cave at the back of the Unganzenji Temple in northern Higo dwelled the Abomination known as the Immortal Swordsman,*" read Bran. "*so called because no living man could remember how long he had lived there, never growing old or sick. The people of…*

144

Kawachi *village describe the Immortal Swordsman as looking almost like any other man, except his eyes were like nuggets of gold, his skin pale, and his teeth blackened like a woman's and sharp like those of a wolf.*"

"That's him!" Satō exclaimed in the high-pitched voice he would sometimes get when excited. "That's exactly what he looked like!"

His sudden cry awoke somebody within the residence. They could hear the shuffling of feet on the wooden floor, and guards shouting.

"We must go," said Satō, "we have stayed here far too long."

"It's all right, we got what we came for," Bran replied, folding the scroll and putting it back on the shelf.

They crept through the fog back towards the lodging house. Suddenly the apprentice halted and stared into the dark mist.

"What is it?"

"There is something... approaching."

"The Crimson Robe?"

The apprentice shook her head.

"I don't think so... It feels like something ancient, stirred from a deep sleep."

"*For once, I agree with the apprentice,*" a voice spoke in Bran's head, "*there is something in those mists that even I wouldn't like to meet.*"

They hurried back to the lodgings. One of the monks, Itsunen, his face grey in the faint light of the stone lanterns, stood in front of the building.

"Noble guests," he said, bowing, "I believe you should leave the temple tonight."

"Why? What's going on?" asked Nagomi.

Bran looked around nervously – the fog was creeping down from the hillside, growing ever denser.

"The hills are restless," Ingen said, emerging from the shadows, "the mist grows thick."

"It's not safe here anymore," added Itsunen, "please hurry."

CHAPTER VIII

The Itō residence at the top of the Sōfukuji Hill was empty. The windows boarded, the doors closed. Sakuma Zōzan watched silently as an old servant, his silver head wrapped in a bandage, locked the outer gate shut and rolled up the *noren* cloth with the Itō crest. There was a sad determination in the way he went about his business.

"*A!*" the servant exclaimed, turning around. "Sakuma-*dono!*"

The scholar nodded politely.

"Where is everybody? What happened here?"

"Ine-*sama* sold the house and is moving to her folk in Nagoya."

"Sold the house… Wasn't there a younger daughter too, the red-haired one?"

"Oh, Nagomi-*sama* is an apprentice now. She lives at Suwa."

"What a pity." Zōzan stroke his pointed beard in thought. *More bad news.* "The Itō were good doctors. There are not many like them left in Kiyō."

The old servant nodded and corrected the bandage that had slipped from his forehead.

"By your leave – I have to deliver these to the harbour," he said, referring to the rolled-up *noren* and a bundle of a few other household items under his arm. Zōzan let him pass and stood for a while yet, watching the abandoned building, trying to think of his next move.

"You seek a doctor?"

A man emerged from under the eaves of the Itō house, his face hidden in a shadow of a dark-purple hooded robe. Sakuma Zōzan stretched his black and white kimono and coughed nervously. He had always felt distraught near strangers.

"Why do you ask?"

"I may be able to help."

"You don't look like a physician."

Zōzan noticed the two sword hilts showing from under the purple robe.

"It is not a physician that your son needs, Sakuma-*dono*."

The scholar breathed in sharply.

"Who *are* you?"

The stranger cast down the hood of his robe, revealing a calm young face adorned with fine whiskers and a thin beard. His dark, slightly popping eyes seemed to pierce through Zōzan's soul.

"Your last hope, scholar."

148

Keinosuke lay on a thick silk futon in a small room on the top floor of the Sakuma Mansion. He would seem to be sleeping peacefully, if it wasn't for a scowl twisting his face.

The stranger leaned over the boy.

"Tell me what happened."

"A deer hunter found him on the slopes of Inasa."

"And he's been like this since?"

"Not a sound."

The samurai touched Keinosuke's forehead and winced. He looked around the room.

"I need to see your library."

Zōzan was taken aback.

"Nobody has access to my library, samurai… I don't even know your name."

"My name is not easily given," the stranger said, "and if you want your son to ever wake again, you'll be doing exactly what I tell you."

The scholar grunted uneasily. It'd been six days since the servants brought Keinosuke home. The boy was dying before his eyes. No physician or priest in Kiyō could help, but what they all agreed on was that he wouldn't last long.

"Follow me," he said, standing up and straightening the creases on his kimono.

The door to his library was locked with a complicated Bataavian lock of brass and steel. Zōzan put the heavy key in and turned. The gears whirred, the bolts moved, the mistfire mechanism hissed and the door slid open.

The stranger entered the room, closed his eyes and stretched his neck out, like a sniffing hound.

"What's in there?"

He pointed to a large locked chest under the wall opposite the entrance.

"That's…" Zōzan hesitated, "that's where I keep my most precious scrolls."

"Open it."

"What – *no*! That's going too far. What does my chest have to do with Keinosuke's state?"

The samurai gave the scholar an impatient look.

"When they found him, was there a lake or a pond nearby?"

"He was found by the White Stag Pool," Zōzan replied, nodding.

"Your son has dabbled in something very dangerous, scholar. I believe he found it inside this chest."

"Preposterous. He wouldn't even be able to open it."

"When was the last time you checked that lock?"

Zōzan approached the chest and touched the padlock.

"It's broken," he stated, astonished. "How…? Why?"

"Show me what's inside." The samurai stood beside him. "Careful."

The scholar lifted the heavy lid with trepidation, but the inside of the chest looked exactly the same as he had remembered it – old scrolls and musty books gathered in a great pile. He saw nothing out of the ordinary, but the strange samurai reached into the pile and pulled out one of the scrolls, a folded length of paper, darkened with age, with red lettering all over it. It smelled of blood and death.

"What's that?" asked Zōzan.

The samurai put a finger to his lips.

"Listen."

Zōzan scoffed, but then heard something. A faint whisper at first, it grew into a voice, annoyed, angry, mean, deep inside the scholar's head.

"Is that you, Keinosuke? You've awakened already? I should've punished you harder. They've managed to take the foreigner away thanks to your fiasco."

"Who…" the scholar started, but the samurai shook his head.

"Well, do you have something to report?" the sinister voice continued. *"I don't have time for this. If you want to be useful, find out what's happened to your sensei. She should be in the shrine…"*

The voice paused and Zōzan felt a penetrating presence in his mind.

"Wait – is there someone else with you? I sense two minds… Sakuma-dono, I'm honoured to meet you at last, and the other one – oh, it's you," the voice seethed.

The samurai crushed the scroll in his hands and the paper burst into flames briefly.

"What was that?"

Master Sakuma stared at the pile of ash on the study floor. He was terrified, but a part of him was also fascinated by the immense power he had sensed in the voice. What magic was this? Why didn't *he* discover the old scroll first?

"Bad news," replied the samurai curtly, "what did he mean by *your sensei?*"

"It's... Keinosuke's magic teacher, the Takashima girl. She disappeared after the accident. The police are searching for her."

The samurai looked up sharply.

"The *accident?*"

He's not from around here. Where did he come from?

"One of Takashima-*sama's* experiments went awry. The house was destroyed, everyone inside perished. A terrible tragedy."

"How long ago was that?"

"Five days."

"So a day after they found your son?"

"Yes... You don't think –"

"I think I need to visit the Takashima residence," the samurai said distractedly. Zōzan could see his mind was already elsewhere.

"But what about Keinosuke?"

The machine-servant pressed a piece of moist cotton wool to Keinosuke's lips until all the water had dripped into the boy's mouth. It then whirred another arm, wiped his face with a damp cloth then returned to a standby position, announcing it with a bell.

Master Sakuma reached for the key at the back and wound the automaton up again. There were more of these machines – *karakuri* – than human servants at his household. He trusted in their reliability and tirelessness. A well-oiled *karakuri* could care for his son all day and night, without respite.

Another automaton arrived on its tiny legs with a cup of tea on a lacquer tray. Zōzan sipped it, observing the strange samurai kneeling over his son, holding Keinosuke's head on his lap, focused in silence.

There was a static snapping sound, like an *elekiter* spark. The familiar smell of ozone spread throughout the room. The samurai opened his eyes and nodded with satisfaction.

Keinosuke stirred and woke up.

"*No, stop*!" he cried out. "I can help…" He looked around astonished. "Where am I…?"

"You're home, son." Zōzan couldn't hold back his emotions. "You're safe."

"He's not safe here – and neither are you," the samurai announced, standing up. "I suggest you move as far away from the city as you can. This isn't your true home, is it?" He assessed the room. "An aristocrat like you…"

"I have an estate in Chūbu, where the boy's mother lives. I only brought him here to study at the Takashima school – but now, with them gone…"

The samurai nodded.

"Chūbu sounds good. And keep him away from mirrors and stagnant water for the time being."

"Will you not tell me what happened to my son? What power was in that scroll?"

"If I told you, would you promise not to seek it for yourself?"

There was something in the samurai's eyes that made Zōzan cower. Unable to lie, the scholar bowed his head in shamed silence.

*The interrogation chamber of the magistrate prison was damp and badly lit.

They made it deliberately so, realised Tokojiro, *so the faces of the criminals seemed even more menacing in the murk.*

The guard guided Lady Kazuko in, her hands bound with a single length of knotless rope, more out of fear of some witchcraft than to prevent her escaping. Despite the gloom, her face seemed illuminated with some internal radiance, still proud and gentle despite her precarious situation.

Tokojiro's cheek and eye twitched nervously. The scar on his face, covered with ugly scabs, blisters and painful inflammation, refused to heal since he had crawled away from the Mogi Temple through the dirt and soil of the pine forest, blind and mad with rage and shame. He kept scratching it, which only increased the irritation.

He was sitting along the wall with several witnesses who were to take part in the cross-examination of the priestess. Two of the samurai who had found him in the forest were also present to confess, the third one, Hibiki, still recovering from his injuries, ironically – at the Suwa Shrine.

I never wanted any harm to come to her, he thought, but another part of his mind mocked him: *You should've thought about it before you betrayed her trust, then.*

He never imagined the authorities getting desperate enough to harass the shrine, much less – arrest Lady Kazuko This was unthinkable. How important was this foreigner exactly?

The priestess sat down on the cold floor in front of the panel made of a chief of local police, the *bugyō* himself and a representative of the *Taikun*'s secret service, the *metsuke*, who had arrived from Edo just the night before. The respect with which each of them was treating the priestess depended on their rank – the poor local *doshin*, Koyata, noticeably out of place among the noblemen with his plain grey coat and flushed jovial face, was all bows and apologetic smiles; the *bugyō* seemed decidedly uneasy, unsure whether to treat her as a prisoner or a friendly guest, while the Edo notable looked at her with the simple disdain he reserved for all traitors. It was obvious he had witnessed many such interrogations in his career.

"I can smell a traitor," he scoffed at the beginning of the proceedings, pointing at his nose, "and it sure stinks here."

The *doshin* frowned discreetly, but said nothing. The *bugyō* smiled politely, trying to keep his face a professionally neutral mask, but his discomfort with the *metsuke's* presence was easily discernible. He started the interrogation as politely as he could, but the *metsuke* interrupted him quickly with a snarl.

"No need to belittle yourself before this traitor, dear magistrate-*sama*. We know all about you in Edo." He turned to the priestess. "We've been watching you for a long time, waiting for something like this to come up."

"What do you mean?" the *bugyō* questioned, raising his eyebrows. "This trial deals only with the matter of harbouring a fugitive foreigner."

"Oh, there's far more going on here than that," the *metsuke* said with a snigger.

The priestess remained quiet, smiling serenely all the time. Her smile unnerved Tokojiro greatly. *Doesn't she know that her life is in danger?*

"By your leave."

The *Taikun*'s spy bowed before *bugyō*, with a slightly mocking attitude, pointing to one of the men sitting under the wall. The chief magistrate nodded grudgingly. The man, whom Tokojiro recognised as one of the lesser acolytes of Suwa, stood up in a half-bow, approached the middle of the room holding a large heavy bundle and unravelled it before the astonished eyes of the *bugyō*.

"We found this hidden inside the inner sanctum of the Morisaki *kami*," said the *metsuke* triumphantly.

"You dared to enter the sanctum…?"

Doshin Koyata gasped, but the magistrate silenced him with an annoyed grunt.

"What is this? I don't see that well."

The man brought the item closer. It was some kind of wooden statue, roughly hewn. Tokojiro could not see the details from where he was sitting.

"I would be surprised if you recognised it, dear magistrate, as it would mean you're not beyond suspicion yourself." The *metsuke* grinned. "It's one of the false Gods of the Heretics, the Lion-Headed One."

Tokojiro gasped, as did everyone in the room except the *metsuke*, his servant and the High Priestess herself.

"Kazuko-*hime*… Did you know of this?"

"Of course she did," the *metsuke* barked, "you don't think she-"

"Let her speak," the chief magistrate ordered, cutting him off curtly.

The High Priestess smiled and nodded.

"But… Why? This is much worse than harbouring a Westerner."

"It's obvious, that entire shrine is-" the *metsuke* started again.

"I said, *let her speak!*" the *bugyō* shouted and the other man fell silent at last.

"Mizuno-*dono*..." The priestess spoke, her gentle voice resonating in the room for the first time. "I remember when you first came to this city two years ago. You may not know everything about the complicated situation of Kiyō. There are tangled webs of connections, relationships, interests, debts of gratitude and vendettas going back as far as – "

"I have been thoroughly briefed on my arrival," the chief magistrate said, raising his hand, "and two years is plenty of time to learn what more there was to learn. I implore you, please tell me the meaning of this statue."

"It is no secret. The Suwa Shrine thrives on its kindness. Most of the city is in our debt, one way or another. The safekeeping of this statue was one such favour, going back to the times of the Shimabara Rebellion. A small act of goodwill, compared with what we did for others at the time. It was a decision made by one of my predecessors hundreds of years ago, so who am I to question it?"

The *bugyō* pondered this answer, scratching the back of his neck.

"And you swear you are not, in fact, a secret follower of the Forbidden Faith?"

"*Magistrate!*" The *metsuke* rose up indignantly. "You can't believe the word of this traitor!"

"You will behave in my presence, *o-metsuke-dono*!" The chief magistrate stood up to full height and glowered at the other man. "You may be the *Taikun*'s representative for the case, but I am his *hatamoto* retainer, and still your superior!"

The *metsuke* sat down, scowling in stifled anger. He bowed an abrupt apology.

"My powers, of which you are, I'm certain, aware, come from the *kami*," replied the High Priestess serenely, ignoring the outburst. "The false Gods of the Heretics are impotent in this land."

"Western witchcraft," mumbled the *Taikun*'s spy.

"I see," replied the *bugyō*, "I shall deal with this later. This is a new matter that I must consider carefully. Now, back to more recent events, I trust your answers will be as prompt, Kazuko-*hime*, and we will be able to go home before nightfall."

The priestess nodded gently.

"You have failed to report the *Gaikokujin* to the authorities. Was this another one of your favours?"

"Rather, an old woman's fancy," Lady Kazuko replied.

"Kazuko-*hime*, the seriousness of your charges..."

"I understand. No, this had nothing to do with the shrine."

"Why then?"

"Even if I could tell you, you would not understand."

Does she want *to die?* Tokojiro struggled to understand. The High Priestess seemed thoroughly resigned to whatever fate held for her. *Is this all part of some greater plan?*

The *bugyō* frowned, obviously as confused as the interpreter.

"What about the outlaw, the Takashima girl? You have harboured her as well."

"The shrine is a holy place. You are well aware we have a right to do that."

"But she's a danger to us all!"

"Oh, and what danger can a wounded, orphaned, seventeen-year old girl possibly pose?"

"A girl who carries a sword," muttered the *metsuke,* "You have tolerated that family for far too long."

"*Doshin-sama.*" The chief magistrate ignored him and turned to Koyata, who looked up in surprise. "Can you tell us the results of your investigation at the Takashima residence?"

So that's why they brought him here, thought Tokojiro. He was observing the interrogation with increasing discomfort. The two men obviously already knew all they wanted about the priestess's crimes, why did they continue with this humiliating performance?

The *doshin* coughed and ran his fingers through thick black sideburns surrounding his round face.

"I… I have concluded that Takashima-*sama* has performed a series of forbidden experiments that resulted in the demise of himself and his entire household."

"And…?" prodded the *bugyō*.

"And that his heir, Takashima Satō, knew about these experiments and was, in all probability, willing to continue them."

"There you go, Kazuko-*hime*. You must admit, all this does not look good for you. An outlawed wizard, a runaway *Gaikokujin*, a *mitorashita* relic in your shrine... Your close familiarity with one of Black Raven's students..."

The magistrate nodded towards Tokojiro, and the interpreter froze. Were they trying to incriminate *him* as well?

"All this points to the highest treason," the *bugyō* continued, "but I hope we can cooperate and explain everything in a satisfactory manner."

Tokojiro felt sorry for the magistrate, who was torn between acting according to the law and trying to save the High Priestess's life or, failing that, her honour.

Lady Kazuko smiled, but did not respond.

"We know you have sent the boy and the girl away from the city on some kind of errand. What was it?"

The priestess turned her head towards Tokojiro. Her eyes seemed to delve into the deepest recesses of his soul.

"You have the interpreter. He knows everything I told the boy. Why don't you ask him?"

"We want to hear it from you."

They trust me less than they trust her.

Lady Kazuko shook her head.

"I have only given them guidance. I don't know which way they took."

"But what is their aim? What are they – and you – trying to achieve?"

161

There was no response. The *bugyō* sighed. Tokojiro felt somebody's eyes upon himself – it was the *doshin* Koyata, observing his reactions carefully. *He suspects*, the interpreter realised and sweat trickled down his neck.

They had interrogated him, of course – as soon as the three samurai had brought him to Kiyō. He told them the boy and the wizardess were heading straight for Satsuma, to seek help at the Shimazu court. The magistrate believed him, having no other source of information. Besides, it seemed like an obvious path to take for the fugitives: Satsuma was the only place more rebellious and friendly to the foreigners than Kiyō.

He did not know why he had lied; he had no reason to. He cared neither for the *Gaikokujin*'s fate nor the Takashimas girl's. The risk, if he had been caught lying, was fatal.

Because you knew what you did was wrong.

"You must see the truth now, chief magistrate," the *metsuke* spoke. 'she is mocking us with her silence. There is treason afoot in the shrine, we've known about it for years, treason of the highest order, or did you think we haven't heard of your precious *Prophecy*?" he enquired, looking at the priestess, who for the first time stopped smiling.

"*Prophecy*? What are you on about now?" The *bugyō* frowned. "Why wasn't I informed of all these things?"

"It was a plan to overthrow the *Taikun*, disguised in divinations. Naturally, its existence was a state secret."

"Is that true?" The chief magistrate turned his glaring eyes towards the priestess. "Does such a Prophecy exist?"

"You have no idea how our divinations work, *metsuke-sama*," replied Lady Kazuko, not looking at the *bugyō*, "these are not the matters of this world. I respond only to the Gods."

"You're not denying it, then?"

"There are many prophecies. It's what we do at the shrine. We heal injuries and foretell the future."

"And protect criminals and fugitives, it seems," added the *metsuke*.

"Kazuko-*hime*..." the chief magistrate began, rubbing his brow, "you're putting me in a most difficult position."

"I am sorry," was her entire response.

"Not as much as I am. I will have to start treating you like a traitor, not merely like a suspect. May the Gods forgive me..." He stood up and nodded at the guards. "I am tired. We will continue this tomorrow. Take her to the Cage."

"The Cage, *tono*?" One of the guards let out a gasp, but quickly composed himself, wary of questioning the orders of his superior. "Understood."

Tokojiro entered the small square room with walls of plain wood and a dirt floor. In the middle of it stood the Cage, a large box of criss-crossing steel bars. It was not big enough for the person within to stand upright. The priestess was sitting cross-legged on the iron floor, her eyes closed. She opened them when she heard the interpreter enter.

Tokojiro nodded at the guard, who bowed back and left them alone. The interpreter was granted a personal visit to the priestess by the *bugyō* himself, albeit grudgingly.

"I will try to talk some sense into her," Tokojiro had pleaded.

"Very well," the chief magistrate had said, waving his hand, "but don't forget you're not completely beyond suspicions yourself. Any tricks and your head will roll."

Tokojiro knew the *bugyō* was well aware of how he had tried to cheat him out of the *Gaikokujin's* capture, but he was now desperate enough to accept any sort of help. The priestess stubbornly refused to provide any information that could save her life and honour, and the search for the fugitives had stumbled at a dead end. It seemed the next head to roll would be that of the *bugyō* himself.

"What is it about this boy, Kazuko-*hime*?" Tokojiro asked, kneeling on the packed dirt before the Cage. "Why are you willing to risk so much to protect him?"

The priestess looked at him with her wise eyes.

"You haven't told them much yourself."

"That's true," the interpreter admitted, lowering his voice to a whisper.

Neither the *Taikun's* nor the magistrate's men were as yet aware of the Ritual changing the foreigner's face or the disguises the three fugitives had donned. When they had found him crawling around the forest, they had little patience for his incoherent babbling. Later, when it came to confessing before the magistrate court, he had omitted these details deliberately. Another lie added to a tower of lies.

"I… I wasn't sure what I should do."

"And yet you did right." Lady Kazuko smiled. "In your heart you knew what was proper. You've never wanted anybody to get hurt, have you?"

"I only wanted the court to notice me…"

Tokojiro shook his head and touched his scar. His hand reached instinctively to his side, where a sword should be. He still could not understand how the boy could outwit him like that.

"I know," the priestess said, nodding.

The conversation took an unexpectedly distressing direction. He had come with hope of extracting information from the priestess, but instead began to confess himself. It was as if he himself was a criminal in the Cage, and she his interrogator.

"Sooner or later they will question me again, and I… I don't understand why I should not tell them all that I know."

"Oh, but you won't. You are not the kind of man who would betray my trust."

But I already have! He wanted to scream, but the priestess gazed at him with her ancient eyes and the words got stifled in his throat.

She had *planned it all. I'm just a pawn in her game.*

"They will torture me," he said quietly.

"Leave the city. They will not bother looking for you in all this chaos. There will be plenty to keep them occupied."

"You *are* a traitor," he said, a sudden understanding dawning on him.

The priestess smiled.

"I have never betrayed my loyalties."

Loyalties to whom? he thought, and stood up.

"I must leave. It's too dangerous for me to continue this conversation. I will have to report my failure to the *bugyō*."

She bowed politely and he bowed back.

"You have a brilliant mind, Tokojiro-*sama*," she added as he was about to leave the room, 'so use it for good. A career at the court is not worth losing one's integrity over... especially in these turbulent days."

He breathed in sharply and slid the door closed behind him.

In the calm sleepy quiet of the night water dripped slowly from the tiled eaves of the magistrate gate into a lazy puddle below. Somewhere in the distance, a cat cried its unfulfilled urges. The wind rang a tranquil melody in the rain-chain gutters.

I should be doing this more often, thought Koyata. *I had forgotten how wonderful the nights in this city are.* He approached the gate and knocked on it with a handle of his *jutte* truncheon. A face with a lantern appeared over the wall.

"A – ! *Doshin-sama*!" the guard recognised him and disappeared.

Wood scraped against iron as the heavy bolt was removed from inside and the thick door lifted open.

"What are you doing here at this time of night?"

"I couldn't sleep," Koyata lied, "so I thought I'd check up on the security of our prisoner."

"Kazuko-*hime* is well guarded, Koyata-*sama*."

The guard looked wounded by the *doshin's* apparent lack of trust.

"No doubt, no doubt, but you can never be too sure, *neh*?"

The guard agreed hesitantly.

"How many soldiers do you have here?"

"Eight at the wall, four inside, and there're Captain Tsukinari's men, of course."

"Good, good," Koyata said, nodding absentmindedly.

He didn't feel good about the numbers at all. If what the purple-hooded samurai had told him was true, it was nowhere near enough...

*The *doshin* was just about to take his evening bath. He disrobed and started to shave himself, leaving the bathroom door slightly ajar as always. He slid the shaving blade along the sideburns; it was a Western fashion he'd picked up from

167

the Bataavians and something he did not trust the town barbers with.

Through the opening, Koyata spotted soft feet clad in black socks treading softly on the tatami mat. *Assassin*, he realised immediately without even looking up. Quietly, he turned the blade around the handle so it changed into a dagger. Dealing with gamblers and smugglers had taught him wariness. As the quiet-footed assailant approached within a few feet of the bathroom, Koyata slid open the door and lunged forwards.

His arm grabbed in a firm clasp, the *doshin's* feet left the floor, his body flipped in the air and he landed with a damp thud on the tatami.

The stranger let out a hearty laugh.

"Formidable reflexes, *doshin-sama*!"

Koyata scrambled up, still cautious, and saw a tall muscular samurai standing in the middle of his room, wearing a purple-hooded cloak over a gaudy blue and yellow kimono.

"Who are you? What are you doing here?" he asked as soapy water dripped down his naked legs in large slow drops.

The samurai turned serious and took something out of the sleeve of his kimono. Koyata tensed, expecting a missile, but it was just a piece of paper, torn off and singed at the edges.

"I believe you have the rest."

The stranger let the piece of paper fly gently down to the floor between the *doshin's* legs. Koyata picked it up and recognised immediately the soft-curved writing of Takashima Shūhan. It was one of the translation pages for the Dragon Book.

"Don't worry, I'm not here to steal it," the samurai said calmly. "I just want to discuss something with you – something regarding the security of the city. Please," he reached out a hand holding the *doshin's* own indigo *yukata*.

"Can you take me to the fire tower?" Koyata asked the guard. "I want to check one more thing."

"Of course, *doshin-sama*, but be careful, it's dark up there…"

The wooden tower rose high above not only the roofs of the magistrate, but above any roofs in the neighbourhood. A brass bell hung from the roof beams, to be used in case of emergency. From this vantage point Koyata could see all the way towards the harbour, the great white ever-burning torch on the top of the wizard spire of the Bataavians and the square island of the Qin, pocked with the tiny red dots of their lanterns. Most of the city slept under the thick familiar cover of the darkness. The deep blue shadow of the holy Tamazono Mountain shrouded the stars to the north, the flat nothingness of the sea spread to the west. He breathed deeply, the salty breeze from the sea tickling his nostrils. Everything seemed as calm and peaceful as it had always been.

Koyata reached into his sleeve and took out a small copper tube enclosed with dark green glass on both sides. He didn't know what the device was called or how it worked

– all he knew was that if he looked through it, he could see everything as bright as day, if slightly tinted green.

It was one of several artefacts he had found buried in the dried-up well in the garden of the Takashima Mansion, along with the Dragon Book. By law, he should've reported them all to his superiors, but he knew they would either destroy it all or sell it back to Dejima, and he couldn't admit to the possession of the devices to anyone else. His situation was already precarious enough after the way he had dealt with the Takashima investigation.

He put one end of the copper tube to his eye and looked down into the narrow streets beyond the stone wall of the magistrate.

A swordsman appeared in the alleyway, crouching, sneaking, and then another. Koyata spied further – they were now coming from all sides, gathering slowly underneath the walls, eight, ten, twelve…

He recognised most of them; petty cut-throats, unemployed household samurai, masterless *ronin*. The usual bunch he had to deal with on a daily basis in his capacity as a *doshin*, but he'd never seen them all gathered together for a purpose. He looked for their leader and found a man clumsily sneaking in front of the first party. For a moment he turned his face straight towards Koyata, easily recognisable due to a great torn scar running halfway through it.

Tokojiro the interpreter… so the *doshin*'s suspicions were right: all this time the interpreter had been hiding his real role in the recent events from his interrogators. But where did he find the means – and courage – to organise such an assault?

Koyata turned around and reached for the bell, but stopped halfway. There was some other movement in the shadows on the opposite side of the magistrate. He raised the copper tube to his eye again. It was another troop of swordsmen approaching from the forest on the slopes of Tamazono. These he did not recognise. They were all wearing the same uniform kimonos, grey and drab in the darkness. They moved more stealthily than the first group, and in order. The *doshin* assessed that these new enemies were much more dangerous.

Forgetting about the bell, he half-climbed, half-jumped off the tower and ran towards the guardhouse.

Both assaults started almost at once. Tokojiro's rag-tag band of cut-throats surged over the wall noisily, running at the guards with naked swords glistening in the light of the torches. As per Koyata's suggestion, the guards feigned a feeble defence before dispersing in a fake retreat. The attack from the forest was a much more immediate threat. Captain Tsukinari and his samurai hid in the shadows along the northern wall, waiting patiently for the situation to evolve.

The grey-clad swordsmen leapt down from the battlements straight onto Tokojiro's band. Both groups stared at each other in confused silence. Obviously neither of them had expected the other. A second passed then another, until at last the leader of the grey samurai, a bulbous-eyed, grim-faced young man – they were all young and grim-faced – growled an order.

"Get him," he said, pointing at Tokojiro, "kill the rest."

171

Koyata observed the battle from behind a stack of building materials piled up in the corner of the courtyard. Tokojiro's swordsmen were more numerous, but they were hardly a match for the grey-clad samurai. Pushed against the wall of the prison, their ranks melted quickly. One by one they were cut down until some of them, having decided death wasn't worth their mercenary pay, began to dash off into the darkness. Soon only a few remained, with Tokojiro standing valiantly in the prison entrance, scowling and waving a dagger – his sword scabbard dangled empty at his side.

At this moment Captain Tsukinari launched his men into an attack at the rear of the grey samurai group. The guards returned simultaneously, this time armed with *naginata* halberds and muskets.

"Round them all up!" Tsukinari ordered over the thunderclaps of the firearms. "Leave some alive."

The commander of the greys turned furiously towards the new threat. He reached for something hanging off his sash and pulled strongly. A round black object, the size of a ripe persimmon, bounced and rolled on the courtyard sand.

"*Look out!*" Koyata shouted from his hideout, but it was too late.

The grenade exploded with a tremendous flash and bang, shrouding everything and everyone in a thick choking cloud of white smoke.

The few remaining of Tokojiro's sellswords emerged from the cloud, coughing and gasping for air. They were quickly subdued by the guards. When the smoke had at last

172

cleared, there was no trace of the grey-clad samurai, only a few puddles of blood remained where some of them had been wounded by gunshot. Gone also was Tokojiro, the interpreter.

Koyata rushed to the prison entrance and breathed a deep sigh of relief. The door was untouched. The prisoner inside was safe – for the time being.

THE WARRIOR'S SOUL

CHAPTER IX

Itsunen stood in the *shukubō's* entrance, observing the street. An odd, hair-raising coldness and the unmistakable reverberating hum of the Otherworld was creeping ever closer. It had been years since he had sensed a presence like this. It felt almost nostalgic.

Together with Ingen they had already woken and escorted all the pilgrims out of the temple – except the three newcomers who had been inexplicably missing from their rooms. When they had finally appeared it was already too late lead them to the main gate, so Itsunen had to explain the way out the back to the raven-haired apprentice while the others packed.

"Through the kitchen to the steel door – it will lead you into the camphor tree grove. There's an old gate there, unused for centuries. Where are you heading?"

"Do you know of a village called Kawachi?"

He froze at the name. *That's no place for a girl like you to look for,* he thought, but then forced a smile. "That old place? There's a path through the fields that will take you around a mountain to the west," he said, "the place you seek is on the other side, on a slope overlooking the sea."

"Try to avoid the main roads," added Ingen, "and the hills."

The girl did not question why. She must have been sensing the oncoming presence herself, Itsunen guessed.

"What about you?" she asked instead.

"Don't worry about us, little apprentice." Itsunen smiled, touched by her concern. "We are the Hosts of the *Shukubō*. Taking care of the guests is our duty."

He watched her join the samurai boy and the servant, and as the three departed through the back doorway he turned to the other monk with a meaningful glance.

"Have you felt it too, Brother?"

Ingen nodded.

"They carry heavy burdens," Itsunen added.

"But the young one carries the heaviest," said Ingen.

Ingen removed a small shrine of Kojin, the three-headed kitchen god, from its stone pedestal and opened a trap door underneath. He climbed inside and started coughing and sneezing furiously.

"I'm sorry, it hasn't been cleaned in a long time," Itsunen said apologetically.

The other monk came out of the dugout carrying two bundles of white fabric and black leather armour. He then disappeared again and brought up a pair of long poles, the ends of which were wrapped in hemp cloth.

"Hurry," he said sternly, "it's close."

"I know."

Itsunen proceeded to put on the old armour made of black leather scales laced together to form a wrap-around coat. He then tied a white cloth cowl around his head and face, and threw a dark cape over his shoulders.

"I hope you were at least sharpening those," Ingen grunted, unwrapping the hemp cloth from the end of his pole, revealing a long glistening blade of a *naginata* halberd.

"Of course, Brother," replied Itsunen, preparing his weapon.

He slashed through the air three times to test the elasticity of the bamboo shaft. The blade buzzed and lit up in a red glow, as if welcoming an old friend.

"Let's see if you still remember how to use this," said Ingen, picking up his *naginata* and heading for the door.

"Your words wound me, Brother Magonojo," Itsunen said, grinning. "Have I not always beaten you in duels?"

"Only because I let you, Brother Motomenosuke," the other monk replied, with a gruesome smile.

The Abbot stood in the middle of the road, misty wisps floating down from the hillside weaving around his short stocky frame. A young man was standing beside him, tall, bald, a staff topped with jingling bells in his hand. His robe was similar to the white cowl that Ingen and Itsunen wore, but jet black, with red pompoms dangling from the sash across his chest and a large conch tied to the waist. A mark of treason was burned into the man's forehead, but he wore it proudly, making no effort to conceal it.

"A renegade," growled Ingen, and spat.

"Not one of us – he's of the mountain hermits," Itsunen said, and turned to the Abbot. "Father, is this really the way to treat our honourable guests?" he asked resolutely. "What about the reputation of our temple?"

"Guests? You mean *thieves*, who sneak into my house at night. Do you know how much it costs to keep the scrolls in pristine condition? I only wanted a little upkeep fee and an offering for a new roof over the archive room." The Abbot spread his hands helplessly. "Was that too much to ask?"

"Who are *you*?" Itsunen asked, referring directly to the silent renegade.

"This gentleman has made a substantial donation to the temple," the Abbot said, "and in exchange he only wished to meet our new guests. Surely you have no problem with that? Please, let us through, there is no need for violence."

"You have dabbled in the dark arts for too long, Abbot." Ingen lowered the humming, glowing blade of his *naginata*. "What's that lurking in the mist behind you?"

"I have done nothing, I assure you. It is all our benefactor's doing."

The man in the black cowl stomped his staff. The bells jingled and out of the darkness emerged a Spirit, white as death, of a great man clad in ghostly armour, wearing a tall conical hat and brandishing a long hunting spear. His eyes burned red like coals, his hair and beard were a blazing flame.

"Behold, the Spear of Shizugatake!" cried the Abbot with glee.

Itsunen stepped back, astonished, recognising the *yōkai* summoned by the renegade.

"Kiyomasa-*dono*!" he whispered in awe.

"You dare to wake the master of Jōchibyō?" Ingen growled. "Have you lost all sense of what is right?"

"Enough of your insolent prattle, I am your Abbot, your superior! Remove yourselves from my path, or suffer the consequences of disobedience."

"May *Butsu-sama* have mercy on your soul, Abbot."

Itsunen raised his halberd above his head, poised to strike.

"You will regret that," the Abbot warned, stepping back. "Move over or you will die!"

"*It is better to live one day with honour than to live to a hundred and die in disgrace,*" Itsunen recited grimly.

The renegade put the conch to his lips and blew. The Spirit of Lord Kiyomasa roared and launched itself upon the two monks in fury.

Even having their way lit by Bran's flamespark and Nagomi's Spirit light, Satō found it hard to navigate in the thick dark mist. The gnarled entwined branches of the ancient camphor trees formed a barely penetrable web of solid black wood.

"There's the wall," she whispered, pointing at a brick surface glimpsed among the trees.

The night around them was completely silent, the mist muffling all sound.

"Then the gate should be nearby as well," replied Bran, "let us venture this way first."

They soon found the remains of the entrance, little more than a pile of wooden beams, blackened with age and rotten to the core. Remnants of gilding on a carved crossbeam were a reminder of the gate's better days. The two planks that had once formed the wings of the door lay buried in the moss, eaten through by time and worms.

Bran reached for one of the planks to heave it out of the way, but Satō stopped him.

"We don't have time for this," she said, "give me my sword." The wizardess pointed the end of her blade at the pile of wood. "*Bevries!*" she cried, and drew a frost rune in the air.

A chain of ice formed around the beams, sharp icicles penetrated inside with a loud crackle. Satō stared into the ice, focusing on the enchantment as the frost spread through the planks, shattering them into splinters in its wintry embrace.

"*Genoeg!*"

She finished the spell, breathing heavily and the ice sublimated, returning its moisture into the mist.

"Most admirable, Satō-*sama*," said Bran. She did not reply to the compliment; the boy may have been impressed, but she remembered how effortlessly the Crimson Robe had shrugged her ice magic off.

"Snuff out that light, we're trying to be stealthy," she said.

A sound of a horn pierced the silence, followed by a blood-curdling roar. The noise of clashing blades came from the direction of the temple grounds. The mist around them thickened. Satō's shoulder burst in pain; she hissed and almost dropped the sword to the ground...

"Art thou all right?"

Bran offered his arm to support her, but she shook her head.

"I'm fine."

Something shifted in the mist behind Nagomi.

"*Look out!*" Bran cried, leaping towards the apprentice and pinning her to the wet ground.

A reddish-grey phantom dashed out and back into the milky haze.

"What was that?" the Westerner asked, staring wide-eyed into the mist.

Instead of replying, Satō raised her sword defensively, the blade covered with hoar frost. The wraith appeared again, and a clawed arm of smoke struck and bounced off the wizardess's sword with an Otherworldly clang. The phantom vanished once more.

"Take Nagomi and run," Satō ordered.

"What... *nay*!" Bran drew his own sword, the runes along the blades lighting up with green radiance. "I shall not leave thee."

"I have trained all my life to fight things like this one." She was adamant. She had not yet recognised the wraith, but could sense its energy. How did the Abbot manage to summon a *yōkai* so powerful? "You stand no chance."

The spectre reappeared from another side, speeding towards them, rolling its eyes and extending its claws. Bran lunged forwards and slashed his sword through the air and through the Spirit's ghostly body. It shrieked and lashed out against the Westerner. He managed to draw back, and the wraith's long red claw merely tore his kimono and lightly touched the skin.

"C-cold!" the boy gasped.

"Western magic is no good," Satō said, blocking another strike of the deadly claws with her icy blade. As she did so, the wound in her shoulder radiated pain again. "Please protect Nagomi. I'll take care of this thing."

Bran nodded and moved aside. The wraith and the wizardess focused on each other.

It was her first real fight, apart from the brief failed encounter with the Crimson Robe. She kept telling herself she had to remain calm and focused, but her hands trembled, her breath escaped her. She was foolish to waste so much energy on those wooden planks when they could have simply been moved away.

Recalling her training, she rolled sideways from under the monster's claws and touched the ground, marking it with a small glowing rune of frost. The phantom followed her, but it was too slow – before it reached her she was already on its other side casting another rune.

She managed to stamp the third magic seal and then the fourth. This was going well. Her father would have been proud of her. Blood in her veins ran hot with the rush of battle and she almost forgot about the pain in her arm – but when she reached for the last spot, she cried out in agony and fell to her knees, piercing darkness momentarily appearing before her eyes. One of the Spirit's red claws reached her back.

The wizardess braced herself, expecting another blow, but it did not come. Instead she heard the ghost shriek, not in triumph or pain, but in helpless anger.

She turned to see Bran standing between her and the enemy. For the moment, with the light of the moon filtering through the clouds illuminating his stark silhouette, he seemed tall, proud and strong, like a real samurai.

A shimmering magic shield separated him and Satō from the monster outside.

"Western magic be no good?"

The boy winked, his green eyes reflecting the pale rays of the moon.

"Where's Nagomi?"

"Safe beyond the wall," Bran replied, "whatever you plan to do, make haste."

Satō froze the fifth rune promptly. The Pentacle of Seimei was finished.

"*Get back*," she cried and, as Bran leapt aside, she cut through the phantom with great force.

The mystic energies of the five points beamed into the blade, and the Spirit vanished with a noiseless flash, banished into the Void.

This time she accepted Bran's shoulder with gratitude.

Nagomi's heart pounded. She ran through the pine forest, down the slope of the hill upon which the temple stood. Behind her, the mist covered the ground with a heavy blanket. Before her there was only night, cold and dark, lit up only by the comforting flicker of Bran's flamespark.

The shadows of the trees loomed above her. They seemed sinister, spiteful. The branches tore at her skin and dress as if on purpose. The silence of the forest pressed upon her like a heavy blanket. There was evil in these woods and she did not know how to cope with it. The Spirits she had learned to commune with were never malevolent. Neutral at worst, like nature itself, they often required coercing to be helpful, but they never posed any direct threat. She trusted them more than she trusted most humans. The *yōkai* – demons – were the stuff of legends, nightmares.

Only now the reality of their endeavour struck her. This wasn't an excursion around Chinzei. *We could die here.* Was this the kind of threat Lady Kazuko had meant when she sent Nagomi along on the quest? But she could do nothing – she was just a burden, as she had always feared; Satō and the

Foreigner had managed the monster well enough on their own.

We should have gone back to the shrine. This is far too dangerous.

The forest ended abruptly and she ran out onto a field of barley. The city below slept, only points of light in the distance marked the watchtowers of the Kumamoto Castle. The thin ribbon of a river reflected the silver light of the moon.

"I think we made it," said Satō, panting.

She dropped her bag onto the ground and sat on it to rest.

"You're bleeding," Nagomi said, reaching towards her with a handkerchief.

"It's nothing," said Satō and wiped her mouth. She had been biting her lips all through the fight.

"Your back," said the apprentice, "you are wounded. Take off that shirt."

"What was that monster?" the boy asked.

The wizardess started to remove her outer garment carefully, hissing. The claw scratch on her shoulder blade was swelling.

"An *enenra*," she replied, 'smoke wraith. I used to train fighting them in my father's school – but those were just illusions, this one was real."

"A *yōkai*…" Nagomi whispered.

"A minor one that must have come down from the mountains. So I was right to fear the mist… What's wrong, Bran-*sama*?"

The boy was staring at the wizardess in astonishment. His eyes focused on the bandages wrapping her chest. When he noticed the girls looking at him, he turned away quickly. His face was red in the light of the Spirit flame.

"Thou… thou art a *female*," Bran mumbled, swallowing loudly.

Satō blinked twice then burst out laughing.

"Oh, of course, you didn't know. You've never seen me in girl's clothes! Was my disguise that good then?"

"It… fooled me," the boy said, still looking away. 'so thou art not… Nagomi-*sama* and thou…?"

Nagomi was the first to understand what he meant.

"*Eeh*? No! We're childhood friends."

The boy grunted something beyond hearing. For some reason he would not turn his face in their direction until Nagomi had finished bandaging the wound, quickly healing under her warm touch, and Satō put on her servant's tunic again.

"I will need to sew it back together when we get to a village," the wizardess said. "You fought well." She nodded at Bran with honest praise. "You have my gratitude."

"It was nothing," the boy replied quietly, looking into the darkness.

"There was something else," said Nagomi.

She could still sense the malignant presence, distant now and weak. The other two looked at her in surprise.

"Even more terrible. It filled the whole place with dread. Did you not feel it?"

Satō shook her head, but Bran spoke slowly.

"'Tis true. I felt… something. The chill, and the humming noise, as if of the Otherworld."

"Whatever it was, we got away," said the wizardess.

"But those two poor monks," Bran said, looking with worry towards the temple, "and the pilgrims…"

"I will pray for their safety," Nagomi said and discreetly stifled a yawn.

"We can't do anything to help them," said Satō, "we're tired and haven't slept all night. We need to rest."

"Is it safe to break camp here?" the dragon rider asked. "We're in the middle of nowhere."

"We won't find a better shelter in this darkness. At least there is cover of trees here."

The dragon rider did not argue. Silently, he nestled himself in a pile of leaves, leaning against the trunk of a massive cedar. Nagomi wrapped herself in the thick travelling cloak and anything else she could find in her bags to stave off the cold. She huddled up to Satō and, exhausted by the long eventful night, fell asleep quickly.

A perfectly round jade glimmered in the darkness, spreading the life-giving light. There was a shadow in the background, a long, serpentine coiled silhouette.

Something – somebody – was lying among the coils.

The green jewel blinked.

A hand gently stirred Nagomi out of her sleep.

She yawned, stretched and looked around. She was the last to wake. The sky was painted pink, the forest rang out with the morning choir of birds and the green barley shoots covered the boundless fields below. By day the landscape was almost idyllic compared to how sinister it seemed in the evening.

There was little as good for one's mood as spending a night in the wild and waking at dawn. The horrors of last night seemed distant and almost forgotten. For a brief moment the apprentice recalled the dread she had felt in the mist, but she shook her head and forced herself to focus on the present. *We can manage. Kazuko-hime trusted in us. But I need to be strong, not just another weight they have to carry.*

"I'm hungry," she complained, rubbing her eyes, "now I wish I had eaten more of that aubergine."

"Nobody could eat more aubergine than you did yesterday," Satō said, laughing.

"What did the monks tell thee about this Unganzenji place?" asked Bran, rummaging inside his satchel.

"It's on the other side of that," the apprentice replied and pointed towards a mountain that rose up from a valley to the west. It wasn't very tall and sloped gently, but it sprawled extensively in either direction.

"I'd say that is easily a day's walk," noted Bran, studying the road ahead through his telescope.

"We're not going to make it on an empty stomach," remarked Satō..

"Why the disguise?" asked Bran, as they descended towards the villages, moving far off the main roads as advised. He was still not sure how to react to what he had learned the night before. The women in the Dracalish military, like Reeve Gwenlian, wore the same uniforms as men and sometimes it was easy to make the mistake – and yet somehow he could not come to terms with the discovery.

"Isn't it obvious? A woman cannot study the art of war," explained Satō, "a girl can't study anything important at all really, unless she's a nun or a priestess. I couldn't wear a sword, couldn't inherit the school… Soon I would have to marry somebody and spend the rest of my days between a lathe and a stove. In Yamato, only men can be truly happy."

"Oh," Bran said simply.

"Is it not that way in your country?"

"It used to be, but not anymore. We have womenfolk in the army and in the Academy. A woman rules all Dracaland from the Dragon Throne – a strong woman."

"Impossible – a female ruler?"

"I assure you 'tis the truth." Her doubt stung him unexpectedly.

"There was a woman *Mikado* in the days of our grandparents," said Nagomi, "and before, in the time of legend."

"Yes, but they never *ruled*. Is your Queen also powerless, Bran-*sama*? Is there a *Taikun* in your country?"

"I'm not sure – who is this *Taikun* exactly? I've heard Tokojiro use this word many times."

"*Eeh*!" She scratched her neck. She seemed surprised that somebody might not know it, even a Westerner like Bran. "He is the true ruler of Yamato. He commands all the armies, controls the ministers, lords over all the *daimyo*."

Bran thought for a moment.

"There are ministers and secretaries in Dracaland, but no man in the kingdom hath more puissance than the Queen."

Satō pondered his words in thoughtful silence.

A small farming hamlet appeared from around the bend. Bran stopped. It seemed as if some disaster had gone through the village. Except one, all of the houses were tiny, single-room huts, even smaller than those in the servants district at Kiyō, and all were half-ruined with neglect and disrepair. High peaked roofs of loose thatch were full of holes and mouldy, as were the walls of bamboo slates tied with reed. The air was filled with the acrid stench of old moisture. Everything looked temporary, more like a gathering of straw-covered sheds than a village. The local shrine was just a box with no offerings, vermillion paint peeling off in patches and the torii gate leaning over to one side. The only road was a narrow path of dirt and mud,

190

overgrown with weeds. A couple of starved cats sleeping in the tall grass and the crying of a child in the distance were the only signs of life.

"So poor…!" Bran was astonished. "What happened here? Where is everybody?"

"Out in the fields," replied Nagomi, leaning over a moss-grown well to draw some water with a cracked pot standing beside it. She tried the water and spat it onto the grass. "It's stale!"

"You mean some poor folk *live here*?"

"Can't be helped," Satō said with a shrug, "it's the mountain soil, not good enough to sustain an entire village. Poor or not, the headman's bound to have some food."

She headed for the largest of the houses, the only building in the village to have a door. Inside they found a plump man with a bushy moustache, counting copper coins on a flat wooden board. The headman stood up suddenly, startled by their appearance, scattering the coins all over the floor.

"*T-tono*!" he stuttered. "To what do I owe… Is it about the new tax?"

"We did not come here from thy master," Bran said, stepping forward. "We became lost on the way to Kawachi. Do you have some – "

"Give us food, peasant," Satō interrupted.

"Of course, of course." The headman bent in a deep bow, his eyes shooting from her to Bran. "I only have some barley gruel, though…"

191

"Are you trying to lie to my master?" Satō asked, frowning. "You're a village headman, I'm sure you can do better than that. Give us rice and saké."

"Right away, *tono*."

"Didst thou have to be so rude to him?" Bran asked, as they finally sat down to the bowls of plain brown rice and pickled onions. The headman disappeared into the only other room in the house, leaving his guests undisturbed.

"Rude?" The girl looked at him blankly. "That's just how you speak to these people. You can't use the language of noblemen. I doubt they would even understand."

He seemed to understand me *perfectly*, Bran thought.

He heard the sound of a horse stopping on the muddy road outside and somebody leaping down onto the mud. A samurai wearing a dark blue kimono, embroidered with an eight-circle crest Bran saw on the tiles of the Kumamoto Castle, barged into the house calling for the headman. He saw Bran and reeled in surprise. He bowed quickly, acknowledging their presence, but remained aloof.

The headman ran out of the backroom bowing profusely.

"Have you seen anyone suspicious passing through the village?" the samurai asked, interrupting the man's flow of polite platitudes.

The headman glanced towards Bran then shook his head.

"No, *tono*."

"There's a fugitive foreigner on the run from Kiyō, we heard rumours he might be somewhere in this area. You do know the punishment for harbouring foreigners, don't you?"

"Of course, *tono*, I wouldn't even dream – "

"Enough. I don't have time to search this whole village. I trust you, Keichi. Keep an eye out for strangers."

"I will, *tono*."

The samurai then turned to Bran.

"And you are…?"

Bran glanced at Satō and Nagomi; they were silent, their eyes turned downwards. A woman and a servant could not reply to a noble born if they weren't asked directly, he remembered. He felt anger stir within him, struggling to break out. He could barely contain himself.

That's no way to talk to a nobleman. Even a pretend one.

He rose slowly. Already a good head taller than the average Yamato, he was now also standing on the slightly raised part of the floor, so he easily towered over the samurai.

" 'tis polite to introduce oneself first before asking another," he said with indignation.

The samurai took a step backwards. For a moment they were staring at each other. At last, the samurai bowed.

"Apologies, *tono*. I am Matsuo, servant of the Hosokawa clan."

"I am Karasu, of the Aoki clan," replied Bran.

"Honoured to meet you, Aoki-sama," Matsuo said. "Forgive me, but… what are you doing here, in this…" he looked around with disgust, "peasant's hovel?"

"We became lost in the mist. This serf was telling us the way to Kumamoto."

"Ah, yes, there was a terrible mist this morning." The samurai nodded. "Please be careful. There is a dangerous fugitive on the loose."

"Well then, thou best be in pursuit," Bran said, losing his patience.

Matsuo bowed once again and backed out of the headman's house. Bran sat back again, sighing deeply. He looked at his hand in surprise – it was clenched around the hilt of his sword. He thought he heard a chuckle deep inside his head.

"For a moment I thought it was Shigemasa-*sama* again," Nagomi looked at him with concern.

"No, I have him under control," he replied, calming down. His heart was still beating fast, his nostrils wide open. *Why did I get so angry?*

"We should be going." Satō stood up. "You heard that samurai. They know we're here."

Bran let go of the sword with some effort. His hand trembled, covered with sweat.

CHAPTER X

His gag had been removed, his hands untied. Shūhan's throat and mouth were so parched he could only whisper; lack of food and sleep had reduced his life energy to the level where he could not perform even the weakest of spells, and, just in case, his fingers had been shattered at the knuckles. The Crimson Robe no longer feared his magic. He was powerless and drained – or so his captors believed.

The wizard crawled up to a thin straw mat he had been given to sleep on, rolled it away and pressed his broken fingers against the packed dirt. He bit his lips, bravely stopping himself from screaming. The pain was almost unbearable, but he had to endure.

The wounds on his hands opened and started bleeding again. His fingers traced a wavy trembling line of scarlet on the floor, joining with other similarly shaky lines into an increasingly complicated pattern.

This was his last resort – the forbidden, hated, cursed practice. He would fight his tormentor with his own weapon. Shūhan recognised the stench of blood magic right away, the demon in the crimson robe must have been its avid practitioner. Every *Rangakusha* knew of its dangers and disadvantages – but also of its daunting power.

The pattern he was so meticulously and painfully drawing was a beacon spell, a distress signal. Anyone sensitive to magic within range would pick up on this call for help. His tormentor would undoubtedly have noticed it too, but Shūhan had no other choice but to risk it. He only hoped it would reach out far enough.

He tried to guess where he was being kept. The only window in his cell opened to the east. In the day he could hear the shrill cries of black kites and at night, the faint roaring of the waves. Sometimes the wind blew the faint smell of sulphur through the window. He gathered from that he was near some source of the volcanic fumes, by the sea – but there were many places like this on the Chinzei Island, assuming the Crimson Robe had not transported him even further.

The door to the tiny prison opened and the guard cast something large and heavy to the ground before shutting the door. Shūhan's weary eyes could not tell what it was at first. He crawled closer and, in the faint moonlight seeping through the narrow window, recognised it as a human being; a young man with the top of his head shaven - a samurai. The newcomer was almost naked, his skin covered in bloody wounds, scars and bruises. A huge, ugly gash split his face, running through his nose and one eye.

The wizard lowered his ear to the stranger's nose. The man was barely breathing. Shūhan gently touched his shoulder with bloodied knuckles. The slightest of shudders went through the man's body, but he didn't wake.

Shūhan hesitated for a moment, but he could wait no longer. The man was bleeding from his many cuts, the blood sinking into the dirt floor; a terrible waste.

"Poor boy," the old wizard whispered, "I'm sure you won't mind... Your blood is precious to me."

He dipped his shattered knuckles into the young man's blood and, as quickly as he could before the liquid dried up on his hands, crept back to his spot.

"I'm eternally grateful," he whispered, half to the boy, half to himself. "Thanks to you I will finish this much faster."

He repeated the procedure several times until the newcomer's wounds were finally covered with dry scabs and became unusable for Shūhan's ritual.

"No matter, no matter," the wizard murmured, "we'll get back to that later."

At noon – or at least Shūhan judged it to be noon from the way the sun appeared in the narrow window – the newcomer awoke suddenly, gasping with pain.

"Poor boy, poor poor boy," Shūhan whispered, crawling towards him, "what have they done to you? Why? Our captor has no need for torture..."

"I... resisted." The newcomer spoke with great difficulty, turning his face towards the wizard. "I meditated... and overcame the *sokukamibutsu's* power."

"What a great feat!"

"I can think… in two languages… that confused the mind-reader."

"You're an interpreter?"

"I am Namikoshi Tokojiro… Black Raven's student. I know you…" The boy pointed at the wizard with a weak hand. "You're that samurai girl's father, aren't you…Takashima…"

"You've met Satō?" Shūhan was enlivened, finding new strength at the mention of his daughter. "Have you seen her? Is she all right?"

"I…" The young man hesitated. Speaking was causing him visible difficulty. "I accompanied her on her journey."

"A journey – what journey?"

"She left the shrine to search for you."

"Poor Satō… She must be so alone…"

"Not… alone… the Westerner - and the red-hair-"

"Nagomi and the boy…? Why is he there? Why is he not kept safe at the shrine?"

"His *dorako*… is somewhere on Chinzei…"

"But how can he travel? He would be captured in an instant…"

"The – ritual…"

Tokojiro dropped his hand and closed his eyes, exhausted.

"*Ritual?* What ritual?"

Shūhan tried to nudge him awake, but the interpreter remained unconscious.

"Yes, yes," the wizard said, patting the boy gently on his scarred back, "sleep, rest. You will tell me – later. Oh look, one of your wounds opened up – back to work, eh…?"

They were brought food – two bowls of thin gruel containing more water and mud than millet, but it was sustenance – and the portions were much bigger than the last time. They were also given water clean enough to drink.

"Eat boy, eat," Shūhan urged, pressing the edge of the bowl against Tokojiro's lips.

The interpreter managed a single gulp before spilling the rest of the gruel on his chin, coughing.

"What *ritual?*" the wizard asked when Tokojiro pushed the bowl away.

"I'm sorry…?"

"The ritual, you said yesterday, the boy and Satō and Nagomi…"

"Oh, yes… it… changed the Westerner's face. He now looks like one of us. They are all disguised."

"Are they safe? Yes, they must be, or he wouldn't torture you," the wizard answered himself before Tokojiro managed to speak. "Is she going south? Is my girl going south like I told her?"

"Y-yes, she is going south."

"Wonderful! Marvellous! Thank you for the good news."

"It's – nothing… What are you doing?"

Tokojiro gasped with pain and shock as Shūhan inserted his hand into a wound in his side.

"Oh, I'm sorry, I just need a little more of your blood."

"*My blood!* What are you…?"

Tokojiro tried to raise himself and crawl away from the wizard, but the effort caused him to pass out again.

"Don't worry, don't worry, I'm not taking much, just a few drops, that's enough…" Shūhan mumbled before noticing his conversation partner was no longer conscious.

The door to the cell opened and the Crimson Robe walked in, smiling broadly.

"I've given you two enough time," he said and clapped his hands once.

The terrifying living mummy entered the room again, creeping slowly.

"It's no use, you still won't break me," said Tokojiro defiantly.

He had regained a little of his strength by now – enough to crawl away from Shūhan to the other side of the cell. The wizard welcomed this development with disappointment. His pattern under the sleeping mat was almost finished.

The Crimson Robe cackled abruptly.

"I did not come for you, my young friend. I've wasted enough time trying to get through that labyrinthian mind of yours."

Shūhan lifted his eyes, as if only now noticing the demon and his undead abomination.

"You've learned everything I know…" he whispered hoarsely as the *sokukamibutsu* approached him.

"Ah, but that was before you so masterfully interrogated the young interpreter." His tormentor smirked. "I knew it would prove useful to spare you."

At last Shūhan understood, and his eyes widened with terror.

"*No, no! Get away, don't…*"

He then fell silent, his mouth drooped. The living mummy began its patient work on his memories.

By late afternoon at last the three travellers had reached the village of Kawachi. This one did not look as shabby and desolate as the one they had seen in the morning. Bran approached an elderly man sitting on a stone bench outside a small, clean house and asked him about the temple.

With some reluctance, the man raised his hand and pointed towards a low spur of the hill to the west.

"We never get any visitors here," he added, eyeing Bran suspiciously.

The boy smiled, trying to seem confident.

"I have a family buried at the cemetery."

The man nodded. He still seemed doubtful but did not dare to contradict a samurai.

I can get used to being treated like a noble man.

The temple turned out to be very small, at least compared to the vast affluent compound of the Honmyōji. There were only two main buildings and a couple of smaller ones, hidden in the unkempt overgrowth of a long-neglected orchard. Of the rest only the burnt out ruins remained. It seemed almost abandoned.

Nobody came out to meet them, so they started exploring the precinct by themselves, trying to find a way to the cave mentioned in the chronicle. There was a path at the back leading up the hill through the forest, lined with stone statues of sitting monks. Following it they came out onto a wide, sunny hillside glade. Bran looked around. Facing west he could see all the way to the sea, while to the east the spur rose in a rocky outcrop staring at them with a single black eye of a cave. The glade was covered with countless more stone statues, hundreds of them, all positioned in concentric rows around the cave, facing towards it. Most of them were overthrown, some broken in two, all incredibly ancient, covered with lichen.

He noticed Nagomi looking pale-faced staring at the bizarre composition.

"What is it? Do you feel something again?" Satō asked, scratching her shoulder.

"Only a faint remnant… These statues were supposed to keep something inside the cave – but it's no longer there."

202

"That's good to hear," the wizardess said.

Is it? Where is it now, then?

The condition of the statues worsened the closer they got to the cave. The ones just before the entrance were shattered into pieces, shards of stone, barely visible in the tall grass. Bran hesitated at the cave's entrance. He laid his hand on the hilt of his sword. The cavern was wide and shallow, and with the sun at his back he could easily see that it was empty, yet he could feel some lingering presence within, as if somebody was still inside, hiding in the shadows.

Satō was the first to cross the threshold, with bated breath as if she was submerging herself underwater.

"Somebody did live here," she said, pointing at a few utensils and accessories, including a pipe and tobacco pouch, scattered under the bottom wall, "and not that long ago."

"A samurai," noted Nagomi.

In one corner of the cave was something like a miniature study room; a low wooden table, writing pad, a whetstone, an iron-bound chest and a black lacquered rack for two swords – empty. Satō kneeled to examine it.

"It's very good quality, but has no markings," she said. "Everything is well kept here. This cave was recently inhabited."

"But by whom?"

"It wasn't the Crimson Robe," the wizardess said. "This rack is for katana and wakizashi, and so is the whetstone. There's nothing here for a sword as big as the one he carried."

"Perhaps this chest could reveal something."

Bran touched the lock on the coffer and tried to manipulate it using his pen-knife. He had a little practice unlocking his grandfather's chests back in Gwynedd, but this lock was of a better quality. Satō asked him to step away, getting ready to use her magic to open the chest.

"No, I can do that," he said proudly and summoned what little power of his dragon he could. He wasn't sure if it would work at all with Emrys so far away. The blue stone on his finger lit up briefly and he suddenly smelled methane and sulphur, the Farlink momentarily enhanced. He channelled the power of the dragonflame through his fingers. It was a feeble flame, but focused just enough to burn through the wood around the lock. After a bit of a struggle the lid popped open with a satisfying creak.

There were papers in the chest in neat bundles, dozens of pages written in thick but elegant calligraphy, and drawings in black ink, delicate yet precise, which even Bran could tell were made by someone with great skill and an eye for nature. At the bottom there was a set of at least fifty drawings of the same peony flower, each slightly better than the last, until the final exquisite image, which somehow seemed even more true and genuine than a real live flower would be – an essence of natural beauty captured on a piece of paper.

While Bran admired the ink paintings, Satō browsed through the rest of the papers.

"These are notes to a treaty on swordsmanship," she announced, "but there is no name or date on any of these pages, nothing that could tell us anything about the author."

"Then we're back to where we started," said Bran, placing the drawings back into the chest.

A voice startled him.

"Perhaps I can help you."

A lonely monk in a white robe stood at the entrance to the cave, studying them with great curiosity.

"Yes, I know the legend of the Immortal Swordsman…"

His name was Sozaemon, and he was, as it turned out, the last monk left to take care of the temple. Those who did not die of old age moved away to larger, richer temples.

"Some say he had lived in the cave for countless millennia. Others claim he had only arrived here when Katō-*dono* started building the castle at Kumamoto."

"Who was he? Why was he immortal?" asked Satō.

"I don't know. I have never seen him – the cave had been empty for long decades when I became ordained at the temple."

"But it's not empty now."

"What you saw is how it always has been. Time seems to pass in a different manner inside the cave; everything always looks like new, untouched. Sometimes we used to store food there – it would never spoil."

"Why was the cave surrounded with those statues?"

"To imprison the Swordsman inside. According to what's written in the temple archives, demons of this kind can't suffer anything holy. Sanctified ground, priests and monks whose faith is strong – all this repels them."

"*Them?*" Nagomi asked. "You mean there are more of his kind?"

"There were… other legends. My predecessor studied them, trying to find a way to cure or defeat the cursed creature. The demons were called variously – *kyūketsuki*, Fanged Ones, or simply *Abominations* – but they seemed to appear in stories throughout the Yamato."

"Did this Abbot leave any writings? Can we see them?"

"Yes, by all means. They're in the library, but… Why are you so interested in an old legend?" The monk eyed them with amusement. "You're too young to be scholars."

"We…" Satō hesitated. "I think I met one of them."

Sozaemon's eyes widened. He opened his mouth and then closed it. He scratched his beard in thought.

"Even so, why would you want to find one again? By all accounts, these are very dangerous creatures."

"What happened to the one in the cavern? Where be he now?" asked Bran, evading the question.

"One day, more than a hundred years ago, the Swordsman came out, destroyed all the statues and broke out of the temple. As to where he is…" The monk shrugged. "The land of Yamato is vast, and it's been so long…"

"And thou knowest of nothing that would help us find him, or one of his kind?"

"I'm afraid that is all I know, young *tono*."

Bran nodded. He glanced outside; it was getting dark. "We must go down to the village for the night. We would come back tomorrow to see thy Abbot's writing, if that's all right with thou."

"Oh, there's no need to trouble yourselves; I can give them to you."

"Verily?"

"There's no point in me guarding these scribblings if you can find better use for them. Nobody ever comes here, and when I die they will fall prey to robbers. Just wait here, I'll bring them to you, I have them just here…" He disappeared into the room at the back for a moment and returned with a bundle of notes. "Here you are," he said, "life's work of the fourteenth High Priest."

Satō read the title page in disbelief.

"The Tale of the Blood Sucking Ghost?"

"I believe that's one of the names the legend is known by in the north," replied the monk. "You can stay here, if you wish," he added. "There are lots of empty rooms, and there is no inn in the village."

"Thou hast our thanks," said Bran, grateful for not having to share an inn room with the girls that night.

"This is all very interesting, but I doubt it will give us any new clues." Satō was holding the fourteenth High Priest's notes in her hand, browsing through them idly. "We don't really know where to go from here, and we can't stay in this village longer than one night – they will find us sooner or later."

"I… I think I may have a clue," said Bran hesitantly. "Dost thou know the crest of a cross within a circle?"

"Of course," said Satō. "It's the Shimazu clan, *daimyo*s of Satsuma."

"Where did you see it?" asked Nagomi.

"Last night, just before you came for me, I had a vision through my dragon's eyes. I saw a man wearing this crest, and sensed great puissance within him."

Satō whistled.

"A Shimazu retainer… That's a bit out of our league, although – "

"Yes?"

"My father did tell me to go seek help in the far south. I believe he had even met Lord Nariakira once. Perhaps we could find friends at the Kagoshima court, like we did in Kumamoto."

"It's worth a try," said Nagomi, "at least this gives us a direction to follow."

"How long will it take us to get there?" asked Bran.

"More than a week," replied Satō. She was the only one of the party who knew her way around the Saikaidō, the network of highways criss-crossing the Chinzei Island. "As long as we don't dawdle along the way."

"Let us not *dawdle* then," said Bran with a smile. "I can wake us up at dawn tomorrow."

208

"Not at *dawn*!" Satō protested. "I will need time to go through these notes."

She'd spent most of the night studying *The Tale of the Blood Sucking Ghost*. She was lying on the straw mat on her stomach, flipping through the pages with one hand, holding a slowly disappearing sticky rice cake in the other.

Nagomi went to sleep early and was peacefully lying on her futon by the wall. The red-haired apprentice was quick to tire, and Satō couldn't blame her – a shrine life was a peaceful one, simple and undemanding compared with what they had endured over the last few days. Nagomi was coping with the strain remarkably well, all things considered. She never complained.

The stories and legends gathered from villages and temples, mostly around Chinzei, differed little in their content from those told about any other kind of magical monster. The Fangeds, as the High Priest referred to them in his work, were immortal, blood-drinking demons invading remote lonely hamlets, killing everyone within and spreading terror throughout the countryside until a Shinto priest or a *Butsu* monk came to exorcise them. An often repeated detail was that the *kyūketsuki* were created from the Spirits and bodies of the dead, animated by a powerful curse, but that, too, was not in itself a unique feature.

One of the pages Satō marked with black ink and put aside read:

The Fangeds were known for wearing clothes of a

peculiar manner, long priestly robes

of a single colour with no markings. An acolyte in the Hachimangu Shrine on the eastern shore of the lake Biwa reported the colour as crimson red; villagers near Funai said they were dark purple or indigo blue; mostly, though, they were said to be wearing the white of death.

In all these tales the Fangeds behaved like all other demons; ruthless, feral, bloodthirsty, mad with rage and lust. A few black ink drawings, made by the book's author, showed googly-eyed, long-fanged creatures hovering in the air, with sharp claws reaching out and black, snake-like hair flowing in the wind. They looked almost comical. They used no weapons, their victims rather slashed to bits with teeth and talons. There was no mention of any greater agenda that would motivate their actions. Satō could find no explanation as to why one of these creatures would suddenly appear in the middle of Kiyō, searching for Bran and attacking her father.

Perhaps they were looking in the wrong direction. Perhaps the man she saw was not a demon after all, or at least not of the kind that had lived in the cave at Unganzenji. It seemed the Westerner and his dragon were still the best chance she had to stumble upon her father's kidnapper.

She put away the papers and rested her chin on her hands in thought. The Westerner and his dragon. She had been so absorbed in the task of finding the crimson robed man that she had almost forgotten why her house had been attacked in the first place. It was surprising how quickly she had become used to the boy's presence. It did help that, for most of the time, Bran sounded and looked so… ordinary.

It didn't matter to her anymore if the boy was a spy. He stood in her defence when he could have just run away from the *enenra*. In her eyes this had proved Bran's honesty. From now on, they were all in this together.

She yawned and realised the better part of the night had passed. It was time to go to sleep. She stood up and unrolled a futon under the window. The night was muggy, clammy, foreboding of a storm. She slid open the paper blinds to let some fresh air into the room.

A shadow of a bat fluttered from under the eaves, startling her for a moment. A lonely night heron crowed in the distance. The nights in the countryside were so different to those which she was used to back in Kiyō - so full of life. She could smell pine resin and the faint scent of dew on wet soil hanging in the air. She could hear night birds calling to each other in the forest, a choir of frogs in the rice fields and a haunting shriek of a fox. There was something primeval in the darkness, but she wasn't frightened of it. Instead, she felt a part of the scenery outside the window, a sense of belonging to some greater whole. She was part of the Yamato – not only the people, but the land itself. This was what the priests must have felt all the time, she realised, what Nagomi experienced. Perhaps this was why the apprentice had kept her calm on their journey. The land itself was giving her strength.

The wizardess unravelled her travel bundle to hide *The Tale...* inside. Something fell out of the baggage and rolled to the floor with a metallic clang. It was the thaumaturgic device Master Tanaka wanted to give her father. She hadn't even remembered she still carried the artefact. The memory of that fateful day appeared before her eyes all over again. The Crimson Robe, the purple lightning, Shūhan's screams... Satō shook her head. No, she had to be strong and focused. That's what Father had taught her. She was certain he was being strong too, not giving up to whatever tortures the enemy subjected him.

She picked up the leather glove and studied it carefully. She twisted a few gears and adjusted a couple of clockworks at random. The glass dial lit up with blue phosphorescence, but nothing else happened. Master Tanaka had written many pages describing the ways to adjust the cranks and gears, but they were now all buried in the well at the Takashima Mansion.

The bronze needle, however, was pretty straightforward. It was sharp, deadly. Satō pricked herself accidentally trying to pull it out. A single drop of her blood was enough to make the gears start whirling, releasing the power hidden within the mechanism. The wizardess almost dropped the device. The dial went up momentarily before dropping back down to zero and the clockwork went quiet again.

She remembered her father's words.

"Blood magic. It's cruel, it's addictive, it's unreliable and dangerous. It changes you. It drains your soul. It drives you mad."

"Then why do people learn it?" she asked.

"Because it is powerful. No magic is more powerful except perhaps the one the priests use – whatever its true nature. That's why it still fascinates scholars, even though it is largely forbidden in the West."

Master Tanaka had no qualms about creating a device utilising the blood magic. Why did Shūhan order an artefact so blatantly defying the unwritten rules of *Rangaku*? What need did he have for something like this?

Curious, she tried the glove on her right hand. It suited her perfectly. Only somebody who had precise measurements of her palm could have made such a snug fit. Satō realised the truth. A new, expensive Matsubara katana, manufactured to her father's precise directions; a device created by a master mechanician according to Shūhan's guidelines and measurements. These were supposed to be her weapons.

Her father was preparing her for a war.

THE WARRIOR'S SOUL

CHAPTER XI

It had taken them another day of climbing up and down the forested hills before they reached a small farming village on the shores of the Shirakawa River that they thought was far enough from Kumamoto to spend a night in. The next morning they took a ferry across and from there a winding road of flat small cobbles led them east, along the left bank of the great river, to a busy crossroads where, among inns, teahouses and little shops selling all sorts of travel accessories, it joined the main highway heading south.

Along the way Bran observed Satō discreetly. He thought he could now sense tiny differences in the way the girl moved or talked, but he was fooling himself. There was simply no way to tell. Satō spoke the brash manly style of the Yamato tongue, walked straight and fast, both the samurai and the servant boy clothes fitting her perfectly.

"Did you know, General?" he asked Shigemasa.

"*Are you disappointed?*" The voice in his head chuckled. "*I did think the boy seemed effeminate — but then, so do you, to me. I thought you enjoyed his company.*"

"Me?"

"*You did say your school was like a Satsuma one.*"

"I didn't know what you meant."

"*All boys, no women... Friendships changing into passions... You must have been an "under", right?*"

"What..." A sudden understanding dawned on Bran. "*No!* I'd never...!" he shouted out loud with indignation.

"You'd never what?" the wizardess enquired, looking at him curiously.

"Nothing," he replied and looked away, "just a bad memory."

There was a road block across the highway, by the watch tower. Across the sandy road, between a rundown teahouse to the right and a sandal-maker's shop to the left, stood half a dozen soldiers, armed with leaf-blade spears and long-barrelled ornate muskets, and one city official, looking nervously at a paper scroll in his hand. He glanced at the travellers passing him by, but did not stop any of them.

The official was a low-ranking samurai, visibly out of his depth as he tried to perform the difficult duty. Bran, taking a cue from what he had learned so far of the complicated system of Yamato ranks and classes, approached the checkpoint at a proud broad pace, pretending not to notice the soldiers. Nagomi and Satō followed a few steps behind, their heads low. The official looked at him, stepped forwards and bowed deeply. His face was supposed to be a mask of formal detachment, but it twitched nervously. Bran stood back, feigning irritation and appal at the man's behaviour.

"What is this?" he asked, as if he had just noticed the checkpoint.

"I beg your apologies, *tono*, but I have orders to question all strangers going in or out of the city."

"Thou didst not stop any of them."

Bran pointed to a group of travellers in front of him.

"I know who they are, respectable *tono*. Your face I do not recognise."

"By whose authority is this interrogation?"

"Lord of the castle and domain, Hosokawa-*dono*."

Bran pretended to ponder his situation for a moment.

"Very well then, ask away," he said, waving his hand in annoyance.

The official coughed nervously.

"I will need your name and your *terauke*."

"Aoki, Karasu," said Bran, presenting a document showing his allegiance to a *Butsu* temple – a hastily falsified version of the paper belonging to the real samurai Aoki.

"You're affiliated to Sōfukuji?" The official raised his eyebrows. "You do not sound like you're from Kiyō."

"I was raised in Mikawa," explained Bran, this time really growing impatient.

"What is the purpose of your journey?"

"A pilgrimage."

"Ah, you must be on your way to Aoi and Kirishima! Yes, the Kuma Shrines are certainly worth the visit."

"Do not tire me with thy boorish talk, fellow. Dost thou have any more queries?"

"I'm deeply sorry." The official bowed even deeper, unsure of what to make of the stranger and his odd, but noble, manner. "Can you tell me who your two companions are?"

Bran raised his eyebrows.

"What possible interest couldst thou have in a woman and a servant? They are journeying with me. That ought to be knowledge enough."

"Nonetheless, my orders are – "

"*The pox and gout on thee and thine orders! My father was Commander of the Guards at Yoshida Castle!* I shall not be questioned by a common townsfolk scribbler. Now let me through or thy head shall roll!"

Bran put his hand on the hilt of his sword and flared his nostrils, making a fierce frightening face. Despite his age, he was a good head taller than the man before him and the wide sleeves of his kimono made his arms seem much bulkier than they actually were. The soldiers murmured and pulled back, clutching their spears as if they were shields, not weapons. The official's forehead became covered with sweat. Bran grunted and stepped forwards. This was too much for the poor man to handle. He dropped to the ground in prostration, whimpering.

Bran stepped over his quivering body and the girls followed, their heads lowered politely, not looking at the soldiers or the official on the ground. They walked for a while in proud silence. The road turned and entered a grove of old bamboos. Bran made sure they were well out of sight of the checkpoint and then stopped, leaned against a bamboo and breathed deeply.

"That was brilliant!" said a beaming Satō, dropping her bag by the same tree to take a brief respite. "Or was that the old samurai guy talking again?" she questioned, eyeing Bran suspiciously.

"No, I told you I have him under control!" he snapped. Satō reeled back. "I'm sorry," he added hastily. He was strangely exhausted. "It was an act. But I did take my cue from how Shigemasa behaved. Truly, I thought no man would be fooled by it. I'm not... 'Tis not my manner," he finished, catching his breath.

"You'll find that most men of power here are either insanely arrogant or cowards," Satō remarked, "and it's almost always better to be the former, or at least pretend to be. Unless you meet somebody who's really uptight, then you have to duel to see who's the more suicidal."

"I shall remember that."

Bran smiled, but inside he was still shaken. *Duel. Death.* Did these people settle everything with blood?

He had lied to Satō. He wasn't certain if the performance at the road block was just an act. *Commander of the Guards of Yoshida Castle...* he remembered. *How did I come up with that?* The general was changing him, slowly, and he wasn't sure if he liked the direction of the change.

Past the bamboo grove, the highway led them straight south across the vast mud plain separating the mountains from the sea. It then climbed onto a causeway, crossing over many smaller and bigger streams, canals and rivulets flowing down from the mountains.

Bran's overwhelming impression of the Yamato countryside was silence, punctuated only by the cries of peddlers, bird songs, the occasional rowdy chants of the women working in the fields or a distant temple bell. The quietude of the villages unnerved him until he realised the reason for it – there was no livestock in this land. No goats or sheep bleated in the green fields, no cows lowed in the pasture, no chickens clucked, no geese honked. There were a few scraggy dogs lazily lying around the households, but even these were keeping themselves quiet, not minding the passers-by in the least. The only other pets were cats, as idle and indifferent to their surroundings as the dogs.

There were no pastures anywhere, as if the locals believed it to be a waste of space. Every free acre of arable land had been turned into fields. Along the way he had spotted barley, buckwheat and broad-leaved lotus plant but little rice – the tide plain soil must have been too poor to sustain it, he guessed. Where there was not even enough dirt for those crops, the peasants grew rush which, as Satō explained, they then used for covering rice straw mats, or reed for weaving baskets and hats. Higher up the hills, in the distance, he could see flowering orchards of persimmon and tangerine trees. No dry spot was left unused by the industrious farmers.

What the countryside lacked in sounds, it more than made up for in aromas and sights. It was crop planting season, so the fields were sprayed with life-giving manure, the heavy stench of which permeated the air. The villages smelled of vegetables pickling in clay jugs, fish drying on poles and home-made liquor fermenting in barrels. The straw mat makers' workshops reeked of wet rushes. Sometimes a fresh breeze brought the brackish scent of the marsh that separated farmland from the ocean.

The villages along the main road were prosperous communities, with well-maintained shrines and large airy houses and people who liked to laugh and sing. The terrible memory of the deprived hamlets in the hills was slowly fading from Bran's mind.

As the sun rose towards noon and the day grew hotter, the peasants they were passing began to wear fewer and fewer clothes. By midday, both men and women were stripped only to their loincloths, and Bran was finding it increasingly difficult to look any way other than the road ahead.

I have to get used to it, he thought. *Everyone else is. I'm standing out too much.*

By afternoon they decided to make a brief stop on a green glade through which a calm blue brook flowed underneath the weeping willows. There were a few half-naked women there from a nearby village, washing their linen, and Satō and

Nagomi decided they wished to take a bath farther upstream. The day was a warm one and Bran agreed without thinking, conscious of the acrid shameful smell of his own sweat. The Yamato people seemed to perspire a lot less than he did, as if they had most of their sweat glands removed at birth.

As soon as they had reached the bathing place, beside a tiny shrine overgrown with moss and ivy, Bran realized his mistake. Satō threw off her servant clothes with an utter lack of modesty. He turned his eyes away quickly, but not quickly enough. Half-consciously he hesitated long enough to catch, for the first time, a glimpse of the girl's entire white-fleshed body. She was built like a boy – which made it all that easier for her to disguise herself as one – narrow-hipped and flat-chested by Western standards, but she was definitely a woman, already well on her way out of adolescence. He felt his face flushing red. Not having any sisters, he had grown up unaccustomed to female nudity. *Don't stare*, he reminded himself, *it's rude to stare*.

The younger girl joined her friend and they both plunged into the water, oblivious of his embarrassment.

"Come on in, Bran-*sama*," said Nagomi invitingly, "the water is lovely."

He didn't know what to say to that. He took off one sandal and a white sock, and put his toes into the stream then pretended to shiver.

"Too cold for me," he said, smiling weakly, "I'll bathe at the inn."

To take his mind – and eyes – off the bathing girls, he proceeded to repack his belongings he carried in the satchel.

By the time they had finished splashing about he had cleaned the lenses on his spyglass and goggles, sharpened the pencil and brushed dust off the dragon figurine.

Satō climbed out of the stream and stood just a few feet away, drying herself with a white fleece towel. She let her hair down, took out a short-sleeved, light-blue *kosode* robe from her bundle and started putting it on.

"A womanly dress?" Bran enquired, when he dared to look at the girl again for longer than a glance. The clothes seemed to fit her worse than the samurai outfit.

"No more servant rags," she replied, chucking the tattered tunic to the bottom of the bundle. "Somebody could still recognise my *Rangaku* uniform and crest, besides, I want it neat and clean for when I may need it."

"Sacchan, you carry more clothes than a courtesan," Nagomi said laughing.

"Wilt thou wish for thy sword back?" Bran asked.

"Not looking like this." She shook her head. "I told you, girls can't be warriors; besides, you look good with two blades. Like a proper samurai."

"Thou thinkest so?"

He looked at himself. It still felt awkward to wear these strange clothes, to feel the breeze blow around his ankles in the split skirt and plod along the dirt road in simple straw sandals. His Prydain sword in its metal scabbard was a bit too heavy to hang loosely in the sash, and the constant fixing of it in place soon became Bran's reflex.

"I do, and it's *do you think so*," she corrected him.

223

She kept doing so whenever she remembered, but Bran was slow to learn the modern way. The general's influence was too strong.

"Why two swords, though?" he asked. "This is a strange custom."

"The katana is for battle in the open field," she said, "the wakizashi is for close quarters, disembowelment and beheading your enemy."

"Disembowelment…?"

He stared at her, his mouth wide open. Satō spoke those cruel words without any hesitation and finished dressing up.

Misreading his surprise, she proceeded to explain.

"Suicide. You stab the blade into your stomach and cut like this," she said, gesturing, "then your second cuts your head off."

"I… I see," he answered, still dumbstruck.

"Not many people do it this way anymore," Satō added, shrugging, "most prefer to take the dagger. These days wearing two swords is mostly just a mark of nobility."

"We should be going," said Nagomi, picking up her bundle. Satō's gruesome tale seemed not to make any impression on her. "We still have a long way to go."

"I only have one room left, honoured guests," the innkeeper said, looking at them as if expecting to lose his head at any moment.

224

"It's all right, we'll manage," said Nagomi before Satō burst into another unbecoming rant.

It was the third inn they had tried that day, and the first to have any rooms free. There was a millet festival in town, and one of the bridges leading south was damaged in a flash flood, resulting in unexpected crowds filling the city's guesthouses.

"It's our biggest." The innkeeper tried to soften the bad news. "We keep it for our most esteemed guests, *and we serve sea trout today*!" he cried after the travellers as they headed for their room.

The accommodation was indeed quite spacious, fit for a large family. The girls settled themselves along the southern wall, leaving the rest of the floor for Bran.

"We knew it would be difficult to travel during the festival season. Besides, it would have been suspicious for us to take separate rooms anyway," said Nagomi.

"I forgot a woman should not be seen travelling on her own." Satō said with a sigh, unravelling her futon.

This was the first night they were to spend together, all in the same room – until now Satō always had to sleep with the servants – and Bran suddenly became aware of his situation when the wizardess started taking off her clothes before going to sleep. She cast off her *kosode* robe just as unashamedly as she had by the stream. Bran turned his eyes away, but again, not fast enough.

Part of him – the one that accepted all the new information given by the old general – knew this was just how things were in Yamato. *It's only natural,* he tried to convince himself, but he was still a Western boy. The wizards of Gwynedd may have thought themselves modern and rational, but their morality had been inherited from that of Rome and the Sun Priests, even if their religion was no longer universally followed. The edicts of the ancient Imperators, separating the sexes in bath houses and gymnasiums still held more sway over his mind than he would have wished. A conflicting mixture of shame and fascination made him want to flee the room – and at the same time, stay close to the wizardess. He struggled to remain calm and unfazed.

"The girl is shapely, I admit," a voice spoke in his head, *"but inexperienced in womanly arts – you will have no use of her, I assure you. Older women are – "*

"If I want matrimonial advice from a ghost, I will make sure to ask," Bran murmured wryly.

The general harrumphed indignantly.

"Are you cold, Bran-*sama*?" he heard Satō enquire, as if from a distance.

He pretended to busy himself with preparing his own bedding.

"No, why?"

"You're going to sleep in your travelling clothes?"

"I…" he hesitated, "I got used to it on the journey." He made up an explanation on the spot. "On a warship you never know when there will be a call to battle."

His eyes now wandered aimlessly around the room, but, despite himself, his gaze was pulled towards the corner where the girl was lying. He sighed, partly with relief, partly with disappointment – she was already wearing a thin, blue linen jacket and shorts, the sleeping clothes of Yamato boys.

"Suit yourself." She shrugged and covered herself with a blanket. The night was chilly. "I think we're pretty safe for tonight, though."

Why am I lying? he thought. *Why can't I just admit this is not how things are in my country? They know I'm foreign, they will understand.*

He said nothing, just turned his face towards the wall and closed his eyes.

That night he dreamt again of the many women from Shigemasa's past. Their arms were welcoming, their bodies eager – and they all had Satō's face.

"Bevries!"

With a loud crackle, the surface of a muddy pool below the bridge was covered with thick bluish ice spreading for about a dozen yards each way.

"Bravo!"

Bran clapped with enthusiasm. Satō turned to him with surprise.

"That is how Westerners express approval," the boy explained. "That's quite a lot of power, but how about precision?"

She accepted the challenge, stretched out her hand, palm up, and focused on it until sweat started trickling down her brow. She weaved a complicated pattern with her other hand. A column of packed snow started to form on the outstretched palm. Bran leaned down to see closer and the skin on his face started wrinkling up as the spell sucked moisture out of the nearby air. He pulled back to a safer distance and watched with admiration as the column of snow turned into a tiny sculpture of a cherry blossom.

"That… is quite amazing." Bran was astonished. "Rarely have I seen such accuracy in Llambed."

"Surely, the scholars in the West…" Satō protested, feeling her cheeks burn. *There I go, showing off again.*

"Wizardry is a crude and rough school," Bran said, "used for blowing up mineshafts or enslaving elementals. The elementalists are not expected to be meticulous and exact in their work."

"It's beautiful!" exclaimed Nagomi. "I never knew you could do such things."

"It's not really what I was trained for," said the wizardess, "I'm supposed to use magic for fighting."

"Thou would easily pass the third year exams at the Academy," Bran said.

"Why not the fourth?" asked Satō, raising her head up. Bran had already explained to her the basics of the tutoring system at Llambed.

"Thou would fail Prydain," the boy said, smiling, and the wizardess grinned back.

"I keep telling you, it's *you*, not *thou*," she corrected him.

She was trying to sound light-hearted, but the show of magic had dampened her mood. It reminded her again of how she had failed to save her father, despite all her training and skill.

She now realised he had always expected some danger to befall his family, but he couldn't foresee the danger having been brought by his own daughter. By saving the Westerner she had doomed her house. It was because of Bran, because she had found him and saved him, that Shūhan had been abducted.

She found it easy to blame herself for the Crimson Robe's attack, but she couldn't condemn the boy. After all, he wasn't responsible for anything that had happened to him since he had been brought to Yamato by the beam of light… but that wasn't all.

She told herself it was only curiosity. There was something intriguing about the boy, a certain mystery in his behaviour towards her. She had no idea how the matters of heart and flesh were resolved in the West. She only knew men from Dejima often took Kiyō girls for lovers – "Dejima wives", they were called – so there had to be some mutual understanding between the two peoples, something universal, overriding all the cultural differences. Satō was aware of the book Bran had stolen from the library, so at least in some respects he was the same as every other boy she knew, but why was he so awkward about it, secretive, as if it was shameful to read it?

He seemed equally awkward about nudity. Even before discovering she was a girl, he had never undressed in their presence and always took a bath separately even if it meant waiting a long time before everyone else had finished. She wasn't sure how to react. Should she start covering herself in his presence? Plenty of boys saw her nude in the bathhouses and neither she, nor they, ever cared about it one way or the other.

She wondered briefly if his awkwardness would have made him an easier target for seduction… Not by her, of course, by some other woman, never by her. She wouldn't even know how to go about it – although she would be eighteen next year, until now she hadn't even thought about boys in that way.

What am I thinking? I must not get distracted from my mission. In a few weeks he'll be gone, never to return.

The first distant shadows of the mountains appeared menacingly on the southern horizon sooner than Satō had expected. It was raining over the jagged ridge, a heavy, dark, torn veil of clouds descending on the forested mountain tops. The rainwater turned to vapour and rose back to the sky in fast moving billows, giving the mountainside a semblance of being on fire, only to fall back to the ground again in another shower a few miles farther north. The south-easterly wind pushed the clouds towards the coast.

"The rain will be here tomorrow," she said, "and it looks like it's going to stay."

"Surely it's not the rainy season yet?" asked Nagomi.

"That's still a few weeks off, but you never know so close to the mountains. The weather here can be dangerous."

As she had predicted, the clouds descended from the mountains by the next morning, covering the sky with an impenetrable layer of grey. She asked Bran to obtain straw cloaks and bamboo hats for all of them in the nearest village and they trudged slowly on under the first drops of cold rain. Midges and mosquitoes soon rose from the marshes and attacked them with tremendous determination.

"I wish we could ride your *dorako* now," she said, waving the insects away and looking at the low-hanging clouds.

Bran nodded, but did not respond, deep in his own thoughts.

"I still can't believe there are scholars of Western magic here in Yamato," he said after a while, using the more modern manner of speaking, as Satō had taught him. "I have never met or even heard of anyone like you since leaving Brigstow. The Qin ignore it - they have their own ways and they don't care for what we do, since they believe themselves superior to any other race. The beast-heads of Bharata are themselves creatures of magic, so they don't need to study it."

"Oh, if only you could have met my old man," sighed Satō sadly. "I remember him conversing with the Overwizards of Dejima like an equal."

"I'm sure Bran-*sama* and your father will have a chance to meet and talk with each other once all this is over," Nagomi said, and Satō was grateful for this attempt at lightening the mood.

"It will be an honour and a pleasure," said the dragon rider, "but if you have Bataavians teaching you and trading with you, why is there so little Western advancement in your country?"

He waved his hand over the fields.

"You must know, Kiyō is a... special place," replied Satō, "because of all the foreigners with whom we meet and trade, we're much more open-minded. Sometimes the attitude of the Yamato people is as distrustful or ignorant as that which you describe in Qin. Believe me, if you started casting spells in the middle of some village in the north, you"d still get pelted with stones – by those who would not run away, that is."

"I see."

"The government hates and fears change," she added with bile. "They only allow a few licensed premises to study the *Rangaku*, the Western sciences."

"It's not just the *Taikun* though, is it?" said Nagomi. "We all don't like things to change too much. The old ways were always better, that's what you'd hear if you asked anyone in these villages."

"I suppose it's the same in villages all over the world," Bran said with a smile, "but the villages don't set up the national policy."

"That may be true, but in Yamato change always brings disaster of some sort; a war or a revolt. We haven't had one for over two centuries. It's enough to get used to how things are run," said Satō. "My old man often mentioned the 'balance of power' between the great lords, which would collapse if any of them tried to change the existing state of affairs," she added.

"Sometimes a change is a good thing," said Bran, looking pensive. "Those poor people in that rotten village, I'm sure they would welcome any change."

"And how would you propose to help them?" Satō asked dryly.

He started telling them of the machines used by the farmers in his homeland, of how magic, engineering and science produced new crops that gave a greater harvest with less work. Satō politely nodded and feigned interest. She did not care about peasants and farming, she much preferred it when he talked about dragons and war.

He's a country boy, she realised, listening to the lecture. *He may come from a more advanced civilisation, but he's been raised in a countryside, among farmers.* Somehow she had imagined everyone in the West lived in great cities – but of course, the Westerners had to grow food somewhere too. *I wonder if he's even a noble born? I never asked him about his ancestors...*

They walked for a while in silence, interrupted only by the sound of their hands slapping at their necks and faces. The rain changed to a light stinging drizzle. The road became muddy and unstable, barely good enough to walk, and their straw sandals badly needed replacing.

They were halfway through their daily distance, travelling now across a land reclaimed from the sea, mile after mile of perfectly flat polders, divided by a myriad of causeways and dams into neat rectangles of swampy rice paddies, lotus fields and rush ponds.

"So the Bataavians are not helping you with these?" Bran asked.

Satō shook her head, dreading another lecture on agriculture.

"We've been doing this for hundreds of years on our own. By ancient law, anyone who reclaims terrain from the sea gets to keep the land."

"Unbelievable. My house in Gwynedd stands near a dyke like that one." Bran's arm arced the horizon. "There are many sluices and dams at Cantre'r Gwaelod, guarding the most fertile land in all Prydain, but it would all have sunk under the sea a long time ago if we had no magic. Bataavians are particularly good at this sort of thing, that's why I thought – "

"There's no need for magic when you have hard working people," she said with pride, which surprised her. She felt the need to defend the Yamato from this Westerner, maybe because of the way she had ranted about their ignorance and backwardness before.

"One day we will learn all the magic we need," she added firmly, "then we'll be able to change not only the Yamato, but the world."

"Or the world will change you," remarked Bran.

Suddenly he hissed, cursed loudly in his own language and started limping. He crouched and examined his feet. The straps of his left sandal were broken and a wide scratch ran along the side of the foot; he must have stepped on a sharp stone.

"That's my last pair," he stated, "now I have to walk barefoot until we can find another shoemaker who can make sandals to fit my feet."

"That won't be easy," said Satō, giggling.

Bran glanced quickly behind then stood up and looked towards the northern horizon with a frown.

"What is it?" she asked.

She looked back too, but the flood plain lay open and empty all around them as far as the eye could see.

"Nothing..." Bran shook his head. "It was just for a moment... I could swear I saw somebody following us, but there's nobody there."

"It would be difficult to hide anywhere in this bare flatland," said Satō, dismissing his concern.

"I must be seeing things in the rain."

The boy shrugged and moved on, limping slightly.

THE WARRIOR'S SOUL

CHAPTER XII

Hosokawa Narimori, the tenth ruling lord of Kumamoto, was sitting by the reading desk in a study room on the third floor of his formidable black castle. The sliding walls of this small chamber were covered with golden foil and magnificent paintings of green cypresses growing on blue mountaintops, river valleys, waterfalls and cedar tree groves. This was Hosokawa's favourite place in the castle, reminding him there was a more peaceful, more beautiful world outside the walls of the busy city below the keep. He had had the straw mats removed from the floor and put a high chair and a reading desk by the window.

The furniture was of Vasconian make, almost three hundred years old. The desk was of solid dark oak, a rectangular top supported by sculpted columns. The chair was of the same set, with a leather seat studded with brass rivets and a back of ebony, carved with scenes of maritime life, fishermen at sea and great trade galleons. The Eagle of Rome spread its wings proudly over the crest.

Lord Hosokawa preferred to sit by this desk and work in a Western manner, rather than at the usual low table with just a flat cushion for a chair. The ancient exotic furniture reminded him of the glory days of his clan, and he found the rigid upright position helped him to focus better – and focus

237

and peace of mind were what he needed the most. After all, he had an entire province to rule, a province vast, populous and rich.

His ancestors had enjoyed the longest period of peace in known history. Ancient armour of the clan's founder stood, its lacquered scales gleaming white, under the wall of the room, reminding him of the violent past, but it was just a copy ordered by Narimori's father in times of prosperity. Polished daily by the servants, it was never to be used in combat.

Narimori had hoped this peace would last at least throughout his time. Unfortunately, recent events made it seem increasingly unlikely.

He was now reading a seven-centuries-old excerpt from the chronicles of Karatsu Shrine, for the third time. It was written in an archaic language, with archaic alphabet, and Hosokawa struggled with deciphering every line. He wasn't even sure if his work would be worth the effort. So far, he couldn't find anything in the old chronicles to help him solve his conundrum.

Lord Shimazu Nariakira, *daimyo* of Satsuma and Lord Hosokawa's closest ally, had asked him personally for this favour.

"I need your books, Narimori." Nariakira referred to the lord of Kumamoto by his first name, indicating how close they were. "I need your grandfather's libraries, your learned monks. I have many books on engineering, economy, agriculture, magic, all very modern and very useful, but your clan has always been more interested in the past, ancient histories, myths and legends. Perhaps we can find some answers there."

How did one deal with a dragon? Sure, the legends gave vivid descriptions of the creature, its dreadful presence and powers of destruction, and told at length of how heroes and warlords fought and defeated them in valiant combat or how priests and monks placated them and persuaded to leave the populace in peace. However, he had found no clue, no hint as to what one should do with a captive sedated beast, like the one Lord Nariakira had shown him a few days earlier.

Killing it was not an option; it was too precious, too important. If tamed, it would have made a formidable weapon against any enemies of the Southern lords. Hosokawa dared not yet think of using the dragon against the *Taikun* himself. For two hundred and fifty years the *daimyo*s of the Southern provinces had been harbouring their grudges and plotted the demise of the Tokugawa regime. The plans never went any further than annual meetings of the resentful *daimyo*, on the anniversaries of the fateful Battle of Sekigahara, where their ancestors had been so soundly defeated. They all drank lots of saké and raised many patriotic toasts – and rode back to their residences harmlessly… But the discovery and capture of the dragon on the beach of Satsuma had the potential to change everything.

If only they knew how to use it.

He stood up from the desk and walked to a larger window on the other side of the room. From there he could see beyond the castle walls and moat, all the way to the Shirakawa River in its serpentine coils, the river harbour filled with boats and ships, and a merchant district that had grown on the other side of the river, opposite the old city. His subjects were getting ready to sleep as the sun set beyond the western sea, painting the horizon bright red.

The sky today is the colour of steel and blood, he thought. *There's a poem in that.*

"*In the first year of the Angen era we got news of the great white Ryū of Kurama Temple in Heian defeated by a young warrior of sixteen years. There was much jubilation, and the* Mikado *declared a day of gratitude throughout the country.*"

A clear, stern voice read out the words from a book that lay on the *daimyo*'s desk. Startled, Hosokawa turned around, pulling out his tantō dagger from a hidden sheath. A pale-faced man with slightly bulging eyes, Vasconian-style whiskers and a pointed beard stood by the desk, looking at the *daimyo*, smirking.

"*You*! You're back!"

The man bowed.

"That's a splendid desk, *kakka*. Not many like it left in the country, I believe."

"I don't know of anyone else who would have one of this quality, and with a matching chair," agreed the *daimyo*. "Have you returned to discuss furniture? I haven't seen you since my father's days."

"You're reading of dragons? That's unusual."

"I have my reasons." The *daimyo*'s voice contained a command and a warning. *Do not ask anymore.*

"I understand." The intruder bowed. "You seem unhappy, *kakka*."

240

"Of course I'm unhappy!" Hosokawa hid the blade back into the secret sheath and raised his hands in exasperation. "My best advisor has just disappeared on some random errand. The magistrate of Kiyō pesters me with demands. My soothsayers see only darkness wherever they look. There's been some kind of massacre at one of the city temples – and now *you* appear in my castle, uninvited, bearing no good news, I bet."

The man's face, twisted in a mocking grin all this time, turned serious.

"Which of your advisors is missing?"

"Yokoi. I wouldn't have anyone else just wander off like that, but I trust his judgment and wisdom too much to question his decisions. Now your face is as sour as mine," the *daimyo* said, laughing wryly.

"I was hoping to discuss something with Yokoi-*dono* tonight."

"Well, I'm sorry to disappoint." Hosokawa scowled. "You will have to settle for me, his less knowledgeable superior."

The samurai scratched his cheek in thought and frowned.

"Are you familiar with the Society of the Eight-Headed Serpent, *kakka*?"

The *daimyo* nodded.

"I understand that they have all been vanquished a long time ago."

"You understand wrongly. They have never been stronger than now, and if we don't stop them, they may soon grow even more powerful."

Lord Hosokawa stared at the intruder for a moment then inhaled loudly.

"Come with me to the Quiet Room. It's the only place in the castle where I'm sure nobody will spy on us."

For a moment everything fell silent. Not a bird chirped, not an insect buzzed. Even the air stood still as the wind paused in anxious heavy expectation.

The earth moved.

That it was more than just another harmless tremor, Sozaemon first realised when the bottle of sacrificial saké tumbled and rolled off the altar. One by one, the tiny statues of the Bodhisattvas toppled over. The bamboo frame of the wall creaked and heaved. The slates started breaking, the paper tore. The ground groaned and creaked, cracked into hairline fissures that grew dangerously wide with every second.

As abruptly as it had started, it all stopped.

For half a minute more there was silence. Then a lonely frog croaked in the pond and the forest around the shrine erupted in sounds, as if nature was trying to pretend nothing had happened.

Sozaemon crawled out from the futon cupboard and assessed the damage. It was relatively minor. He picked up the statues and fixed the altar trappings. The paper panels would need more work, and money. He dreaded looking at the roof – there were spare tiles under the veranda, but he hated the idea of climbing all the way up.

He sighed. Was it really worth it? There didn't seem to be anybody who would appreciate his efforts. Even the villagers rarely visited, and then only to pay their respects to the local *kami* enshrined in a vermillion chapel behind the Worship Hall. He couldn't remember the last time anybody had made a substantial offering for the upkeep of the temple.

He was the last of the line, the sixth of the Sozaemons. There used to be three Guardians of the Unganzenji – Brother Sozaemon, Brother Magonojo and Brother Motomenosuke – but the other two clans eventually had neither the will nor the means to appoint new heirs to the insignificant, impoverished temple. Now he was alone in the big house. Maybe it was time to shut the door and move on. He could become an itinerant beggar-monk or go back to Honmyōji. He had heard the old Abbot had died recently, so maybe there was still a vacancy for the position?

Sozaemon opened the offering box to see if he could afford to buy new paper for the walls. There was the usual handful of small coins and, shining like the sun among the clouds, a single piece of gold. It must have been left by the three travellers who came looking for the Abomination. They were a strange group – the boy spoke rarely and with an accent he had never heard before, the servant boy behaved like a samurai. They reminded Sozaemon of an old play he had once seen, in which the warrior Yoshitsune and his faithful servant, Benkei, traded places to fool the pursuing guards. He chuckled. Whatever the nature of their

243

mission, they had paid real gold. The coin he rolled in his fingers would be more than sufficient to pay for all the repairs.

The discovery put him in a better mood. Maybe *Butsu-sama* had not abandoned him yet.

Sozaemon climbed up the forest path towards the cave, to see what damage the earthquake had done to the stone statues. He didn't dream of fixing them, he was simply curious. A few large trees lay across the path, felled by the tremors. Having to bypass them made his journey more arduous and longer than usual. By the time he came out onto the glade, he was panting and sweating, out of breath and cursing the moment he had the idea to make the trip.

Four or five more statues had toppled and sunk into the liquefied ground, but the rest had held up remarkably well. He noted with regret that a large crack had appeared across the head of one of his favourite sculptures – the disciple with a peony flower. It would not survive the next quake. He patted the statue on the head, like an old friend, and headed towards the cave.

Nothing ever changed in the cave. The monk came here so often that he now knew the position of every item, every accessory. He could see the disturbances done by the three travellers – some papers rustled, the chest burnt through around the lock - but other than that, everything was as usual. The writing pad on the table, the sword stand by the wall, the smell of tobacco smoke…

He sniffed again. This had never happened before. It was the unmistakable scent of a freshly lit pipe. He looked quickly at the place by the bedding where the pipe and tobacco pouch had always lain. They were gone.

He felt a presence behind him; a dreadful, cold presence. If he had any hairs left unshaven, they would have stood on end. The cold sweat of terror replaced the sweat of fatigue.

"Who…"

"Don't turn around," a voice spoke, icy and sharp like the blade of a sword.

Sozaemon did not repeat the question.

"You came back," he stated the obvious.

"Where is Kiyohide?"

"The fourteenth Abbot? He's been dead for years."

The shadow behind him hissed impatiently.

"I forgot how short-lived you people are."

"Can I… can I sit down?"

Sozaemon was feeling increasingly weary in the presence of the dark being. He *felt* the creature nod, and sat cross-legged on the cave floor.

The Abomination spoke.

"There was somebody here."

"Travellers," he said with a shrug.

"More than that. Where are they now?"

"Why do you care? They didn't take anything from the cave."

"It would be shrewd of you not to question my motives and just answer me."

The voice cut him like a knife and the monk swayed as if he had been physically hit. His heart pounded madly. He felt like a mouse facing a snake. He wondered what it would be like to turn around and look the Abomination in the eyes. Were they really golden, like the legends said?

"They were asking for the best way south, beyond Kumamoto."

"That's better. When did they leave?"

"Two days ago. I… I gave them Kiyohide-*sama*'s writings," he added, sensing it was somehow important.

"I see – interesting."

"Please don't hurt them. They are just some kids," the monk pleaded.

"I will do as I see fit," the voice said calmly, trickling like a wintry waterfall.

There was a pause in the conversation and Sozaemon heard a puffing sound. A cloud of robust sharp tobacco smoke enveloped him.

"Do you still train in the Five-fold Way?" the creature asked, its voice now milder and warmer.

"I… Not as much as I used to," the monk admitted.

The question had surprised him, but only a little.

"That's no good. You should always train. It keeps your mind sharp and your body fit."

"I know, I just – "

He didn't finish. The air around him was not so cold anymore, and he could take a deeper breath. He turned around. The creature was gone, only the scent of tobacco remained, and two sets of wooden prayer beads on the cave floor.

Sozaemon wiped the sweat from his brow and stooped to pick the beads. They were marked with the crests of Magonojo and Motomenosuke clans. He sensed something terrible had happened to their owners.

He sighed. Now he really was all alone. The first drops of rain moistened the bald heads of the statues outside.

A powerful blast shook the brick wall. A soldier dropped his musket and fell down from the battlement with a shriek, but the thirty-foot tall rampart held.

The spider-machine swayed on its thin iron legs, rotated the wooden turret against another target and the long, ornate bronze cannon fired again. This time the cannonball smashed through the wall of a whitewashed steeple on the northern corner of the bastion. The curled pointed roof tumbled to the ground in smoke, and the rebels in and around the machine let out a triumphant cry.

Dylan observed the battle from the safe distance of the Concession, holding the spyglass in his left hand, his right arm in a makeshift sling. The Heavenly Army surrounded the circular walls of the Old City completely, cutting it off from the river to the east and the foreigners' district to the north. It was a matter of days before Huating was taken, but the rebels left the Concession alone. Where else would they get ammunition and fuel for their hellish machines if not from the Western Barbarians?

The Foreign Concession in Huating was a far cry from the splendour and luxury of the Thirteen Factories. Here, the district inhabited by the Westerners was just a random jumble of low wooden buildings, on a malaria-ridden island in the middle of the marsh. Only the headquarters of the trading company in the centre was constructed of local brick and limestone.

But the place had access to a good river harbour, and was much closer to the great cities of the northern Qin than Fan Yu. Dylan was certain it would grow to become a great port one day. *If there is anything left of it*, he thought, as another cannonball whistled over the ramparts and exploded near a tall, yellow-plastered pagoda.

There was a triple knock on the door. Dylan put away a map of the river delta and looked up.

"What is it, Banneret?"

The Tylwyth Teg entered, stamping his heels and nodding.

"It's Reeve Gwenlian, Sir."

"Leave us."

She entered the office limping slightly and sat down on a rickety chair.

"Any luck?"

She shook her head. Her black hair was cut short now that they were in a war zone, but still beautiful.

"The villagers know nothing, or so they say. We tried the Southern camp, but it was too well defended."

Dylan looked at her sternly.

"No casualties, I hope?"

"Nothing but flesh wounds."

He ran his fingers through his scraggly beard. He hadn't shaved since the *Ladon's* disaster, too busy and distressed to think of such minor details.

"I told you not to risk the soldiers for my sake. The boy is in a safe place."

"I'm sorry, Dylan —*Ardian*," she corrected herself hastily, "but, how can you be so sure?"

"You studied in Brigstow, didn't you? So you won't know how the Seal of Llambed works… Trust me, Bran's whereabouts are the least of our worries."

"If you say so."

"How is your leg?"

"I will live," she replied, grinning.

"That's as much as any of us can hope for," he said, nodding.

"What about you? You look as though you haven't slept for days," she said, her black eyes filled with worry.

"I don't sleep that well lately," he agreed. "I still dream about the disaster."

In his long career as a soldier and spy, Dylan had seen his share of death and suffering, but he knew the screams of his men and crew of the *Ladon* being boiled alive in the raging flaming waters of the Qin Sea would haunt him until the end of his days.

There was nothing he could have done to help them. He was the leader of his soldiers and had to make a decision, however difficult it would prove to be. They were over a hundred miles from the nearest land, and the dragons were already tired with battle – some were injured. If they were to have any chance of survival, the squadron had to fly away from the mayhem, unburdened, leaving the poor souls to their doom.

He had never learned what had caused the terrible explosion, but he could guess it was no accident. Only a skilled, well-prepared saboteur could have sunk the greatest ship ever built with one blow. How did he get past the guards? Were there traitors among the crew? He would never know for certain.

At least Bran was safe. Of that he was sure. He had witnessed the white pillar of light pierce the night sky over *Ladon* and knew instantly what it meant – the Seal of Llambed. He had circled over the chaos once to make sure – the boy was nowhere to be seen and his jade green dragon was flying away into the darkness, in the opposite direction to the land, too far to try to catch it. *Good riddance*, Dylan had

250

thought, angry with the dragon for not trying to save its rider. In the end it was just a selfish coward like all its kind.

Nonetheless, he knew Bran's fate was only his own fault. If only he had been more forceful in Fan Yu! He should never have agreed to the boy's demand, and then, just before the explosion – did he have to lose his nerve and enchant Bran with Binding Words? What it must have been like for the boy to see the ship fall apart around him and not be able to move... Still, he was proud of how his son managed to stay calm enough to invoke the power of the White Eagle. He could only hope the Seal's magic did not carry him all the way to Gwynedd. Dylan would never be able to face his wife again.

"I'm sure I could help you forget," the Reeve said with a coy smile.

"Thank you for the offer, Gwen, but I'm afraid I will be too busy tonight."

"Don't overexert yourself, Ardian. We will need all your strength and wits if the battle comes our way."

"Let's hope it won't come to that."

The squadron – whatever was left of it – had landed in Huating at the break of day the morning after the disaster. There was no time to mourn their fallen comrades. By afternoon they realised they were in the middle of a war zone. The right wing of the rebel army besieging the Southern capital moved against the harbour town, defended only by a handful of imperial soldiers and the tall walls of red brick and dark sandstone.

The rebels seemed as numerous as the grains of sand, but even more fearsome than their numbers were their fighting machines. Like the whirligigs of Fan Yu, these monstrous automata were built of bamboo, leather and rope, powered by cranks and gears turned by the arms of men. They were as big as houses, armoured with studded cast iron plates, armed with cannons and pipes spewing Roman Fire. The garrison at Huating had nothing that could even touch the machines.

"If only we still had the *Ladon*," said Edern, standing beside him at the wooden palisade surrounding the Concession — a boundary mark more than a fortification. "One broadside would wipe this entire battlefield clean."

He was also wounded — his left side was tightly wrapped with blood-soaked bandages, but his Faer organism was strong and quickly regenerating. The Ardian and his Banneret suffered their injuries on their first — and, so far, last — patrol over the front line. In an uncharacteristic mistake, Dylan had underestimated the rebels and their ability to quickly gather a strike force against a couple of Western dragons. There were only five of them on patrol and at least fifteen rebel *long*s, white as alabaster, topaz yellow, and green like fresh grass, spewing poisonous mist and lightning. They fought bravely and cast all fifteen from the skies, but failed to come out of the skirmish unscathed. Four of them returned with injuries, the fifth, ensign Dunstone, was thrown off his mount and captured.

Dylan wondered if his son had suffered the same fate — imprisoned by the rebels. There was no way of knowing. No message could get in or out of besieged city except a carrier wisp they had managed to send out on the first day, before the rebels disrupted Huating's ley line.

"The Crown must have already sent reinforcements," he had told Edern, "they should be here in a matter of weeks."

"Will we hold out that long?"

"They wouldn't dare touch us."

"They already have. That's why we're here."

"That was subterfuge. We have no proof of the identity of the perpetrators. It could have been any of the Dracaland's foes. An open attack against a colonial power would bring down the wrath of the entire Western world upon their heads. They must be aware of this."

"I hope you're right, Ardian. *Ho*! There's something flying from the city!"

Dodging the musket shots, zigzagging around rockets and deflecting the rebels' arrows, a fragile whirligig was approaching swiftly across no-man's-land and the marsh separating the Old City from the Concession. It was a large vehicle, powered by at least three men, armoured with silver plate and decorated with the imperial colours.

"What a *twp*," Dylan shook his head. "Flaunting the flag in this situation – are they trying to get themselves killed? Prepare the landing glade."

The vehicle was almost over the palisade when a stray flare hit one of its bamboo propellers. The whirligig turned over and fell to the ground with its landing legs sticking up like a dead beetle.

"*Jawch*! Edern, get the medics!" shouted Dylan, jumping off the palisade.

CHAPTER XIII

A broad-shouldered, balding man with a long oval face stood in front of the cage, peering inside. His eyes were close set and clever. A large cross-and-circle crest adorned his elegant, rich off-white kimono and vest.

"Marvellous," he said quietly, "amazing, and, dare I say, quite terrifying."

"The *dorako* are known to induce irrational fear in anyone unprepared, *kakka*," the lanky man in horn-rimmed glasses said, stepping forwards, "even when they are dormant like that."

"There's nothing irrational about it, my good wizard," the aristocrat said, laughing. "It's as big as a whale and has teeth bigger than a shark. I'm certain this little cage of yours will avail nothing if the beast wakes up."

"We are doing our best to prevent this from happening, *kakka*," the wizard said with a bow.

"Are you prepared for the transfer to Kirishima?"

"Almost, *kakka*. The oxcart will be ready tomorrow."

"Good. We can't wait any longer. I need my daughter to be on her way in a matter of days."

"You will not be accompanying us?"

"I need to sail to Nansei. There's a report of some black-winged monsters I need to investigate."

"More *dorako*?"

"If only we were so lucky!" the aristocrat said. "No, I don't think – " He stopped abruptly, leaned nearer to the cage and stared closely at the dragon. "Look at its eyes, Heishichi. The beast is not asleep at all – it's watching us."

The wizard frowned then clapped his hands twice. Two more men appeared, reaching their hands out towards the dragon. Together, all three chanted a brief incantation, then the man in glasses puffed a handful of white dust into the air. The dragon's head dropped to the floor of the cage with a thud.

Bran awoke from a half-dream, half-trance. It was the middle of the night and the rain outside the inn's windows lashed in a monotone. The blue light on Bran's finger faded fast, just like the memory of the vision, and soon both the room and his mind were again enveloped in total darkness.

The floor was trembling strangely as if it was alive. At first he thought it was just another part of the dream, but then realised the tremors were real, though now barely felt. The whole thing lasted for less than a minute and he soon fell asleep again, quickly forgetting about the odd experience.

The boat was long, narrow and wobbly, but the oarsman knew his job and the shoddy-looking vessel soon started moving up the Kumagawa at the pace of a brisk walker.

The great Kumagawa, Bear River, tumbled down the mountains into the Yatsushiro Sea, forming the southern boundary of the flatland. On Bran's map the only way farther south was by the sea – a route which they could not choose, fearing the harbour guards might spot them – or up the river, across the wild hills that quickly became ominous rocky summits, hemming the Kuma Valley in between walls of granite and basalt.

An oar-powered boat... Bran had never seen one of this size; the only oar boats he knew were leisure coracles and canoes used for recreation on the rivers and *camlas* of Gwynedd. He remembered the great canal barges, transporting elementals from the Southern mines to the industrial centres of the north. Most of them had mistfire engines, although some were still pulled by kelpies. The Yamato had neither technology nor magical beasts to ease their lot, and the oarsman – just like the palanquin porters, Bran remembered – had only his strong muscles to push the boat against the swift current.

He pondered Satō's words about "changing the world". *She may have been boasting, but there is some truth in it,* he thought. The polders through which they had travelled were an astounding feat for a people who used neither magic nor machines. How many hundreds of years had it taken to reclaim the marshland and turn it into fertile fields? How many thousands of people had struggled against the elements throughout the centuries? The potential of these people was staggering. It seemed once they decided to do something,

257

they would spare no time, effort and resources to achieve it in the best way possible.

The way they performed magic, once they got into it, was amazing too. The Yamato have managed to turn even Western wizardry into art. He wasn't just flattering Satō with praise - with the power and control she exhibited, the girl would have been a star of any school of mystic arts. She said her father was even more talented! Yes, these people had the capacity to change the world, if they were stirred enough to do it. But to what end? He remembered Satō explaining nonchalantly about suicides and executions and a shudder went through his spine. And she was supposed to represent the enlightened ones...

The river meandered across the valleys, canyons and gorges, through deep, dense humid forests of tall proud cedars and spry cypresses. Their trunks shot straight upwards like pillars supporting the skies. He had never seen trees like these, and he would often cry out in admiration at a particularly awe-striking specimen.

"It's just trees, what's so great about them?" asked Satō.

"In my country we cut most of our forests down," he replied sadly. "The Dracaland fleet needed a lot of timber. Only in the mountains the old wood remained, but nothing like this..." he paused, gazing at the striped bark with awe.

"Many great Spirits live in these forests," said Nagomi piously.

The other two looked at her in surprise, as she'd been keeping quiet all day.

"I can sense them. The great trees speak to each other in the rustling of the leaves, the howling of the wind."

"The trees?"

Bran eyed the forest suspiciously. There was a time when he would have dismissed this talk of Gods and Spirits as superstitious nonsense, but now he was curious.

"Of course, look!"

She pointed at an enormous gnarled cedar, its trunk bound with hemp rope and paper tassels, a gate of vermillion logs before it. Bran had seen these decorations many times already and often wondered what they meant.

"This one is old beyond measure, and many come from afar to revere and admire it. Its spirit is ancient and wise. Do your people not worship the mountain and the forest?"

"Our Gods are different, more… distant," Bran replied. He was vaguely aware that there were nature worshippers living somewhere beyond Midgard, but for the most part those faiths had been eradicated by the Sun Priests. "We do not commune with the Spirits as closely as you."

"What does the forest say?" asked Satō.

"They speak of the beginning of the rainy season, of how much water they'll get this year and how great the ocean winds will be in the summer. Some trees will die in the typhoons, and some will be born from their seeds – but the forest will prevail."

"How disappointing - I thought there would be some news."

"The great trees do not concern themselves with mortal matters," Nagomi admonished her friend then her face turned pale and serious.

"What is it?"

"There are also evil Spirits here. They speak of hunger and pain and death," she said shuddering, and turned her back to the forested riverbank.

"Do you think there are some white foxes still left here, or racoon dogs?"

"I don't know," the apprentice replied uneasily, "could be… Perhaps the Yōkai War did not wipe out *all* the magic creatures in the deep forests."

"Goblins maybe?"

"I don't know," Nagomi repeated firmly.

"What was the Yōkai War?" Bran asked.

"It was a war against the creatures of magic," explained Nagomi. "It lasted twenty long years, and the result is the Yamato you see today – only humans and dumb animals remain."

"What? But, why…?"

Bran remembered the Faerie people of his own land. Some of them could have been a menace, but he couldn't think of anyone wishing harm to *all* of them.

"The first Tokugawa *Taikun*s waged it to bring peace to the land, protect humans from demons," replied Nagomi.

"Or so they said," added Satō. "I don't know what harm the foxes or racoon dogs bring to ordinary humans, apart from the occasional prank. I think they just couldn't stand anyone who didn't respect their authority. The Yōkai have always ruled themselves, independent from humans."

"Is this what happened to Yamato's dragons?" Bran asked, dreading the answer.

Satō shook her head.

"The *ryū* were hunted to extinction in the times of legends. The chronicles say they were last seen flying in the Genpei War, and that was six hundred years ago."

"Nothing since? Not even from Qin?"

"If there were any others, they are not mentioned anywhere. The dragon lore is forbidden. My father was the only scholar of the subject that I know of. Still is," she corrected herself quickly.

"What about those Fangeds? Aren't they magical creatures?"

"I don't know," replied Satō, pursing her lips.

"And you really have no other creatures left?"

"Nothing that would have a body that could be killed, but there are still ghosts, Spirits, lesser *kami*..."

Bran listened to this, baffled. To exterminate all races was an idea as preposterous as it was terrifying. One might as well consider destroying all animals. Again, the casual cruelty of the Yamato shocked him, but what intrigued him more was how had it been possible for the *Taikun* to achieve his victory without advanced magic or technology?

"What magic creatures do you have in your land?" Nagomi asked.

"Oh, there are plenty. Apart from dragons there are wyverns, lindworms, kelpies, selkies… all manner of beasts. Then there are the Fair Folk, Tylwyth Teg, and the small ones, Corianiaid, but they are only a little different from us."

"What are they like?"

"The Corianiaid are short and stocky, long-eared and narrow-eyed. The Tylwyth Teg are very tall and slim, their hair is golden or silver – but not what you usually call that, it looks like actual gleaming metal. Their eyes are like those of a cat and they can see at night. One of the Tylwyth was a soldier on *Ladon*. I wonder if he survived the disaster…"

His voice trailed off as he gazed at the cypress grove in quiet contemplation. What happened to the soldiers of the Second Regiment? Were their dragons able to fly all the way to the mainland? They must have been tired after the battle with the rebels. And what of his father? Was he now fighting in the siege of Jiankang or trying to find his son? No, Dylan always put his soldier's duty before family. Bran could only count on himself – and his new found friends.

On a sudden impulse, he reached out, put his hand on Nagomi's shoulder and smiled at her. The girl was startled at first. People in Yamato did not touch each other, he had noticed, except the closest of families. He didn't care. What he did seemed natural enough to him. She smiled back, uncertain. They looked at each other in silence.

The boat halted for the night at Haki, a small timber port built at a confluence of Kumagawa and another unnamed mountain stream. The Kuma River flowed a bit wider here, dark mountains reflecting ominously in its calm shimmering waters.

The riverside inn at Haki was a simple one, used to welcoming lumberjacks and mountain hermits, not samurai, and the landlord would not stand up from his prostration until Bran and Satō told him that it was all right for him not to have the finest horse meat – the specialty of the region – on the menu.

"So tell me, the book from my Academy in Gwynedd," Bran started, as all three settled to a meal of rice, local pickles and dried taro tuber, "how did it find its way here to Yamato?"

Satō sprinkled her rice bowl with some shredded taro before answering.

"If truth be told, I don't know. My father always had smugglers bringing strange things to the house, but they were almost always Bataavian, from Dejima, sometimes from Qin. The man who brought us the Dragon Book... He spoke with a strange accent. I don't believe I have ever heard it before, or since, come to think of it."

"You don't remember what he looked like?"

Satō shook her head.

"I could only hear the conversation between him and my father from my hideout – I was never allowed near the smugglers. I don't think the man realised how valuable the book was, as he was satisfied with just a regular fee. He did

263

seem to be in a hurry, but then thieves and smugglers always do."

"What happened to the book?" asked Bran.

"Oh, it's buried in the well, along with everything else. I figured you can teach me everything I need to know about the *dorako* anyway," the wizardess replied, smiling.

Bran nodded.

"I'm not sure if I will make a good teacher, but I can certainly try to answer any questions you may have."

"I have plenty, don't worry about that! Finish your rice and we can start the first lesson. That taro gets chewy when it's cold."

He reached for the chopsticks, but a sudden trembling of the floor caused him to drop them.

"*It's happening again!*" he exclaimed. 'so it was not a dream!"

"What, you mean the tremors?"

"You can feel it too?"

"Of course, it's just a small earthquake."

"Earthquake…?"

Bran felt cold. He imagined the terrible death and devastation he had associated with the word. The Ruin of Olisippo, the Fall of Ragusa, the Devastation of Trinacria… Eithne had studied earthquakes a lot, he remembered. It had always been the geomancers' main ambition to predict and prevent these disasters. How could Satō be so calm about it?

"Nothing to worry about; the worst that can happen around here is a landslide," the wizardess said with a shrug. "Now look, your taro is completely cold. You should order another one."

On the third morning of the cruise the boat emerged from the deep narrow canyon hemmed in between tall walls of granite onto a wide flat valley where several other mountain streams joined Kuma River as it spilled lazily over the flood plain.

"Who rules from this castle?" Satō asked the tiller, pointing to a large sprawling keep on a flat-topped mound across the river, surrounded by a small trading post town. Unlike all the other castles they had seen since leaving Kumamoto, this one was not a ruin and still seemed to be in use.

Instead of answering, the man laughed broadly and burst into song.

Koko no Hitoyoshi

Yu no deru tokoro!

Sagara otome no

Yuki no hada!

This here is Hitoyoshi

The place to go for a hot bath!

The beauties of Sagara

Have skin white as snow!

"Sagara clan," the man added merrily, "and they have done so for the last seven hundred years."

"So we're not in Satsuma yet?"

"It depends on whom you ask. The Shimazu like to think this land is under their control, but in truth the border lies across these mountains to the south."

The boat moored at a busy harbour across the river from the castle, where countless barges waited for the load of timber from the forested slopes surrounding the valley. Workshops and manufactories lined the shore. Satō sniffed; the air smelled sweetly of fermenting rice. Her mood improved at once.

"There's a hot spring!" Nagomi rejoiced at the sight of a small building with yellowish steam billowing from beyond the bamboo fence.

"You go and have a bath, I'll find us an inn," Bran said, and sneezed. It had been raining since morning and his clothes were all soaked.

"You should go to the hot spring too," said Satō, curious of his reaction, "or you'll catch a cold."

"I'll come in later. I'll go arrange our lodgings first."

Half an hour later they found Bran just outside the hot spring entrance. He tried to seem as if he had just arrived from the inn, but Satō knew he waited deliberately until they emerged from beyond the bamboo fence, in fresh *yukata* gowns, their skin clean and flushed with heat.

"You must try it," said Nagomi, pulling him to the counter.

"Where's the inn?" asked Satō. The hot spring was excellent; a good cold drink would make a perfect ending to the evening. Who'd have thought there was such a nice town so deep in the mountains?

"Across the road from the big shrine," Bran explained, pointing east to where a mighty thatched roof rose high above the houses and bamboo tops.

The Aoi Aso Shrine in Hitoyoshi was the most ancient building Nagomi had ever seen.

Its thick thatch, blackened with age, resembled a giant haystack stuck on top of a wooden frame. The wood was painted black instead of the usual vermillion. She didn't know much about art or architecture, but even she could tell the style in which the shrine had been constructed and decorated was much older than anything she was familiar with.

At every stop since leaving Suwa the apprentice had made sure to visit a local shrine. Some were tiny and poor, chapels served by itinerary priests, where a local *kami* accepted even the merest of offerings. Others were grander, town or castle shrines, dedicated to protectors of clans, great chieftains or the Heavenly *Kami* – Gods of Yamato.

Nagomi prayed at all of them. She prayed for her parents' and Lady Kazuko's health, she prayed that Satō could save her father and Bran would find his *dorako* and a way home. She never asked for anything for herself; she trusted in the protection of the *kami*.

Everywhere around her, in the stones, in the trees, even in the old brooms and sandals she felt their the presence. She was never alone, but now she was *lonely*. She missed her parents, Ine and, most of all, the High Priestess. Unlike Satō, she was used to having people around her. There were always crowds at Suwa, pilgrims, priests, *miko*, servants... Even if some regarded her as a freak and outcast, at least they were *there*.

For many days now they had to hide, flee and avoid people. She endured, with the support of *kami,* but this was not enough. She needed more; she needed something the Spirits could never give her.

She sighed and finished her prayers. As she stood up, she saw a young priest looking at her with a bright smile.

"Rarely do we see such devotion as yours, young priestess-*sama*."

"I'm just an apprentice," she said.

"Which shrine, if I may ask?"

"Su…" She hesitated. Should she be saying that? She was never sure how to behave. This was another thing Satō was better at, having grown up in a household full of plots and conspiracies. "Suwa," she said at last.

"*Eeh*! Suwa!" The young man clapped his hands joyously. "You must see something. Come, *come*!"

She followed him to a building at the back, standing between two great black pines. It looked even more ancient than the rest of the shrine, covered with an thicker layer of thatch. Inside it was dark, damp and filled with strange smelling fumes.

"These are vapours that come all the way from the Aso Mountain," said the priest, seeing recognition in the apprentice's eyes. "They say they are even more potent than your Waters of Scrying."

"Have you tried them?"

"I don't have the Gift," the young priest replied, shaking his head sadly, "do you?"

"A little…"

"*Really*?"

He looked at her with honest admiration. She felt her face redden.

"Would you like to try our mists? I've never seen anyone scry before…"

"It's not that easy…" she started, but his eyes gleamed with such anticipation she could not resist. "I suppose it can't do any harm…"

"Excellent! Please, stand here, priestess…"

"I'm only an apprentice," she reminded him, "and my name is Nagomi."

"This mirror is what the Scryers of old used… Nagomi-*sama*."

"And what are these?"

She pointed to a set of three strange masks carved into a pillar, high by the ceiling, painted white. They were disembodied heads of a child, an adult and an old man.

"I do not know," the priest admitted sheepishly. "They have always been here. This shrine is old, full of things nobody remembers anymore."

She positioned herself in front of the bronze mirror and breathed in. The fumes were stronger than at Suwa, more odorous.

"Do you – do you need anything?" the young priest asked.

"No, just… peace and silence."

What am I doing? Scrying is dangerous. Kazuko-hime isn't here. This boy will have no idea what to do if anything goes wrong. Why did I agree to this?

She could feel the onset of the vision surge through her body, like slowly building lightning. Her hair stood on end, her skin was covered with goosebumps. Everything around disappeared, only the mirror remained – and the three carved heads.

One of them, the head of a child, suddenly opened its eyes and looked straight at Nagomi.

Something appeared in the mirror. The vision, but unlike any she had ever experienced. It was not symbolic or dream-like, it was crisp, vivid and showing something real, familiar.

270

She saw herself and Bran on the beach in Kiyō, the boy reaching out his hand to touch her hair; then at the infirmary, him looking at her with unabashed curiosity.

"I like your real hair better."

She was reminded of Bran's quiet words at the inn on the day of their departure from Suwa, the dragon figurine from his satchel, the strange markings on the base, neither Yamato nor Bataavian runes. She felt his hand on her shoulder at the boat.

Nagomi did not understand. Why was she shown all this? This was no vision, just memories. She had seen all this before. What kind of scrying fumes were these?

The mirror dimmed and she was ready to step away when the second mask, the one of an adult, turned towards her with a mischievous grin. She was entranced, unable to move. The polished bronze surface revealed another image.

This one was not from her past. It showed the courtyard of the Kiyō magistrate, a rectangle of sand surrounded by a low stone wall. The cherry trees on the looming slopes of Tamazono were dressed in green, waving in the gentle wind. The courtyard was filled with onlookers, many priests and priestesses among them, standing silent, waiting.

A group of men marched out of the magistrate building with an older woman in tow. It took Nagomi a while to recognise Lady Kazuko with her hair uncombed and wearing a ragged gown. She seemed tired and her face was even more wrinkled than usual. The men were all armed and looked hostile. As the entire group reached the middle of the courtyard, the men stopped. One of them unrolled a silk scroll sealed with the mallow crest, and started reading.

"By the order of the great and illustrious *Taikun*, His Excellency Tokugawa Ieyoshi, we sentence one Hosoki Kazuko, former High Priestess of the Suwa Shrine, to death by sword for conspiracy with enemies of the court, harbouring fugitives and treason against the Divine *Mikado*."

The people gathered in the courtyard were ashen-faced, but none dared so much as to gasp. The High Priestess looked up into the sky as if searching for something.

The vision ended, but the apprentice was still entranced. She could feel tears falling slowly down her cheeks, but she couldn't wipe them. The third mask opened its eyes. They glowed red.

The mirror showed her a wide empty road running through the middle of a forest. Tall walls of mountains rose on both sides. A narrow path branched out to the left, into the woods, barely visible, overgrown by ivy and fern. The vision led Nagomi down this path, deep into the dark heart of the forest, until it reached a circular open glade.

A ring of stones surrounded the glade, and in its centre was a mysterious, mound-like construction, walls of flat boulders covered with a thick cap of dirt, moss and grass, with a single narrow entrance leading inside.

There was a man sitting inside with his back to her. She could not see much detail in the darkness of the barrow, only that it was a samurai in elaborate, old-fashioned clothes. The man slowly turned his head. His face was an oval of blackness.

The vision ended. All three masks closed their eyes and rotated back to their positions under the eaves. The shrine around her emerged from the darkness and the young priest ran up to support her as she swayed backwards.

"You seem very distressed… Was it a bad vision?"

"I – I cannot tell you," she said, wiping the tears from her eyes.

"Of course, I understand." The boy's voice betrayed his disappointment. "Shall I take you to the inn? You can barely walk."

"No, thank you, I can manage," she said. She pushed him away and ran out of the shrine.

THE WARRIOR'S SOUL

CHAPTER XIV

Ozun raised himself up on one elbow and gazed admiringly at Azumi's young athletic body. His fingers traced the outline of a *kirin's* horned head tattooed in red, green and blue ink on her arm. The rigid muscles rippled under the smooth taut skin, the magical beast's scales flickering in the light of an oil lamp.

The girl opened her eyes and bashfully covered herself with a straw blanket.

"Don't look at me like that," she said, smiling innocently.

Ozun laughed and bit her gently on the shoulder.

"I can't help it."

"It's almost dawn."

"I know."

He reached his arm around her, but she writhed herself from under it.

"*Stop it!* We need to prepare ourselves."

Ozun sighed and sat up with his arms around his knees. Those fleeting moments where they only had each other were much too brief for his liking.

275

The bright crimson light of the sunrise peered through a small square window.

"It almost looks like the house is on fire," he remarked.

Azumi shuddered, pursing her full lips.

"Don't say that."

"Oh, I'm sorry. Sometimes I forget."

He reached out to her, but she rolled away, swift like lightning, then jumped up, flipping backwards and landing on her feet behind him without making a single sound. Her hand was on his throat, ready to punch in his windpipe.

"Show-off." Ozun laughed, awed by her supple nakedness.

"Don't be fooled by a woman's tears, hermit," she said, giggling. "I've forgotten all about Koga. I have a new life now, by your side and the Master's."

"I'm also not a mountain hermit anymore," he replied.

"That means you're no longer celibate." She leaned down and kissed the mark of a renegade tattooed onto his bald scalp. "And this makes me the happiest girl in Yamato." She straightened herself abruptly and glanced towards the door. "He's coming."

"Are you sure? I can't hear anything."

"What if he's going to punish you for the failure at Honmyōji?"

He gnashed his teeth. *Those damned pious monks. And I could not even take their spirits.*

"I'm not one of his monsters or sellswords. He can't just – "

The paper panel slid open suddenly and their master appeared in the doorway, his crimson robe seeming almost purple in the shadow. He looked at the two naked lovers indifferently.

"I have a task for you, *kunoichi*," he said to Azumi. His voice carried no emotion.

"Just me, Master?"

"Yes. Hopefully you will fare better than your hermit."

Ozun tensed feeling the cold stare of the golden eyes.

"Be careful," he whispered to the girl as she grabbed her clothes and followed the Master. A faint nod was her only response.

A small, white-furred wolf trotted up and down the side of the causeway, snout close to the wet ground, sniffing. It paused and nudged a piece of dirt with its nose.

"What have you got there?"

Azumi crouched and investigated. She picked up a single long black hair. She tasted it and spat.

"*Dyed.*"

She opened a gourd and poured some saké over the hair. The black dye dissolved, revealing bright red, glistening like pure copper.

"It's beautiful," she whispered with a hint of jealousy. Her own hair was thin, drab, cut neatly at neck-length. "Well done, Inuki."

She scratched the wolf behind the ears. The beast rolled its eyes in bliss. Azumi stood up and blew softly into a bamboo whistle strapped to her sash. The wolf vanished into the mist. A small strip of paper with the character "wolf" written on it floated to the ground.

The *kunoichi* picked up the paper carefully, rolled it up and inserted into one of the many containers at her sash. She then drew the bamboo hat over her face, grasped the iron-ringed staff that completed her mendicant monk disguise and moved on down the road.

She set up her tent on an island of grass in the middle of the marsh, far away from the main road and the prying eyes of passers-by. She much preferred it this way. An assassin needed to be wary of other assassins, and being enclosed within four walls and a roof always made her uneasy. Only when she was with Ozun could she sleep inside a building without waking up in the middle of the night, sweating, remembering the terrible night when the *Taikun*'s father had decided to destroy the Koga assassins – *shinobi* and *kunoichi* - once and for all.

A small bat fluttered in the shadows. Azumi reached out her hand and the creature swooped onto her palm. It chirped quietly, and the *kunoichi* listened, nodding.

"A boat, I understand. Thank you."

She smoothed the tiny hairs on the bat's head and gave it a single cherry. The animal sunk its teeth into the plump flesh of the fruit gratefully.

The bat, like the wolf, Inuki, was a gift from her beloved hermit. She herself had no powers other than her *kunoichi* training, but she had discovered an affinity to communicate with Ozun's Spirits. It was this successful partnership that compelled their Master to endure Ozun's insolence. "Once a rebel, always a rebel", was the hermit's motto.

This time, however, Azumi feared he may have gone too far. He had let the prize get away, and had returned from Honmyōji with nothing. The Master tolerated disobedience in his most trusted servants, but only as long as it was proving effective. A failure put too much strain on his patience. It was now up to her to make up for her lover's shortcoming.

The earth beneath her feet shuddered gently, the tent swayed. The tiny bat was startled and, with the cherry still in its mouth, flew away into the night.

She sighed.

Bran passed hesitantly under the green cloth hanging across the doorway leading into the open air bath.

He knew what hot springs were, but was reluctant to use them. The girls had often reminisced about their favourite bathing places along the journey. He was not yet ready for bathing together with the girls – certainly not with Satō.

279

He put his clothes in a straw basket and began to wash himself. He examined his feet; three days of rest on a boat helped to heal the blisters a little. Criss-crossing purple lines, however, still marked where the straps of the straw sandals, much too small for his size, cut deep into skin. *Tomorrow we walk again*, he thought with a sigh. *How much farther, I wonder?*

There was only one little old lady in the spring, submerged up to her neck in the steaming water, her eyes closed. With great care Bran stepped into the bath, a large rectangular pit surrounded by cold flat stones – and suppressed a yelp. It was as if he had descended into a cauldron of hellfire. The splash awoke the old woman and she was startled for a moment, but then just smiled and moved aside to make place for the boy. He nodded in silence.

After a while he got used to the heat and started enjoying the soak. His arm and leg muscles relaxed, his sinuses cleared. He could feel the cold perish from his body. He started falling asleep.

"Where are you from, boy?" a squeaky voice asked.

The sudden question stirred him from slumber. It was the old lady, looking at him with interest. She was munching on a thin curly cucumber she had produced from somewhere.

"Mikawa."

"*Oh*! All the way from Mikawa to our little spring! How curious!"

"I'm on a pilgrimage," he explained.

"Ah, of course. The shrines of Satsuma seem quite popular these days."

"How so?"

"There were two girls here earlier who are also on their way to the Southern Shrines, and a troop of samurai passed through the city yesterday, going in the same direction."

"*Samurai?*"

"Yes, about thirty of them, all well-armed and very haughty looking. Their commander stopped to take a soak in this spring and I chatted with him for a while, a very dashing gentleman."

"Do you live in this spring?"

Bran chuckled and the old lady giggled.

"At my age there are few diversions to be had, young man. If you're on a pilgrimage, you should visit our shrine, Aoi," she added a moment later. "*Aoi Shrine gate, best in all of Kuma!*" she sang, and giggled again at the screechy sound of her own voice. "It's very ancient and revered. Not as much as Kirishima, of course. You are going by way of Kirishima, I assume?"

"I suppose," Bran replied vaguely, though the name stirred something in his mind, as if he had already heard it before.

"It's the greatest shrine in all of Satsuma! You must visit it! That's where those samurai were going, by the way."

A troop of samurai going to Kirishima... Bran tried to ponder the news, but the relaxing heat of the pool and the faint smell of rotting eggs disturbed his thoughts. The more he looked at the old lady, the more he noticed there was something odd about her. Casually, trying his best not to show he was doing anything unusual, he cast True Sight and stared at the woman.

In her place he saw a green, reptilian, tortoise-like creature, covered with scales, with a long snout filled with sharp teeth, and webbed feet and hands. It looked at him with the same curious eyes, still snacking on a cucumber, unaware of his penetrating gaze.

"W-what are you?"

The creature realised its true form had been revealed and dived into the water, either out of embarrassment or fear. Bran jumped out of the spring, trying to peer at the creature through the mists and vapours.

"Pleasse, don't kill me!" the creature gurgled from under the water, hissing like a snake. "I am bound by the priestss of Aoi to never harm anyone!"

"I have no intention of hurting you, but – what manner of being are you?"

"Don't you know a *kappa* when you ssee one?" The creature's head, covered with seaweed-like dark hair, emerged onto the surface. "A great *onmyōji* like yoursself surely would recognise a water ssprite."

"How did you survive the…" He struggled to remember. "Yōkai War?"

"The good priestss of Aoi provided a refuge to a few of the magical creaturess. The war passed uss by."

"*Us?* How many more of you are there?"

"I'm the lasst of my kind. There could still be ssome goblinss and white foxess hiding in the highesst reaches of the foresst. Pleasse don't let anyone know you've seen me! You must promisse!" The creature swam up to Bran's feet and stared at him eagerly. "Promisse!" it repeated.

"I promise, but you must tell me one thing. Did those samurai say why they were going to Kirishima?"

"They mentioned something about escorting a princesssss."

"And they did not say anything about… other magic creatures?"

"No, but – "

"Yes?"

"Ssomething arrived in the mountainss a few days ago, ssomething new and powerful. The foresst iss frightened, there's never been anything like thiss before. Iss that what you sseek?"

Whilst dressing, Bran discovered something round and heavy in the folds of his travelling kimono. It was a golden coin. He smiled to himself, thinking how fairy creatures the world over seemed to have the same idea of rewarding kind strangers.

Just before the inn he saw Nagomi, running from the shrine down the steep bridge spanning a lotus pond. She was pale, trembling.

"Are you all right?"

He reached out to lay his hand on her shoulder, as he had done on the boat. Nagomi shook her head.

"I'm fine, just tired," she said, but then she wrapped her arms around him and broke down in tears, her whole body shaking with sobs.

He awkwardly patted her on the back then just hugged her tightly. He didn't ask, and she wasn't saying anything. She stopped after a short while, swallowed and wiped the tears from her face.

"Thank you," she said very quietly.

"It's... fine." He rubbed her shoulder, trying to think of a way to comfort her. "Everything will be fine."

"Yes."

They entered the inn. Satō was holding a stone flask in an unsteady hand, pouring clear liquid into the cups of some newly found companions, her clothes dangerously dishevelled. A couple of village entertainers were performing a shockingly bawdy song about a housewife and dried eel, with the locals – and Satō – joining in at the rudest parts of the chorus. There was only one other traveller among the revellers. A samurai in a garish purple and yellow kimono was sitting in the corner, quaffing liquor straight from a flask and smoking a long bamboo pipe, grinning broadly.

"Ah, you've come at last!" the wizardess shouted at Bran and Nagomi over the din. "Come on, join in the fun! Try the famous Kuma Shōchu!"

Nagomi drank a little cold *cha* and excused herself with a headache. Bran glanced at her worriedly, but said nothing. Satō grunted something unintelligible and burst into a song about unfaithful samurai wives and the virile men of Kuma.

The apprentice rolled out the futon, changed into her sleeping clothes and lay down on her back. She sniffed. There was a very faint smell of sulphur lingering above the floor. Did the fumes from Aoi Aso seep through even here?

Sleep found her quickly, thick, heavy, like a cotton-padded blanket, merciful. She dreamt she was at Suwa again. Her room was empty, just as she had left it. Dust had settled on the straw mat floor. *Somebody should clean this up*, she thought.

The door slid open and Lady Kazuko entered the room. Nagomi gasped with delight and ran up to her, embracing the woman.

"I thought you were dead! I had this vision..."

The High Priestess caressed the girl's copper hair silently. At last Nagomi stepped away.

"Kazuko-*hime*? Why do you not say anything?"

Only now did Nagomi notice a thin red scar running around Lady Kazuko's neck. She understood.

"You *are* dead..."

"Do not distress yourself, child. I will soon be joining my ancestors," the priestess said quietly and softly. She seemed completely at peace with herself. "I have been ready to meet death for a very long time, since before you were born."

"But... What about the shrine? What about me...?"

"The shrine will endure and so will you. I came only to tell you this – you must continue with your mission."

"I... I don't think that we – that I have the strength..."

"You *have* to," the priestess pressed, "it is even more vital now, since I cannot be there to help you."

"I'm just an apprentice."

"Not anymore. I ordained you before my death."

"But I'm too young! I have not performed the rites!"

"The dying words of a High Priestess mean more than any rites. You are now a priestess of Suwa. Everyone in Yamato will recognise your new position."

"Oh, Kazuko-*hime*." Nagomi wept, the reality of what happened finally reaching her. "Is the *Gaikokujin* really worth all this suffering? First Satō's father, now you – how much more will we need to sacrifice to help him?"

"Somebody else asked me the same question recently…" the priestess said, smiling. "It's not about the boy. It's about the future of all of us, the fate of Yamato – I can see it clearly now..."

"*Fate*? I can't..."

"You can't do it alone, I know. That's why you have each other. Do not distress yourself with my doom. Death is just a transformation. In a way, I'm happy my life ended like this – at least I managed to do something good in the end."

"Everything you did was good."

"If only that was true." The priestess smiled sadly then looked up. "My time has come. I will become one with the *kami*. Remember me in your prayers, child."

"Always."

"You have always been my favourite apprentice," Lady Kazuko said, patting the girl's head one last time, "and the most beautiful."

"You were the only one who ever thought that."

Nagomi smiled through her tears.

"Maybe I was," the priestess said, nodding, "but it will not always be so."

"What do you mean?"

The priestess did not respond. She closed her eyes. A bright, white blinding light filled the room and caused Nagomi to shield her eyes with her hands.

A faint voice reached her from the light, over the distant hum of the Otherworld.

"Oh, of course, I can see it clearly now!" The High Priestess spoke one last time with a dire sense of urgency. "Listen, Nagomi, things are not what they seem. The man you will meet – you must…!"

The vision perished. Bran and Satō stumbled into the room, waking Nagomi abruptly.

"Sorry," muttered the boy.

The wizardess barely managed a mumble.

The way into the Westerner's consciousness lay wide open. The jade dragon snored loudly at the crumbled gates.

Shigemasa did not plan to run this time. He had grown too curious of the Westerner's fate. He decided to wait and see what came out of all this while he waited for his own destiny to unravel.

He still had urges that needed fulfilling, though, needs that had lingered dormant for two hundred years. The Spirits had no life other than the timeless existence in the Cave of Scrying, but once he had possessed the boy's body, the unquenched passions awoke with increased strength.

The general stepped through the crumbling gate and took a deep breath. The air was crisp and moist – and real.

He came down to the common room. The landlord looked up from the counter. Shigemasa presented the golden coin given to the boy by the kappa.

"The maidens of Hitoyoshi," he asked, "are they truly as white as the songs say?"

The landlord rotated the coin in his fingers and licked his lips, greedily.

"For this I can find you Oyuki-*hime* herself, *tono*."

"Good. Bring the woman to my room, and give me thy best shōchū – believe me, I shall know the difference."

The landlord bowed deeply and disappeared into the back.

"You gave a very moving performance tonight, boy."

Shigemasa turned around. The samurai traveller was still sitting there, his bamboo pipe in one hand and a shallow cup in the other, looking greatly bemused. "I haven't heard the *Warrior of Kuroda* being sung in these parts for… oh, many long years."

The general strode the length of the common room in several, quick long steps.

"*Thou*," he said, "I know thee."

The samurai turned serious. He looked deep into Shigemasa's black eyes. At last, he bowed, slowly.

"It is a strange and fateful meeting, Taishō-*dono*," said the samurai.

"What art thou doing here, Swordsman?"

"I heard rumours. I wondered if they were true."

"What rumours?"

"That an ancient prophecy came to pass and the last Shard has returned to Yamato. That the Eight-headed Serpent is awake. That the dragon child is coming."

"Hmph," Shigemasa grunted, "and thou thinkest this boy is the dragon child?"

"I do not know. Perhaps."

Shigemasa grunted again.

"You are displeased, Taishō-*dono*."

"I had hoped the boy would be just a vessel that I might use for my own purposes, to settle whatever holds me to this Earthly plane."

"It still might be true, Taishō-*dono*. Perhaps your path is entwined with the boy's."

Shigemasa contemplated the samurai's answer in silence.

The tavern door opened and the landlord walked in, leading a fragile-looking woman wearing the flowery robes of a courtesan.

"Are you certain of this?" the samurai enquired. "The boy has had a rough night already."

"He is young and strong, and I have waited two hundred years. Do not worry, I shall return the boy to bed long before dawn."

"I'm certain he'll appreciate it."

The samurai sipped from his cup and puffed on a pipe.

The woman proved more than satisfactory. Her eyes were large, brown and unafraid, her skin surprisingly smooth for a woman in her late thirties, perfectly white and glistening with tiny droplets of sweat on her long neck and back. She was politely quiet and patient throughout the ordeal as Shigemasa mounted her awkwardly, unused to the barbarian's long legs and arms. It did not take long before he reached the shuddering explosion he had longed to feel for so many endless years. The woman beneath him squeaked and panted in unison. He knew she pretended, but was impressed that she knew how to do it so convincingly. When he finished, she complimented him on his potency and prowess.

"Do not go yet," he said, as she started picking up her clothes in silence.

She bowed and sat down, covering her nudity modestly with a bunched up red *yukata*.

"Thou hast been trained in a city?" guessed Shigemasa.

"I have, *tono*. My family sold me to a place in Kumamoto."

"What happened?"

"I bore a child... with one of my customers."

"*Ah*! Most unfortunate."

"If I may be so bold, *tono*," the woman said, lifting her eyes, "it is rare to find a boy of your age with such... refined taste."

Shigemasa laughed.

"Thou may travel the length and breadth of Yamato and thou wouldst not find another youth like me," he boasted.

A hint of alarm appeared in the woman's brown eyes as she sensed something odd in the general's voice, and she started rising to her feet. Her fear excited him.

"Do not fear me, woman. I am merely a boy! Come." He reached out his hand. "I can feel this young body regaining its vigour already. Oh, 'tis good to be alive!"

The snow-skinned woman dropped the *yukata* to the ground and stepped forwards, her face becoming the impenetrable mask of politeness and resignation Shigemasa knew so well.

THE WARRIOR'S SOUL

CHAPTER XV

The precious passenger salvaged from the wreckage of the silver whirligig turned out to be the Governor of Huating – incidentally, the nephew of the viceroy who had perished on *Ladon*. He was recovering from concussion, lying on a mattress at the makeshift infirmary prepared in one of the tea warehouses – the Western medics, guarding their precious neutrality, had been treating the injured on both sides of the front line as long as they were paid to do it.

"What on Owain's beard were you trying to do?" Dylan bellowed.

The doctor bandaging the governor's head winced, but said nothing, knowing Ardian ab Ifor was not a man whose anger one could hope to placate.

"Huating… will fall," the governor whispered. "I need your help."

"What makes you think we can help you? We're as trapped here as you are. I have only a dozen dragons and a few hundred armed men behind the palisade. Good enough for a breakout, maybe, but not to relieve a besieged city."

"There are more… coming."

"More Dracalish soldiers?" Dylan moved closer. He wrinkled his nose at the heavy, sweet smell of the Cursed Weed. *An addict, even at such a high position. Our tradesmen have fared exceptionally well in this area.* "How do you know?"

"Last night – a messenger came through the enemy lines from Jiankang. Your Queen... is sending another ship."

"A ship, you say?" Dylan scratched his scar. *At last some good news!* "A troopship? A frigate? Is it ironclad?"

"I do not know. It will come too late to save the city, but with luck you can use it to recapture it..."

"I can use it to get out of this mosquito-infested island!"

"You must help the city," the governor whispered weakly. "If it falls, the Concession is next. I know that's what the rebels are planning. They now feel strong enough not to care about your trade."

"Strong? I admit there are many of them, but they're still just a bunch of rag-tag – "

"No – listen... The messenger did not come just to tell me about your ship. He came bringing news about... Jiankang..."

The man heaved and started retching bile into an enamelled bowl.

"Please, this poor man is obviously – " started the doctor, but Dylan pushed him aside.

"What is it? What about Jiankang?"

"Jiankang…" the governor said, raising his eyes with the effort, "has fallen."

The triangular red flags of the Heavenly Kingdom – as the rebels demanded it to be called – hung from the ramparts and turrets of Huating Old City. The defenders were brutalised, tortured. All officials had their pigtails cut off, and their precious robes torn off in a public humiliation. The common townsfolk were driven away in a long column across the causeways, over the marsh, into the unknown.

Dylan observed all this from the back of Afreolus, using the lull in the fighting to spy on both sides of the conflict. The rebels were too busy with looting the city to pay attention to the silver dragon above their heads. Only when he got too close to the labyrinthine Yunan Gardens, where the rebel commander had established his headquarters, was Dylan shot at by one of the spider machines. The cannonball whizzed past the dragon harmlessly, but Dylan decided he had seen enough.

Heading back to the Concession he passed a lonely *kirin* rider approaching the wooden palisade with the flag of the Heavenly Kingdom at the saddle of his mount, a snow-white horned horse with hooves of flame. The emissary of the rebels was bringing the conditions of surrender.

Dylan entered the brick headquarters and climbed the stairs to the dining room. The Intendant of the Concession and his councillors had already gathered, discussing the message presented by the envoy.

"They are letting us go free!" the Intendant exclaimed, waving a piece of paper. "*We're saved!*"

"On what terms?" asked Dylan, frowning.

"We leave all weapons, munitions and supplies, taking only enough to get us all back to Fan Yu…"

"And…?"

Dylan sensed the intendant had not told him everything.

"And your dragons," another councillor explained.

Dylan banged his fist on the table.

"*Ludicrous!*"

"Ardian, we appreciate your input, but you're not an authorised member of this council," the intendant reminded coldly.

"I've just seen what they did to the people of Huating. If you think they'll just let us go, you're deluded. It will be Gandhara Retreat all over again."

"I understand your concern, but I can't risk the lives of civilians. We're merchants, Ardian, not soldiers. If we have a chance to get away with our health, we must take it."

"They say their leader believes in Mithras. They can't be all that bad," added another councillor.

"Their leader believes he *is* Mithras," Dylan said, eyeing the councillors with narrow eyes, his scar twitching unnervingly. *They can't be serious.*

The Intendant coughed.

"Does anyone else have anything to add?"

The Intendant never managed to give his reply to the rebels. Within half an hour, all councillors were arrested by the soldiers of the Second Dragoons. Dylan effectively took over control of the Concession.

At first he pretended to consider the proposition of the surrender. In reality, he was playing for time, still hoping the ship promised by the messenger from the Southern capital would materialise sooner rather than later.

Two days had passed on fruitless negotiations and the rebels were at last done with waiting. The Heavenly Army began to unravel its lines, surrounding the marsh island from the west and south. To the east was the Huangpu River, and to the north a flooded canal. The walking machines moved forwards, the footmen readied themselves at the rear. The *long* riders patrolled the sky over the Concession, making the dragons of the Second Dragoons agitated and irritated, but largely helpless.

The relief was nowhere to be seen. A few merchants sneaked out of the island in the hope of fleeing, but it was too late to count on the rebels' mercy. The Heavenly Army captured every one of them and cut their throats in front of the wooden palisade, in mockery of the Sun Priests' rituals. After this display, the remaining civilians swelled the ranks of Dylan's tiny army. They preferred to die fighting than to be slaughtered as slaves.

"We are breaking out," Dylan decided at last, "east along the river and then north. All the way to Ta Du if need be."

"It won't be easy," said a grinning Edern.

"It never is."

Dylan turned to his men to give them final orders, when suddenly a barrage of powerful explosions shattered the air, followed by a roar of thunderbolts and a whistle of rockets flying above their heads.

He looked over the palisade to the east. A mighty ironclad battleship, black like the night, chuffed at full speed up the river, cannons blazing, funnels steaming. It was followed by a large stable-ship and a couple of escort vessels. The Queen had sent them not just one ship, but a whole flotilla!

A dozen dragons launched from the deck of the stable-ship. The Qin riders tried to fight them briefly and futilely, overwhelmed by the combined might of flying beasts and the rapid guns of the escort. The marsh to the west of the island filled with smoke and flame, scattered wrecks of the walking machines and bodies of the slain soldiers. The rebels were not yet ready to retreat from the battlefield, but they were certainly much less eager to attack.

A silver dragon landed in front of Dylan and his marines. It carried two men. One of them – a flaxen-haired Seaxe boy - remained mounted, while the rider, a young, brown-eyed soldier of Prydain stock with the shiny new Leader insignia upon his epaulets jumped off with heavy grace and saluted. Dylan noticed the Seal of Llambed on the soldier's chest. *He looks about Bran's age. I wonder if they knew each other.*

"Flight-Leader Hywel ap Cadell, Twelfth Light," the soldier said with a strong Llyn accent, "hope we're not too late."

"Ardian Dylan ab Ifor of the Royal Marines, and interim Commander of the Huating Concession," Dylan said, returning his salute. "You're just in time. First time in combat?" he added, recognising the tell-tale signs in the boy's face, the flushed excitement and hint of fear.

"Green as spring grass, Ardian, but eager," replied Hywel with a grin. "I'm sorry we're not the Guards, but we were the best the Empire could procure at short notice."

"You will have to do." Dylan smiled back. "Whose ship is that?" he asked, nodding towards the black ironclad.

"This fine frigate, Sir, is *Wintoncaestre*, the flagship of Rear Admiral Reynolds of East Bharata and Qin Station."

"Rear Admiral, eh?" Dylan raised an eyebrow. "Come, Flight-Leader, I believe we have a lot to discuss."

The Flight-Leader turned towards the Seaxe.

"Get her to the stables, Wulf. Make sure she's got a nice stall this time!"

"Yes, Sir," replied the blond rider quietly, with only the slightest hint of venom in his voice.

The large sturdy cage of iron bars was much more robust than the previous one. Three men stood around it, feeding a barrier woven closely of many Binding spells. They were wearing vermillion robes with the crest of a circle and cross on their shoulders. He sensed their terror and the immense effort with which they struggled to keep him from breaking out.

Suddenly, with a wild roar, he stood up, stretching his back and wings, shattering the bars of the cage like matchsticks. The wizards tried to fight back, but to no avail. He lunged towards one of them and, in a blink of an eye, snapped his mighty jaws on the man's midriff. Hot warm blood gushed into his starved throat.

Bran woke up strangely sore. His thighs and stomach muscles ached, his shoulders were covered in scratches. He wasn't rested at all, as if he hadn't slept all night. His head was pounding. He remembered scraps of dreams, vivid images. The women from Shigemasa's memories were there again and once more they all had Satō's face. For some reason it annoyed him greatly.

There was something else… a vision of the dragon. Bran could not recall the details of the dream, but could not shake off the feeling that something terrible had happened. He tried to focus and reach out with the Farlink, but received nothing except faint signs of life. The beast must have still been asleep. Perhaps it hadn't eaten for too long – hungry dragons in the wild would sometimes fell into a kind of hibernation, preserving energy until an opportunity to feed presented itself. He dared not to think of another reason for the dragon's silence.

Slowly, he dragged himself from the flat mattress and put on the bottoms of his travelling clothes. With great effort he staggered down to a vegetable garden at the back of the inn, looking for the well.

The mountains around the valley were steaming. The rain had stopped and the dew rose, filling the garden with a milky mist. In the midst of it, by the well, stood Nagomi, looking at her reflection in the dark water, her hair covered with a fresh layer of the black gunk. She nodded and smiled at him weakly. Bran was delighted to see her relaxed and in higher spirits than the day before.

"How do you feel?" she asked.

Before answering, Bran took a bucket of the cold well water and poured it over himself.

He was slowly remembering the events of the previous evening. Satō had been so exhilarated with the opportunity of having a proper night of revelry, she had decided to buy everyone in the inn a round of best local shōchū – then another. With every round, more people had come into the inn, until eventually the whole neighbourhood joined in the merrymaking. One of Satō's golden coins was more than enough to cover the bill.

It had been almost a year since Bran had spent a night at a tavern. He was never big on parties, but this time was different. Was it because the local liquor was stronger, the people more cheerful and friendly – or because Satō's clothes seemed to magically loosen a little bit more with every cup she had gulped?

During the day, as he had already learned, all the conduct of the Yamato people was guided by strict rules. Their manner of speaking, manner of walking, even gestures and facial expressions were always controlled and subdued. However, after a few cups of saké, all this was changing. That night everyone, rich and poor, had joined in singing, dancing and joke telling.

Bran had observed Satō showing off her wealth with concern. She was making them conspicuous. Everyone at the inn had warned them of travelling farther south through a wild mountainous region. As if the rumour of bandits was not enough, there was the water sprite's mention of malevolent creatures hiding in the forests – and Nagomi's strange behaviour a few hours earlier. All of this was very unnerving.

By the end of the night the wizardess had been hanging off Bran's arm, unable to stand, her face deep red. He had dragged her to the room she shared with Nagomi and laid her gently on the futon. For a brief moment she had wrapped her arms around his neck and looked into his eyes daringly, singing in a drunken drawl.

Ima wa ima wa ima wa

Okoran bai ka?
Shita kota gozansan!

Now, now, now,

Why are you angry?

Nothing's happening down there!

Before he could guess what the song meant, she had closed her eyes and was sound asleep.

"I feel fine, thank you," he answered Nagomi's question at last. "Did you sleep well? I'm sorry for waking you up..."

"That's all right." She shook her head. "I slept long enough."

Shadows under her eyes belied her words. Her skin had a greyish, tired hue. Bran felt a pang of guilt. *I should never have allowed the party to last that long into the night*, he thought. *We're far from safe. What if we have to fight today? I'm weak and tired. But she was having such a good time… I haven't seen her so happy before.*

The girl in question appeared in the courtyard. She was wearing her *Rangakusha* clothes, tightly bound this time. She didn't look in good shape, the unfortunate effects of last night's revelries reflected in her tired face and baggy eyes.

A couple of locals staggered towards the well. Bowing clumsily before Bran, they glanced towards Satō and exchanged a few giggly indecent comments. The wizardess clutched the collar of her robe tightly and stared coldly at the men.

Bran dried himself off, threw the towel around his bare shoulders and bowed before the wizardess.

"*Bore da!*" he welcomed her in Prydain.

"How could you have drunk that much and still wake up before me?" asked Satō, wincing. "Is that your soldier training?"

"To be honest, I find your drink rather weak," he boasted, although the back of his head still hurt.

"How long did the party continue after I left?" she asked.

"Not that long." He tried to remember. "In the end only that samurai in the purple kimono remained drinking. He was even tougher than me – flask after flask, as if it was water. He didn't talk much. At last even the innkeeper wanted us to go to sleep," he laughed, but not very loudly.

"I'm not really that used to alcohol, myself. Father always frowned when he saw me drink saké. He said it muddled one's talent."

"He may well have been right. I'm certainly in no mood for spell casting today," he said, laughing again even more quietly. "I had no idea the Yamato were so fond of drinking and singing," he added. "It was almost like one of the nights in a *tafarn* back home, with a harper by the fireside and cold *cwrw* in the tankard..."

His voice trailed off wistfully.

"I had no idea you knew any Yamato songs."

"That was... Shigemasa," he admitted. "The *Kuroda Warrior* was the last song he performed before his death – I felt it decent to let him replay it again."

"Are there many songs in your land, Bran-*sama*?"

"Please," he said, raising his hand, "it's about time you started to call me simply *Bran*. It is a custom in my country that those who drink together, as we did, do not need to refer to each other by anything more than a name."

"Very well," Satō agreed, "are there many songs – *Bran*?"

"Oh, yes," he replied, "children in Gwynedd learn to sing before they learn to speak!"

"You'll have to sing for us one day then"

Oh great, look what your boasting got you into...

"We should be moving," Nagomi said. "The innkeeper said the next lodging place is more than half a day away, in this weather."

"Weather changes quickly in these mountains," remarked Satō, "and I have no intention of staying in this place any longer." She cast a nervous glance at the two locals, who were now swaying their way back to the inn. "I think I would like my sword back today," she added, looking at the wild dark forest rising menacingly over the southern edge of the valley.

Satō was furious with herself. Furious and ashamed.

What she could remember of the last night now was absolutely appalling.

I should never have drunk that much.

It had felt strangely enticing to reveal herself before the foreigner's captivated eyes. It was a new thing for her. The men, she had learned from poems and books, were supposed to be excited by poetic subtleties, the red lining of the *kosode*, the blackened teeth, the purple peony in her hair. But something as common as flesh?

How did the night end? What did she tell him? What did she do? She remembered them struggling up the stairs to the room, her arms around Bran's neck. He smelled so nice… What happened next? Oh no, did she sing *that* song? She hoped he did not understand its real meaning… Had she brought shame to her family?

No, nothing happened. Nagomi was there and Satō would know from her accusing eyes. Bran just left her alone, sleeping on the cheap uncomfortable *futon*. He was that chivalrous, or naïve, or maybe he preferred the company of other boys, like so many young samurai sons she knew…

Stupid, *stupid* girl! All this for what? A few spellbound glances and one drunken embrace. *Get a hold of yourself, Takashima Satō*, she kept reproaching herself as the party climbed the forest road, ever deeper into the dark mountains. *If you need a man, there are plenty of proper Yamato boys. No need to waste your time with this odd, uncouth barbarian.*

She cast one last look at the valley they were leaving behind as the road climbed back into the forest. The sun was still shining at Hitoyoshi, its friendly households and terraced fields, dancing merrily on the tin roofs of the workshops and silver waters of the Kuma River below; but there were heavy clouds gathering around the tops of the mountains and up the hill where she stood the rain started anew – a drizzle at first, but Satō knew it would not end at that. She pulled the hood of her rain cloak tighter and followed Bran and Nagomi up the forest road.

This was the one part of their journey that truly troubled her. Past the last of the lumber mills started a wild country she knew nothing about. The only road winded up and down, left and right, in zigzags and spiral turns through the deep, dark, mystic ancient wood. The trees up here grew even denser and taller than they had along the river, barely touched by a woodcutter's axe, only enough to keep the dirt road passable. There was no sign of any lodgings in the distance and they had not passed a single traveller since leaving the village. By the end of the day the mist started rising from the ground and quickly got so thick she could barely see further than twenty feet or so. The sky turned dark. The evening was fast approaching and the rain became an unpleasant drenching shower. The road narrowed to a slippery path. Her *hakama* was covered in mud.

"It's no use," Bran said. "We'll have to find some shelter for the night."

"Just a bit more. Maybe there will be some lumberjack hut or hermitage," said Satō.

"Or a forest shrine," added Nagomi hopefully.

This was the first the apprentice had spoken since leaving the town. *She's very gloomy today. We're all tired but there's something else...*

She almost bumped into Bran who stopped suddenly. A large tree was lying fallen across the road. The boy moved forwards to look for a way around it, but Satō grabbed him by the sleeve.

"Look out," she said, "they did warn us about the bandits…"

"And quite right they were," a mocking voice spoke behind them.

A tall muscular hulk of a man emerged from the mist. He wore a white tunic, torn at the bulging forearms, and brown trousers. A red band tied his black unruly hair. He held an iron mace, longer than a sword, studded with nails, slung loosely over his shoulder. A little blue electric light wandered along the length of the weapon.

"Well, well, *what is this*?" he boomed loudly, twirling a bushy beard in his fingers. "Three kids on a mountain path? Are you lost? Where are your parents?"

Again a blue flame flickered along the length of the iron mace. The bandit smiled cruelly and scratched his chest with dirty fingers. His tunic spread apart, revealing a tattoo of a five-pointed, interlaced star.

"He's an *onmyōji*!"

Satō pointed at the pentacle on the man's chest.

"*Onmyōji*? What's that?" Bran asked.

"Our own native magic – "

"Have you finished?" the bandit interrupted them. "I don't think you're quite as scared of me as you should be!"

He came a few steps closer, swaying arrogantly, the mace still on his shoulder. Satō pulled out her sword with a metallic whistle. Bran put his right hand on the hilt of his Prydain sword and locked the index and middle fingers of the left hand together.

308

The bandit stopped and observed them carefully, squinting. He snapped his fingers and out of the forest came three other men, dressed and armed like the samurai, but without any markings on their ragged clothes; *rōnin* – warriors without masters, lethal swords for hire.

The boat hobbled up to the pier, frightening a lazy heron, and the passengers began pouring out. First to disembark were four swordsmen in grey uniforms, grim-faced and silent. The *kunoichi* was the last to step out of the boat, still in her beggar monk's clothes. The ferryman helped her down and bowed with his hands clasped – a devout superstitious man. Azumi bowed back, reaching out with her bowl. No real itinerant monk would pass an occasion like that. A couple of copper coins jingled into the black bowl.

"May *Butsu-sama* bless you with a long life. Tell me, good man, what decent inns are there in this town?"

The ferryman looked at her quizzically, but gave her directions to several establishments.

"We have rich temples, monk-*sama*," he added proudly. "I'm sure they will be happy to accommodate you."

"Saké loosens purses," she said.

"*Ah*, I see!" His face brightened up in a wide honest smile. "How silly of me."

She feared she would be too late again. The boat had trudged so slowly up the mountain river she wondered if it wouldn't be faster on foot, but the ferry moved relentlessly through the tall canyons from dawn to dusk and she needed to be rested for the confrontation, if there was to be one.

It wasn't hard to find the right guesthouse. The memory of the party and the three young travellers was still fresh in the minds of the locals.

"Do you know when they departed?" she asked the landlord.

They couldn't have been more than half a day away – the sun was still high.

"Departed?" The man laughed. "I do believe they haven't even woken up yet!"

Azumi couldn't believe her luck. Could they really have been so reckless?

She hid behind the corner of the inn, opened one of the numerous ivory compartments hanging at her sash and, unrolling a piece of paper, summoned a lizard messenger.

"Tell them to come to the inn by the riverside," she ordered, and the spectral reptile skittered away to where the samurai in grey uniforms were awaiting her orders.

Four skilled swordsmen and herself may have been deemed an overkill, but the *kunoichi* could not afford a failure, and these three kids had defeated an *enenra* already. Two of them knew magic. She wasn't taking any chances.

She watched in astonishment as the three youths passed her by, no more than a few feet away. The youngest – a shrine apprentice, Azumi recalled – even dropped a few pieces of copper into the alms bowl. Azumi bowed and muttered her thanks. They were silent and seemed tired, despite sleeping so late into the day, but they were moving fast even so, and the four swordsmen for whom she waited failed to appear. The children were already on the narrow bridge over Kuma. In a few minutes they would leave Hitoyoshi altogether.

The *kunoichi* could not wait any longer. She merged into the shadows and began to follow the travellers as discreetly as only a trained Koga assassin could.

What had happened to her men? *A betrayal? Impossible, unless...* Was the Master toying with her, testing her? Was she supposed to finish the task by herself to prove her worth? She could do it, she was certain, now that she had seen the targets up close. They were easy targets, unaware of their surroundings, unprepared for a fight. All she had to do was wait until they were out of the town, out of sight of witnesses. This could be one of her easiest assignments yet...

Her keen senses picked up a sudden presence. *She* was being watched. *Who dared...?* She looked around, but could not see anybody. *A Spirit?* No, it had to be a man. She froze, blending even further into the shadows among the cedar trees. The children moved out of her sight, but she didn't mind – the road led straight south through a dense forest, they could not escape her now. The new threat required more immediate attention.

A samurai in a purple robe thrown over a flowery kimono stepped onto the road, looking straight at her. He was brandishing two naked swords, their plain black hilts contrasting with the gaudy colours of his unfashionable outfit. How had she missed him in these clothes?

"Come out, monk," he said, pointing at her with one of the swords.

The blade was caked with fresh blood. She obeyed. There was no point in hiding anymore.

"I know you," she said, remembering at last. "You were in Yatsushiro, by the harbour, but you haven't been on the boat."

"I walked," the samurai stated simply.

It was impossible. He must've travelled day and night without respite to have reached the town before her, and he showed no trace of fatigue.

"What do you want with me?"

"Go back to your Master, monk. These three are *my* prey."

The air around them grew noticeably colder. Azumi shivered. This was not an ordinary opponent. She knew now whose blood was on that blade.

Slowly, within the folds of her robe, she bent the palm of her left hand, reaching for a

hidden blade strapped to her wrist. The samurai's eyes darted towards that hand. He winced.

"Please don't. I don't enjoy killing monks. Even pretend ones."

Smoothly and noiselessly, she let the hidden knife fly towards her enemy's chest. Even as the blade still flew, she pressed a hidden spring on her pilgrim's staff. It split in two, revealing a three-foot long iron chain concealed inside one of the halves, with a weight at the end. Another secret blade popped out at the end of the other half. Hot blood rushing through her veins, she charged at the stranger silently.

She managed to stand against him for several long seconds, and she knew then that this was her greatest moment, the fight she would be most proud of until the end of her days – if she survived the ordeal. His swords were like snakes, living creatures with minds of their own, ribbons of steel, flashes of metallic lightning. The two blades whistled around her a sweet song of triumph and skill, but the samurai's face remained impassioned all through the duel, as if he was trimming a garden.

She felt droplets dripping down her face and she couldn't tell whether it was sweat, blood or tears of exasperation. With a clang, her weapons were torn from her hands, disappearing into the ferns. She tumbled back, just as one of the two inhuman blades whizzed past where her neck had been a fraction of a second earlier. She reached for the smoke grenade and threw it at the samurai, but he cut through it with such force that the air buffeting off the blades dispersed the poison. He was unstoppable.

A white wolf jumped on the samurai's back, snarling, reaching towards the man's neck with its teeth. Azumi didn't have time to think from where the beast had come – it was not her companion… This was the one moment of distraction she could use. Weaponless, she did not consider another attack, but she could still run, and run she did, into the forest, into the mist as far away from the terrifying swordsman as she could.

THE WARRIOR'S SOUL

CHAPTER XVI

"Now," the mage spoke in a calm voice, "you have something that I would very much like to have. Give it to me and I will spare you. I have no desire to hurt children."

"I don't know what you're talking about," Bran replied. Something told him the bandit was not after Satō's gold coins.

"The blue stone, the sapphire shard. This – " He pointed at Bran's left hand. "It is much too precious a thing for a youth like you to carry around these forests."

"This?" Bran looked at his finger with surprise. "My grandfather's ring? Why would you want it?"

The bandit chortled.

"If you don't know what it does, you won't miss it, will you?"

"Tell the Crimson Robe to come and get it himself!"

The bandit blinked in confusion.

"I have no idea who this Crimson Robe is."

Then who – ?

"Come now, this is taking too long," the bandit interrupted his thoughts, "I really only want the jewel, but if you trouble me any longer, I am willing to take your gold too, as compensation."

"Three swordsmen and a mage against three kids?" mocked Bran. He was already observing the scene of battle with True Sight and noticed the three *rōnin* had no magical weapons. This filled him with confidence. "Not taking any chances, eh?"

"You have swords," the bandit replied, shrugging his muscular shoulders. "I like my face unscarred." He rubbed his bearded chin. "Let's finish this, the rain is most annoying. I have given you enough warning."

He stepped forwards and swung his mace, aiming for Bran's head. The strike seemed fatal but Bran stood steady, unwavering, watching the iron weapon buzz off his *tarian* without effect, the shield's surface shimmering softly in the rain.

Satō raised her sword threateningly and the mage pulled back. The three *rōnin* looked at their boss but he shook his head.

"What now?" Satō whispered.

"He can't get through. Not without a Soul Lance or an Unravelling spell," Bran replied confidently.

"A *kekkai*, huh? I see you know a few tricks. So do I…"

The bandit scratched his scraggy beard. From a fold of his shirt he pulled out a strip of paper with Qin characters

written on it in black ink. He threw it at the shield. It burst
with blue flame. Bran swayed and felt the barrier's collapse
around him almost like a physical blow.

"W-what?" he gasped.

"*Get them!*"

The mage waved his hand and the swordsmen rushed
to capture the three travellers.

Satō cried out a spell word and slashed the air twice
with her sword. Arches of ice struck the closest two
opponents in their chests, throwing them backwards. The
third swordsman hesitated.

"I knew it!" the *onmyōji* cried. "You're *all* wizards!"

Bran snapped out of his astonishment. His blood
rushed in expectation of combat, accelerating his reflexes,
but his poise faltered. Without his dragon he was like a
cavalryman turned footman. He was trained to rely on
shields, Soul Lance and the link with Emrys, but the Farlink
was overstretched and could maybe provide him with one or
two bursts of dragon flame, and his shield turned out to be
useless.

He pointed at the still standing warrior and spoke
Binding Words. He put little power into the spell, but it was
enough to halt the man's movements completely. He then
spread out his palm and tried the same with *onmyōji*, but the
mage only smirked and shrugged the spell off.

The dragon rider cursed and drew his sword. A row of runes
lit up along the blade. He was not a keen swordsman and the
weapon in his hand felt unfamiliar, unwieldy.

"Are you sure you know what you're doing?" a voice called in Bran's head.

"Leave me be." The boy struggled to push the general's spirit away. "I have everything under control."

"He doesn't look that tough. I could cut him down if you"d only let me."

"You've chosen a bad time to try your tricks. I need to focus, so be quiet!" the boy cried in his mind with great energy.

The general fell silent, watchful.

The *onmyōji* swung his mace sideways at Bran. The boy leapt up and forwards, quickly calculating the curve of his enhanced jump above the mage's head. He landed hard and turned around, cutting backwards, but the jump had carried him too far and his blade swished through the air futilely. He lost his balance and struggled not to fall face-forwards into the dirt. The Enchanted Acrobatics had failed him once again.

The mage spun around. Bran opened his left hand and summoned dragon flame, spewing a spiralling tongue of fire from between his spread fingers. At last the *onmyōji* stopped smirking as the air filled with the stench of burning skin and hair.

The mage grunted, annoyed. He clearly had not expected to get hurt. He smashed his mace into the ground with full force and the earth around him shook violently.

Bran staggered, dropping to one knee. He attacked with dragon flame again, but this time the mage bit his teeth and endured the pain as the blaze enveloped him. He threw his mace high up into the air then clapped his hands together and murmured a quick mantra before catching the weapon as it fell.

A five-pointed star appeared glowing on the ground around Bran. The dragon rider tried to jump away, but he bounced off an invisible wall – he was trapped within the borders of the pentacle.

The mage towered over Bran with a stern face. His shirt burned to tatters, the five-pointed star tattoo on his chest was fully visible, dancing on rippling muscles. The skin on his torso was covered in fast reddening blisters, but the mage seemed to pay no attention to what must have been a terrible agony.

With lightning speed he swung his iron mace high above his head to bring it down upon the boy, but Bran was just as quick. He dropped his sword and summoned the Soul Lance between his stretched out arms. Blue lightning crackled as the mace clanged against the lance's shaft of solidified life energy. Bran moaned, his shoulders nearly breaking, but the lance held where the sword's blade would have no doubt shattered.

The mage laughed and pushed further against the lance, confident in his pure physical strength. Bran resisted valiantly, but his weapon flickered under the strain and suddenly vanished. The *onmyōji* lost his balance momentarily. The iron mace missed Bran's head by an inch and fell with great force upon the boy's left shoulder, smashing through the collar bone with a loud, nauseating crack.

"*Gwrthyrru!*"

Ignoring the excruciating pain, Bran hit the mage's chest with a Strike of Repel. The enemy launched a few feet into the air with a surprised expression on his face and fell on his back, splashing the mud around.

The road, the forest and the grey sky revolved around Bran, shock quickly overcoming his consciousness. He saw Satō running to his help and then there was nothing but the red darkness.

The fight was too easy. The bandits may have been skilled swordsmen, but they were no match for her magic. She had already frozen two of her opponents to the ground; the third one was struggling to set himself free from Bran's spell.

Satō would have preferred to fight the *onmyōji*. She was curious how her Takashima School training would aid her in a fight against what many wizards perceived as a natural foil to the *Rangakusha* – a native mage, skilled in channelling the destructive aspects of the *kami* power – but the bandit chief focused his efforts on Bran, leaving her to deal with his meagre minions.

She raised her sword to strike the nearest of the swordsmen, when his eyes lit up with red glow and his face twisted and transformed into a blazing demonic mask. He shrugged Bran's enchantment off. The other two men underwent the same metamorphosis and the ice shackles holding them shattered with a loud crackle.

"*Shikigami!*" Satō scowled.

The demonic familiars in human guise! Now the fight became serious. She leapt back as her enemies jumped at her from three sides. She put her left hand to her lips and whispered a quick incantation. Three ice lances shot from her fingers. The demons let out otherworldly howls, but kept on approaching, ignoring their wounds.

This was no good, she realized. She put more energy into her next shot and launched one powerful javelin-shaped missile against the nearest of the assailants. It tore right through him, leaving a gaping hole in his torso. Still the *shikigami* moved forwards as if nothing happened. She parried one blow of his sword, then another, but there seemed to be no stopping the demonic swordsmen. Suddenly she heard Nagomi cry out.

"Sacchan, look out – Bran…!"

Glancing beyond the three demons, the wizardess saw Bran slip and fall down under the pummelling of the *onmyōji's* mace. She noticed the five-pointed star glowing in the sand and cursed loudly.

Fighting the familiars was taking too long and her reserves were draining fast. And now she had to do something to help Bran out of the mage's trap. Desperate, she reached into the sleeve of her vermillion kimono and took out the glove given to her by Master Tanaka. She slid it hastily on her right hand and pressed on the spring. A thick needle popped out, piercing her palm. Blood spurted in a thick stream. The glass dial twitched and lit up brightly as Satō's life energy poured into the enchantment.

"*Bevries!*" the wizardess cried at the top of her lungs.

The nearest bandit immediately turned into an ice statue, frozen solid from head to toe. Satō was as surprised with the result as the other two.

"*Bevries, weder*!" She cast another spell, and another demonic swordsman was stopped in his tracks, his limbs encased in ice. "Blood magic..." she whispered, fascinated by the amount of power she was able to generate.

But that was almost the limit of what the device was capable off. The grip of her sword was slippery with blood and the energy gauge was running low. Worst of all, the wound in her shoulder once more began to throb with pain.

She hissed through gritted teeth, trying to ignore the ache.

Satō dodged a blow from the last swordsman's blade. She pierced the *shikigami* with her sword, but the demon pushed on. Slashing sideways, she sliced the enemy across the stomach. The swordsman glanced at his innards pouring out of the gash, confused. He made a clumsy step forwards and his legs wobbled. Satō pushed him aside and ran towards Bran and the *onmyōji*.

The bulky mage picked himself up off the ground and raised his dreadful mace over Bran one more time. She released all her remaining power, hoping to hamper his movements with strong ice chains. She managed to turn his attention on herself for a moment.

The *onmyōji* swirled his weapon over Satō wildly. She ducked and cut the enemy across the stomach, but her sword bounced off an invisible shield. The mage had his own *kekkai*! Was there no limit to his powers? She lunged forwards, dodging another blow. While the bandit struggled against her icy shackles, the wizardess reached Bran.

She tried to lift him but the boy's body slipped from her grasp. She heard and felt the last of her enchantments shatter, the *onmyōji* breaking free behind her. She turned around and raised her sword feebly, in an attempt to block the final blow from the terrible iron mace as it came crashing down towards her. Parts of the sword covered with frost, but she was too weak to embed the entire blade in ice. Her shoulder was almost paralysed with the agony spreading from the bronze dagger wound.

She stared straight in the mage's eyes, ready to face death…

The moment the three *rōnin* turned into demons, Nagomi hid behind a tree, shivering with terror. She had never experienced such fear in her life, not even when they had to flee from the Honmyōji. She prayed to all her ancestors, but they offered no guidance. She prayed to Lady Kazuko, but the priestess did not appear before her, did not come from the Otherworld at her time of need.

She was on her own and helpless. Again there was nothing she could do but watch her friends struggle, lose and die. Bran was already down, Satō fighting on her own. Still the Gods did not come.

"I must do something," she whispered in despair, "*anything!*"

She felt something warm in her sleeve and reached into it. The Spirit light beaker lit up with the merry orange flame, as if trying to comfort Nagomi in her distress.

"I'm sorry," she whispered and threw the beaker at the *onmyōji* with all her might and little hope.

The hulking bandit's back made for an easy target. The tiny, fragile clay pot smashed against his burly frame and the Spirit light, set free, immediately engulfed the mage's body in flames.

The *onmyōji* howled loudly. He dropped the mace and clasped his hands to his face. Faint pale wisps of bright orange flame whirled around him, penetrating magic defences, scalding his blistered burned skin. The mage reeled to the side of the road.

Satō saw Nagomi standing in the middle of the road with her eyes and mouth wide open, breathing fast, her trembling hands clutching her paper-tasselled wand. Shards of her Spirit fire beaker were scattered on the road. The wisps of shining orange fog spread all over the mage like fiery insects and leapt onto the stumbling *shikigami* behind him, who began to howl and crawl in the dirt just like its master.

But the icy tombs holding the other two were shattering from inside. There was no time to wonder about the miracle. The wizardess pulled Bran up by his right arm, herself still numb with pain.

"Nagomi!"

The apprentice shook off her astonishment and ran up to help raise the boy from the other side. Bran grunted weakly, his consciousness slowly returning.

"There's a hidden path behind that big tree," Nagomi whispered.

The wizardess nodded and the three stumbled into the humid darkness of the misty forest. The undergrowth seemed to part before the girls and, as they carried wounded Bran farther down the narrow muddy path, the woods closed behind their backs defensibly, keeping them safely out of sight.

For all Nagomi knew, they could have been carrying the boy straight into the bandits' lair, but there was no time to think of a better plan. The path was definitely the one she had seen in the revelation the day before. Every fern, every cypress tree, every moss-covered boulder was the same. She could only hope she had interpreted the vision correctly.

She could hear the enemies in the distance, trying to find their way through the dense forest, then there was only the silence of the deep wood and the sound of rain battering on the leaves. Eventually the path ended before a round open glade, surrounded with a circle of roughly hewn, moss-covered stones. Exactly as she had seen in the bronze mirror, in the middle of the glade was an ancient earthen mound with a stone-lined narrow entrance. Remnants of an old straw rope lay in front of it, and a dilapidated wooden door frame showed the inside was still in use long after the mound had been raised.

Nagomi hesitated, remembering the rest of the vision, but there wasn't anyone inside and Satō was urging her to move quickly. They were both at the edge of their strength. The girls entered the mound and put Bran on the floor of flat hard limestone. The chamber was surprisingly dry and warm. Satō sneaked outside to cover up their tracks, while Nagomi sat down by the unconscious boy.

There was very little daylight seeping through the entrance. Nagomi wished she still had her Spirit light with her. Its loss was disheartening. She had been carrying the merry orange flame with her ever since she had become inducted as an apprentice. It had kept her company in any darkness, reminding her of the happy times she had at the shrine. Now her loneliness was even more palpable.

She focused on examining Bran's wounds. The boy's shoulder was dark purple, quickly turning black, swollen to twice its normal size. When she touched it, she could feel the bits of crushed bone move sickeningly underneath the skin. She felt queasy, but at least *now* she knew exactly what to do. She started her healing chant, quietly at first, bowing repeatedly, shaking her wooden wand and sprinkling his arm with dew and rainwater gathered from the floor. There was very little effect – the bleeding did not subside, the swelling remained in place, the shattered bones refused to mend.

"Ooh, it's not working! Why doesn't it work?" she complained. "You're not old enough to be so resistant!"

Bran opened his eyes and looked at her. His pupils were as black as night.

"*His Ancestors are not with him.*"

326

The guttural roar of the Otherworld coming from deep within the boy's throat accompanied the words spoken by General Shigemasa.

Nagomi backed away, shielding herself with the wooden wand.

"*The boy has great innate resistance*," the old samurai said, "*even to thy healing power.*"

"What… what do I need to do?" Nagomi whispered.

"*I shall endeavour to open the conduit. Thou wilt have little time, so do thy best.*"

Bran-Shigemasa closed his eyes. A bright blue light surrounded his body and on that cue Nagomi started her chanting once more. The wound started to heal, contract, the bleeding stopped, the swelling receded. The bones and muscles moved around within the flesh and joined together, mending. Soon all that was left was only a dark bruise, a faint memory of the battle. Nagomi leaned back against the wall, panting, exhausted to the very edge of her strength. She had never felt so weak and tired in her life.

"Thank you, Shigemasa-*dono*," she managed a faint whisper.

"*The boy is no good to me dead. If he perishes out here in the wilderness, I become a wandering Spirit.*"

"You will… not be trying to control him now?"

"*Not today. There would be no honour in that.*"

"I… I don't believe you. He warned us about… your tricks."

The general chuckled.

"He was right, but the Barbarian deserves this little respite. He fought bravely today – almost like a true samurai. I can appreciate that."

Satō barred the narrow entrance with the remnants of the door and sat down next to her friend. The chamber was shrouded in darkness, light barely seeping through the cracks between the stones. The wizardess, too, was tired and dishevelled, her forearm covered with dried blood, her shoulder hanging loose, limp. She loosened her kimono and undid the breast wrap to catch a deeper breath.

"How is he?"

"He should be fine. Do you need that cut looked after?" Nagomi raised a feeble hand but Satō caught it gently and put back on her lap.

"No, it's just a scratch. Don't worry."

"And the… arm?"

"The Suwa priests already did everything that could be done. What about you? You seem exhausted."

"I'm… I'll be all right. I just need to rest."

Bran stirred, opened his eyes and slowly sat up.

"I'm alive," he said.

"For now," said Satō grimly. "They're still out there somewhere."

"Odd…" He rubbed a bruised arm. "I thought it would be crushed to bits."

"It was," the wizardess told him, "you're lucky Nagomi's such a talented healer."

"A healer...?"

"Any priestess would do the same," Nagomi protested shyly.

"I don't understand."

"Nagomi *healed your wound*," repeated Satō slowly as if talking to a child, assuming his mind was still muddled by the shock of the fight.

"But how could she...?"

"*Oh*, you – don't you have healers in the West?"

"No! I've never heard of such thing. Do you mean medicine?" he asked.

"No, that's not it. Your medicine is great when it comes to dealing with diseases and internal ailments," replied Satō, "but for battle wounds or injuries, we have the Spirit healers."

"But... is this true? This is a fantastic power! How did you manage to keep it a secret?"

"*A secret?*" Satō seemed genuinely surprised. "Nobody's keeping it a secret. I thought everyone knew about Spirit healing."

"I assure you if the world outside knew... The Bataavians are certainly not letting this information out." Bran stopped and looked around the dark chamber. "How did we get here? I don't remember..."

"You passed out with pain and we carried you into the forest."

"We've defeated them?"

"No." Satō shook her head. "But we did manage to run away, thanks to Nagomi's sacrifice."

"How do you mean?"

Despite the darkness inside the tomb, Nagomi could feel Bran's incredulous eyes fixed upon her. She avoided their gaze and looked at the floor, wringing the end of her *obi* sash in her hands.

"It wasn't… I didn't…"

"She used her Spirit light to distract the mage," said Satō, patting her gently on the back, "am I right?"

Nagomi nodded.

"Thank you," whispered Bran, "and thank you for the… healing. I still can't – such power…!"

"It's – nothing, really." She felt her throat closing in.

The boy looked around.

"Are we safe here? What is this place?"

Maybe if I could purify this place and make an offering, its kami would yet return…

"The Ancients?"

Bran flicked a faint flamespark. The hollowed-out chamber was lined with flat limestone flagstones, its surface smooth and cool to touch.

"People who used to live here before the Yamato came," explained Satō.

"*Used to* live? What happened to them?"

"Never mind the history lesson – it was thousands of years ago," Satō said impatiently, "what did those bandits want from us? From *you?* Why were they after your ring?"

"I wish I knew. I thought it was just a curious memento my grandfather retained after his…" He hesitated. "His journey to Yamato. But those bandits thought that shard of sapphire was a more interesting prize than your roll of gold coins."

Nagomi bit her lips. A shard of sapphire… The High Priestess did ask her not to tell anyone about the Prophecy for fear of reprisals – but surely they could not find themselves in a more desperate situation. The priestess was dead, and they were all pursued by some terrible monsters – and all, she guessed, because of the Prophecy; that strange disturbing vision she had saw so many months ago. *They had the right to know.*

Before any of them managed to say anything, a twig cracked and a bush rustled outside. Bran immediately vanquished the flamespark.

"They've found us," Satō whispered in the darkness.

Bran joined the wizardess by the narrow entrance, observing the *onmyōji* and his weird companions. There were now six of them, approaching the tomb quietly through the fog in a fan-shaped formation.

Bran reached for the sword readying himself for another battle, but the scabbard was empty. The Prydain blade lay abandoned somewhere in the dirt of the road.

Satō drew her katana with trembling arms.

"I… I don't think we'll make it," she whispered. "I thought I'd covered us well enough. I failed again."

"You did all you could – we're only human," said Bran, trying to console her. "Maybe we can still sneak out…"

She shrugged his hand off.

"I'm a samurai!" she said firmly, "and if I can't fight like one, at least I can die like one. I've been running away long enough. *Takashima!*"

"No, wait…!"

Before anyone could stop her, with a fierce battle cry on her lips she kicked out the door, raised her sword and leapt outside, ready to charge to her death.

Suddenly a blade flashed in the fog behind the bandits' backs, then another. One of the enemies collapsed face down without a sound. Before the others could react, the second also fell victim to the unseen swordsman. The blades flashed once more like twin lightning strikes, and the third tumbled down, flailing bloody stumps of arms. The swords skipped from one enemy to another like two steel vipers hiding in the mist. Within seconds, only the mage remained alive. The *onmyōji* turned to face the enemy and raised his mace with a defiant roar, but it was already too late. The two mysterious swords flashed one last time in a neat, flawless strike and the mage's head rolled slowly off his body, leaving a trace of bloody spurts in the grass.

Silence fell like a death shroud upon the forest.

THE END

THE WARRIOR'S SOUL

CHAPTER XVII

The night was hot and uncomfortably muggy. Yezaimon Kayama stirred uneasily in his sleep, throwing off the thin quilt. He had been suffering from nightmares ever since the *Taikun*, in his great wisdom, had resolved to make him the Governor of Defences of the Uraga Channel. The heat and humidity of early summer nights only made the anguish worse.

The position, although ostensibly prestigious, was a burden in the best of days. His wife was right to warn him not to accept it, but it was impossible – nobody refused a gift from the *Taikun* and lived. The domain consisted of miles of empty shoreline, dotted with ancient forts built in times immemorial to thwart some invasion of a forgotten foe. There were no pirates on these seas, no invading fleet sighted in centuries.

Boredom and useless chores filled Kayama's days as he travelled up and down the coast, hopelessly trying to build up some pretence of defence. The local samurai feigned effort only for as long as they could feel his eyes on their backs. Money was short, the treasury almost empty. The breaches in the walls of the coastal forts were covered with grey cloth instead of stone. The cannons remembered the days of the first Tokugawa *Taikun*, some of them had barrels

335

made of wood, painted black to imitate iron. It was all make-believe, a theatre stage with outdated props.

Nobody ever threatened these shores. The Divine Winds protected the islands with a tight impenetrable maze of storms and twisting currents, passable only in one secret place south of Chinzei Island. Once every ten years or so, a barbarian ship tried to break through, but always failed. Sometimes the waves would cast away a few hapless survivors. The regularity with which the barbarians attempted the landings baffled Kayama's mind. Did they not know that as long as the *Taikun*s ruled from their Edo castle, the Gods themselves protected the Sacred Soil of Yamato?

Recently, if the rumours were true, another foreign ship had been sighted off the Nansei Islands, heading north. Like so many times before, the governor had to make sure at least some of his cannons were able to shoot more than blanks, and that a few of his archers and arquebusiers were stationed at their proper posts, in the unlikely event that the barbarians would somehow succeed.

The obviously exaggerated rumours of the size and strength of the barbarian flotilla did little to ease his anxiety. For the last few nights he'd been dreaming of great monsters emerging from the waters of Uraga Bay and devouring towns and villages along the shore. These were ominous menacing dreams and he sincerely wished that the foreigners would already come and go, and leave his poor soul in peace.

The desperate ringing of gongs coming from the beach awoke the governor from an uneasy slumber. Kayama pulled himself off the rice hull-stuffed mattress, grumpily.

"Enough already," he mumbled, "you call yourselves samurai? I thought I'd trained you better than this."

Without haste, he put on his everyday clothes, a plain grey *haori* jacket and sand-yellow, pleated *hakama* skirt, thrust two swords into the sash around his waist and opened the door of the coastal outpost in which he was spending the night.

The ringing continued. He inhaled deeply and instead of the usual scent of sea and wind, he smelled soot and smoke.

Intrigued but not yet worried, Kayama gazed over a high cliff overlooking the port of Kurihama, the gateway to the Uraga Bay. In the pink glow of dawn, a scene of chaos and destruction was unfolding before his eyes. The town was ablaze. The gongs of the military were by now joined by the loud booming drone of the temple bell and the clanging little bells of fire guards. Raging flame was devouring houses along several of the streets, feeding on the wooden frames and thatched roofs. People were running towards the hills in panic, leaving all their possessions to the fire.

Before he could take all this in, a bewildering sound came from the sky, as if a giant lion roared in the clouds. Kayama looked up and reeled in terror. For a moment he thought he was still dreaming or had gone mad. Above the town, far beyond the range of any cannon, bow or matchlock, circled four giant black beasts, like enormous eagles, slowly beating their great wings and weaving long serpentine tails. One of them was greater than the other three, flying higher, as if commanding all this destruction. Every so often, one of the lesser monsters spewed a ball of flame from its mouth which fell into the sea with a deafening blast and a hiss of steam.

There was nothing Kayama could do but admire the destruction from afar. He was, after all, an educated samurai, and could find poetry even in death and ruin. The monsters, he understood quickly, were no doubt Gods or their messengers, coming from the sea to inflict punishment on the unsuspecting sinners. The famines and earthquakes were just a prelude: this was what the prophecies and divinations of the priests had been all about. Kayama sat down on the ground, resigned, as the unbelievable beasts continued to circle above the harbour.

Oh, poor Yamato, the shadow of black wings portends thy doom!

In his head he began to compose the first stanza of an epic poem *On Destruction of Uraga Harbour* when, to his surprise, the black monsters stopped their circling and swooped towards him. As they soared above Kayama with tremendous speed, heating the very wind before them, he noticed tiny silhouettes of men riding atop the beasts, two on each except a lonely figure on the largest one, their faces hidden in the shadows of grey hooded cloaks.

They weren't Gods, he realised with relief, which quickly turned into renewed terror. They were human beings – invaders. They were heading straight for Edo, and he could do nothing to stop them…

THE END

APPENDICES

GLOSSARY OF TERMS

(Bat.) — Bataavian

(Yam.) — Yamato

(Pryd.) — Prydain

(Seax.) — Seaxe

aardse nor *(Bat.)* spell word, "Earth Tomb"

amazake *(Yam.)* a traditional sweet drink from fermented rice

ardian *(Seax.)* the Commander of a Regiment in the Royal Marines

banneret *(Seax.)* the Commander of a Banner in the Royal Marines

bento *(Yam.)* a boxed lunch, usually made of rice, fish and pickled vegetables

bevries *(Bat.)* spell word, "Freeze"

biwa *(Yam.)* fruit of loquat tree

blodeuyn *(Pryd.)* spell word, "Flowers"

bugyo *(Yam.)* chief magistrate of an autonomous city

bwcler *(Pryd.)* magical shield covering a fighter's arm, a buckler

cha *(Yam.)* green tea

chwalu *(Pryd.)* spell word, "Unravel"

Corianiaid *(Pryd.)* a race of red-haired dwarves from Rheged

cwrw *(Pryd.)* beer

dab *(Pryd.)* creature, thing or a person

daimyo *(Yam.)* feudal lord of a province

daisen *(Yam.)* chief wizard

dap *(Pryd.)* the same size and shape as something

dengaku *(Yam.)* a meal of grilled tofu or vegetables topped with sauce

denka, —denka *(Yam.)* honorific, referring to the member of the royal family

derwydd *(Pryd.)* druid

dōjō *(Yam.)* school of martial arts or fencing

dono, —dono *(Yam.)* honorific, referring to a noble man of a higher level

doraco *(Yam.)* Western dragon

doshin *(Yam.)* chief of Police

dōtanuki *(Yam.)* a type of katana, longer and heavier than usual

draca hiw *(Seax.)* spell word, "Dragon Form"

draigg *(Pryd.)* a dragon

duw *(Pryd.)* a swearword

dwt *(Pryd.)* a young child

egungun (Yoruba) a holy spirit, also a shaman dancer representing Egungun

enenra *(Yam.)* a spirit born of smoke

faeder *(Seax.)* father

fudai *(Yam.)* an "inner circle" clan; one of the vassals of the Tokugawa Taikun before the battle of Sekigahara

futon *(Yam.)* a roll-out mattress filled with rice husks

gaikokujin *(Yam.)* a foreigner, non-Yamato person

genoeg *(Bat.)* spell word, "Enough" (to mark the end of a continuous spell)

gornestau *(Pryd.)* magical duel

graddio *(Pryd.)* school graduation ceremony

gwrthyrru *(Pryd.)* spell word, "Repel"

hakama *(Yam.)* split trousers

hamon *(Yam.)* visual effect created on the blade through hardening process

haori *(Yam.)* a type of outer jacket

hatamoto *(Yam.)* the Taikun's retainer, samurai in direct service to the Taikun

hime, —hime *(Yam.)* honorific, referring to women of high position

igo *(Yam.)* a board game for two players, using identical black and white tokens

ijslaag *(Bat.)* spell word, "Ice Layer"

inro *(Yam.)* a wooden container for holding small objects, hanging from a sash

inugami *(Yam.)* a dog spirit

jawch *(Pryd.)* a swearword

jutte *(Yam.)* police truncheon

kabuki *(Yam.)* a form of classical dance theater

kagura *(Yam.)* a type of theatrical dance with religious themes

kakka *(Yam.)* honorific, referring to lords of the province or heads of the clans

kambe *(Yam.)* a shrine servant taken from an adjacent village

kami *(Yam.)* God or Spirit in Yamato mythology

kanpai *(Yam.)* Cheers!

kappa *(Yam.)* a water sprite, reptilian humanoid

katana *(Yam.)* the main Yamato sword, over 60cm in length

kaya *(Yam.)* a bright yellow wood used for making igo boards

kekkai *(Yam.)* a magical shield, similar to tarian

kimono *(Yam.)* official layered robe of the noble class

kirin *(Yam.)* a chimerical creature of Qin, body of a deer and the head of a dragon with a large single horn

kodachi *(Yam.)* a short Yamato sword, less than 60cm in length

koenig *(Seax.)* the monarch of the Varyaga Khaganate

kosode *(Yam.)* basic, loose fitting robe for both men and women

kun, —kun *(Yam.)* honorific, referring to young persons of the same social status

kunoichi *(Yam.)* a female shinobi assassin

kuso *(Yam.)* a swearword

lloegr *(Pryd.)* Dracaland east of the Dyke

llwch *(Pryd.)* spell word, "Dust"

long (Qin) Qin dragon

mam *(Pryd.)* mother

mamgu *(Pryd.)* grandmother

Matsubara *(Yam.)* the family of katana swordsmiths

metsuke *(Yam.)* inspector representative of the Taikun

mikado *(Yam.)* the divine Emperor of Yamato

mikan *(Yam.)* fruit of tangerine tree

mithraeum (Latin) temple of Mithras

mitorashita *(Yam.)* worshippers of Mithras

mochi *(Yam.)* a sweet made of rice gluten

mogelijkheid *(Bat.)* magical potential

monpe *(Yam.)* workman's trousers

naginata *(Yam.)* a polearm formed of a katana blade set in a bamboo shaft

nodachi *(Yam.)* a large, two-handed sword, over 120cm in length

noren *(Yam.)* a curtain hanging over the shop entrance, with the logo of the establishment

oba (Yoruba) chieftain

obi *(Yam.)* a silk sash wrapped around the waist

obidame *(Yam.)* a buckle for tying the obi sash

oden *(Yam.)* a type of stew

omikuji *(Yam.)* fortunes written on a strip of paper

onmyōji *(Yam.)* a practitioner of traditional Yamato magic

onmyōdō *(Yam.)* traditional Yamato magic

oppertovenaar *(Bat.)* overwizard of Dejima

swyfen *(Seax.)* a swearword

tabako *(Yam.)* tobacco

tadcu *(Pryd.)* grandfather

tafarn *(Pryd.)* tavern, inn

tafl *(Pryd.)* strategic board game, played on a checkered board

taid *(Pryd.)* grandfather

taikun *(Yam.)* military ruler of Yamato

taipan (Qin) leader of a trading company

Taishō *(Yam.)* field marshal, commander-in-chief of all the forces in the field

tarian *(Pryd.)* magical shield surrounding entire body

tengu *(Yam.)* a forest goblin

tenpura *(Yam.)* small fish and vegetables fried in batter

teppo *(Yam.)* a "thunder gun" — hand-held lightning thrower

terauke *(Yam.)* a passport produced by an affiliate temple

tono, **—dono** *(Yam.)* honorific, referring to a noble man of a higher level

torii *(Yam.)* wooden or stone gate to the shrine

tozama *(Yam.)* an "outer circle" clan that was forced to become the vassal of the Tokugawa Taikun after the battle of Sekigahara

tsuba *(Yam.)* a handguard of the katana

twinkelbal *(Bat.)* sparkleball; a stone used for thaumaturgy practice

twp *(Pryd.)* insult, "stupid, simple"

tylwyth teg *(Pryd.)* Faer Folk, a race of tall, silver- or golden-haired humanoids

THE WARRIOR'S SOUL

waelisc *(Seax.)* (slur) Prydain

wakashu *(Yam.)* an "unbroken" youth, a virgin

wakizashi *(Yam.)* a short sword used as a side arm, 30-60cm in length

xiexie *(Qin)* "thank you"

y ddraig goch *(Pryd.)* Red Dragon

yamabushi *(Yam.)* an ascetic mountain hermit

yōkai *(Yam.)* evil spirit, demon

yukata *(Yam.)* casual summer clothing, simple light robe

GLOSSARY OF CHARACTERS

GWYNEDD

CANTRE'R GWAELOD

DYLAN AB IFOR o Cantre'r Gwaelod

b. 2566 a.u.c. Ardian of the Second Dragoons Regiment of the Royal Marines. Married to Rhian ferch Rhys.

Mount: Highland Silver, Afreolus (*Unruly*)

BRAN AP DYLAN o Cantre'r Gwaelod

b. 2590 a.u.c. A graduate of Dracology at the Llambed Academy of Mystic Arts.

Mount: Rhos Jade, Emrys (*Ambrosius*)

ROYAL MARINES

EDERN mab Gwyn

b. 2526 a.u.c. Banneret of the Second Dragoons Regiment of the Royal Marines. A Tylwyth Teg.

Mount: Highland Silver, Nodwydd (*Needle*)

GWENLLIAN ferch Harri

b. 2577 a.u.c. Reeve of the Second Dragoons Regiment of the Royal Marines.

Mount: Highland Silver, Tywyll (*Dark*)

WULFHERE of WARWICK

b. 2589 a.u.c. Ensign of the Twelfth Light Dragoons, descendant of Richard Warwick the Kingmaker.

Mount: Highland Azure, Eolhsand (*Amber*)

HYWEL AP CADELL o Llyn

b. 2590 a.u.c. Flight-Leader of the Twelfth Light Dragoons

Mount: Eryni Ruby, Taran Goch (*Red Thunder*)

BROUGHTON REYNOLDS

b. 2542 a.u.c. Rear Admiral of East Bharata and Qin Station

YAMATO

KIYŌ

MIZUNO TADANORI

b. 2563 a.u.c. *Bugyō* – Magistrate of Kiyō. *Hatamoto* retainer of the Taikun.

KOYATA JŪMONJI

b. 2570 a.u.c. *Doshin* – chief of police – of the Merchant's District in Kiyō

ISHIDA TAKUYA

b. 2566 a.u.c. Lieutenant of *Doshin* Koyata

HIRATA MITSUYU

b. 2574 a.u.c. Lieutenant of *Doshin* Koyata

TSUKINARI SHIGEZAEMON

b. 2578 a.u.c. Captain of the guards of Kiyō Magistrate

BLACK RAVEN SOMERLED

b. 2577 a.u.c. Cast-away, teacher of Dracalish

TAKASHIMA

TAKASHIMA SHŪHAN

b. 2544 a.u.c. A *Rangaku* scholar, head of the Takashima School of Wizardry.

TAKASHIMA SATŌ

b. 2589 a.u.c. Heir of Takashima School of Wizardry.

SUWA SHRINE

HOSOKI KAZUKO

b. 2567 a.u.c. High Priestess of Suwa Shrine.

NAMIKOSHI TOKOJIRO

b. 2581 a.u.c. An interpreter of Dracalish language.

ITŌ NAGOMI

b. 2591 a.u.c. An apprentice at the Suwa Shrine.

IKŌ

A servant girl at the Suwa Shrine

SAKUMA

SAKUMA ZŌZAN

b. 2564 a.u.c. A scholar of *Rangaku.*

SAKUMA KEINOSUKE

b. 2594 a.u.c. A student at the Takashima School of Wizardry.

SATSUMA

SHIMAZU NARIAKIRA

b.2562 a.u.c. Daimyō of the province of Satsuma, lord of Kagoshima Castle.

SHIMAZU ATSU

b. 2589 a.u.c. Adopted daughter of Shimazu Nariakira, princess of Satsuma.

TORII HEISHICHI

b. 2557 a.u.c. *Daisen,* Arch-wizard of Satsuma.

KUMAMOTO

MAGONOJO ITSUNEN

b. 2579 a.u.c. A monk at Honmyōji temple, host of *shukubo*.

MOTOMENOSUKE INGEN

b. 2570 a.u.c. A monk at Honmyōji temple, cook of *shukubo*.

IPPONIN

b. 2538 a.u.c., d. 2606 a.u.c. Previous abbot of Honmyōji temple

CHIZONIN

b. 2565 a.u.c. Current abbot of Honmyōji temple

SOZAEMON FURUHASHI

b. 2567 a.u.c. Fifteenth abbot of the Unganzenji Temple

KATŌ KIYOMASA

b. 2315, d. 2364 Founder of Kumamoto Castle, general, one of the *Seven Spears of Shizugatake*

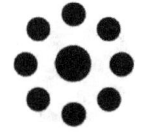

HOSOKAWA

HOSOKAWA NARIMORI

b. 2557 a.u.c. Daimyo of Kumamoto domain, tenth lord of Kumamoto Castle.

HŌJŌ

YOKOI SHŌNAN

b. 2562 a.u.c. A scholar and reformer at the Hosokawa's court in Kumamoto.

ITAKURA

ITAKURA SHIGEMASA

b. 2341, d. 2391 a.u.c. Daimyo of Fukōzu Han in Mikawa Province, commander of Taikun`s forces during Shimabara Rebellion.

TOKUGAWA

KAYAMA YEZAIMON

b. 2547 a.u.c. Daimyo of Uraga, commander of coastal defences of Edo Bay

MORIYAMA EINOSUKE

b. 2573 a.u.c. Interpreter of Dracalish at Edo court, school friend of Tokojiro Namikoshi

EIGHT-HEADED SERPENT

OZUN

b. 2581 a.u.c. A renegade Yamabushi priest

AZUMI

b. 2585 a.u.c. The last of the line of shinobi assassins of Koga

Thank you for reading *The Warrior's Soul*.
If you enjoyed it, why not leave a comment on Amazon or Goodreads?

The Year of the Dragon cycle contains the following volumes:

The Shadow of Black Wings

The Warrior's Soul

The Islands in the Mist

The Rising Tide

The Year of the Dragon: Books 1-4 Delux Edition

THE ISLANDS IN THE MIST

PROLOGUE

The white silk of his robe was stained with the blood of his brethren.

Wet sand squeaked under his bare feet. At the break of dawn the sea was silent, cold and dark like the swords which slaughtered the priests at the Mekari. His brothers had thrown themselves against the blades to protect him and that which he carried away.

The Jewel was not for human hands to hold. The orb of white crystal burned his skin and flesh like a glowing ember. He bit his lips and endured.

The black line of gnarled, twisted pines moved closer with his every breath. He dared not look back; he knew the grey-clad assassins were near. He hoped to lose them in the dark forest growing on the windswept seaward slopes of the nearby dune ridge. If he could only make it to those trees…

Out of the corner of his eye he glimpsed the falling blade and instinctively raised his hand to shield himself. The sword clanged harmlessly. The white sleeve of his robe fell, revealing an arm covered with black scales, glinting in the first rays of the rising sun.

He grasped the blade and snapped it in two. The swordsman stared incredulously at his broken weapon, then at the long, sharp claws reaching for his eyes.

He left the howling assassin to bleed out onto the sand and kept on running. The trees were now less than fifty paces away, their safe shadows beckoning him invitingly. The others were now so close behind he could hear the shuffling of their feet. He stumbled, losing precious seconds. Thirty paces. Twenty. His aching calves cried for him to stop, but he ignored the pain. His heart pounded as if trying to break free from the ribcage. Just a little more effort. Just a few more steps.

He glimpsed them standing among the trees, swords drawn, and realised all was lost. He slowed down and stopped. The men behind him stopped too, waiting, patient. He turned around. There were three of them, all in the same grey, unmarked uniforms, solemn faces without a trace of emotion. Two more approached unhurriedly from the forest.

They could see the Jewel clearly, shining like a beacon through his right hand and the white silk sleeve, but, for the moment, were more concerned with the left hand, armed with its deadly claws. Wary of the fate of their comrade, the swordsmen bid their time until, at last, the first one leapt towards him with the weapon raised. There was no war cry, not even a hastening of breath.

The sun rising over the dunes painted the sea as crimson as the blood of the five men lying in the sand and the robe of the long-haired, gaunt faced man standing before him.

"I'm impressed," the man said, grinning to show his sharp, black teeth. His eyes glinted like nuggets of pure gold. In his right hand he was holding a giant sword, almost four

pilipala *(Pryd.)* spell word, "butterfly"

proost *(Bat.)* Cheers!

rangaku *(Yam.)* "Western Sciences", study of Western magic and technology

rangakusha *(Yam.)* a practitioner of Western magic

reeve *(Seax.)* the Staff Sergeant in the Royal Marines

rhew *(Pryd.)* spell word, "frost"

ri *(Yam.)* measure of distance, approx. 4 km

rōnin *(Yam.)* a masterless samurai

ryū *(Yam.)* a Yamato dragon

Saesneg *(Pryd.)* (slur) Seaxe

sakaki *(Yam.)* a flowering evergreen tree, used to produce **sacred** paraphernalia

sama, —sama *(Yam.)* honorific, referring to peers of the same social status

sencha *(Yam.)* popular kind of tea

sensei, —sensei *(Yam.)* honorific, referring to teachers and doctors

shamisen *(Yam.)* a three-stringed musical instrument

shinobi *(Yam.)* assassin

shōchū *(Yam.)* strong liquor (25-35% proof)

shōgi *(Yam.)* strategic board game similar to chess

shukubo *(Yam.)* accommodation for temple pilgrims

sokukamibutsu *(Yam.)* a self-mummified monk

stadtholder *(Bat.)* the ruler of Bataavia

feet in length. "So, this is how the last of the Sea Dragons fights."

The priest said nothing, saving his strength. Two of his claws were broken, his left eye gouged, his stomach and chest cut with many deep wounds but, somehow, he was still standing. He no longer felt any pain, only weariness.

The man in the crimson robe drew his sword and threw away the plain wooden sheath.

"This is where you should say something poignant," he remarked and raised the weapon horizontally above his head. The priest wondered if it was too late to pray to the great Watatsumi for help.

With a sudden roar he lunged forwards. The man in the crimson robe stepped back and brought the sword down. The blade struck the priest's right shoulder, slicing the arm cleanly off his body, but the claws pierced deep into the enemy's chest. No blood pulsed in the swordsman's veins; no heart beat inside the ribcage.

The demon laughed and pushed the priest away. He reached down and wrestled the Jewel, clutched in the hand, though the arm was cut clean off. A frown marred its pale face as the gem's white light burned through the parchment-thin skin.

"That's not right," he murmured to himself. The priest tried to crawl away, slipping and stumbling, but the demon grabbed him by the folds of the white silk robe, turned effortlessly and, with a swift stab, pierced his chest.

With dying eyes, the priest watched as his own blood stained red the Jewel of the Ebbs, turning the stone from a white diamond into the purest of rubies.